Judy Astley was freque... ...ff for day-dreaming at her drearily tradiu... school but has found it to be the ideal training for becoming a writer. There were several false starts to her career: secretary at an all-male Oxford college (sacked for undisclosable reasons), at an airline (decided, after a crash and a hijacking, that she was safer elsewhere) and as a dress designer (quit before anyone noticed she was adapting *Vogue* patterns). She spent some years as a parent and as a painter before sensing that the day was approaching when she'd have to go out and get a Proper Job. With a nagging certainty that she was temperamentally unemployable, and desperate to avoid office coffee, having to wear tights every day and missing out on sunny days on Cornish beaches with her daughters, she wrote her first novel, *Just for the Summer*. She has now had eight novels published by Black Swan.

Also by Judy Astley

JUST FOR THE SUMMER
PLEASANT VICES
SEVEN FOR A SECRET
MUDDY WATERS
EVERY GOOD GIRL
THE RIGHT THING
EXCESS BAGGAGE

and published by Black Swan

NO PLACE
FOR A MAN

Judy Astley

BLACK SWAN

NO PLACE FOR A MAN
A BLACK SWAN BOOK : 0 552 14764 8

First publication in Great Britain

PRINTING HISTORY
Black Swan edition published 2001

3 5 7 9 10 8 6 4

Set in 11pt Melior by
County Typesetters, Margate, Kent.

Black Swan Books are published by Transworld Publishers,
61–63 Uxbridge Road, London W5 5SA,
a division of The Random House Group Ltd,
in Australia by Random House Australia (Pty) Ltd,
20 Alfred Street, Milsons Point, Sydney, NSW 2061, Australia,
in New Zealand by Random House New Zealand Ltd,
18 Poland Road, Glenfield, Auckland 10, New Zealand
and in South Africa by Random House (Pty) Ltd,
Endulini, 5a Jubilee Road, Parktown 2193, South Africa.

Printed and bound in Great Britain by
Clays Ltd, St Ives plc.

David Snelling, like it or not this one's for you.

One

'Any thin Celts?' The waitress was standing so close that Jess Nelson could smell fabric conditioner on the floppy sleeve of her white blouse. Comfort, Bounce or possibly Lenor? Jess sniffed delicately, like a cat scenting distant mouse, then remembered she'd been asked a question, a peculiar one.

'Sorry, what was that?'

'I *said*, can I *gechew* any *thin Celts*?' The girl was speaking loudly and slowly, perhaps assuming, as they were in a Gatwick Airport coffee shop, that Jess was From Abroad. The question still seemed absurd and an assortment of skinny Cornish and Welsh nationals marched through Jess's mind. She frowned, then smiled as some sort of understanding took over. 'Oh I see! Right! No thank you, I don't need anything else, I'm fine.' The waitress sighed, tore off a slip of paper from her pad and slapped it smartly down next to Jess's empty coffee cup. 'Pay at the desk,' she ordered and strode off, leaving a wake of laundry scents.

Jess picked up her bag, paid for the coffee and began the long trail back through the airport to the short-stay car park. All around her people were shopping manically as if this was their last-ever chance, darting in and out of the Body Shop, cramming on straw hats in Monsoon, hanging about in Knickerbox eyeing the slinky underwear and browsing in Waterstones seeking something to read that wouldn't disappoint on a sun lounger. How easy it must be to forget you were supposed to be travelling somewhere, to forget that the plane now standing at Gate 31 was waiting to take you away from all this. With all the passengers' brains lulled into shopping-mode no wonder there were so many exasperated tannoy announcements along the lines of 'Will the last remaining passengers for flight whatever *please* make their way *immediately*' etc. etc. Jess and the family used to be just the same: the three children geed up dangerously close to tantrum point with excitement, Matthew sensibly telling them all to slow down, they'd got a long fortnight ahead, no point in squandering holiday money on stuff you could get in any high street at home. And Jess herself would be silently going through lists in her head, had they got toothpaste, remembered Lomotil just in case, would she need Tampax, Nurofen, Calpol, Elastoplast . . .

Oliver hadn't let a mundane little thing like shopping hold him up today. Classing himself grandly as a Traveller, superior to the dallyings of a mere Tourist, he'd quickly checked in his backpack and raced straight through to Departures with no hanging about to let Jess do her mumsy last-minute routine on him. In his eyes she'd detected no faltering doubts about this long, rite-of-passage trip, more a barely concealed terror that she'd fall to the floor sobbing and pleading with him not to go, not to abandon her to the mercy (what mercy?) of The Girls. There'd barely been time to say 'Call us when you get there,' when he'd hugged her briefly and made a bolt for Passport Control. She tried to fix that last view of him in her mind. The turned head, the fast rangy walk, the wide grin full of perfect teeth, the dark floppy hair that would probably be six inches longer and tied back next time she saw him. She also tried, as she sped along the moving walkway back to the car, to fix for herself an accurate idea of his height: just that small bend as he hugged her, that made him, what, about two inches taller than that man over there with the battered leather briefcase? Or was he even taller than that? It was always a slight surprise to her, just how much space her once-baby son now occupied. There'd been that strange teenage growth-spurt time, four or five years back, when one morning he'd ambled downstairs and she could see quite clearly that the 5'5" that had gone up to bed the night before had come downstairs as 5'7". He'd walked across the kitchen and banged into a chair because his accustomed number of steps took him that bit further than they had the day before. What happened to nineteen years? How come a year was so luxuriously long when you were nineteen yourself but so breathlessly brief when your eldest child was that age?

Jess settled herself into the Golf's driving seat, firmly trying to convince herself she was not inclined to tears. You had to let your children go – their independence was proof that you'd got their upbringing right. If only it didn't happen so fast though, not quite so suddenly. Couldn't he have gone to live in say, Devon, for a few months instead? Why race off to the furthest continent? The car still smelled faintly of Oliver, a mixed scent of Lynx deodorant, Marlborough Lights and new trainers. She looked around quickly, half expecting to find a forgotten essential item, perhaps the All-Australia bus pass that Matt had bought him as a last-minute surprise or the *Rough Guide to Oz*, that backpackers' bible. He'd left nothing though, apart from his pack of chewing gum which lay among the petrol receipts and her own Starburst wrappers in the cubbyhole in front of the gear stick.

Eventually, mindful that she'd already paid for the parking and couldn't hang about, Jess started the car and wearily began the drive back to London. She switched on the radio and joined the middle of a discussion about ovarian cysts. '. . . Easily the size of a grapefruit . . .' she caught someone saying in alarmingly comfortable tones, before she speedily pressed buttons and settled for some house/techno sound that Oliver would have liked. She definitely didn't want to hear about female ailments: thirty seconds into it and she'd be prodding her side as she drove, wondering if there was a strange new lump or if her insides always resembled a loose bag of apples. Discussions like that, along with Facing the Menopause, The Empty Nest and Midlife Men: The Far Side of the Crisis, reminded her of the depressing fallibility of increasing age. So far Jess had escaped pretty well, health and looks more or less satisfactory. She went to the gym three times a week (with glamorous neighbour Angie, who provided, with only half the effort that Jess put in, a figure to aim for). When she read about *middle* age it had never occurred to her, so far, that this was *her* category. Oliver setting off on his travels was only the first of what was likely to be a string of mind-muggings waiting round life's shadier corners. Still, she thought as she headed for the M26, at least this week she wouldn't have a problem deciding on what to write. Nelson's Column in the *Sunday Gazette* (page four, the Comfort Zone supplement) would be about the first Gap Year departure from her household. It would be funny, frivolous and probably contain just a little bit of self-satisfaction. She wouldn't write about feeling bereft: readers could have their amusement but they weren't allowed into her soul.

'So can I have his room?' Natasha, being fifteen and therefore as yet with no instinct for the right time to ask for this kind of thing, was standing in Oliver's doorway checking over the stuff he'd left scattered around. From her teenage point of view, far from being bad timing, she'd picked this vulnerable just-back-from-the-airport moment quite deliberately, getting in quick before her sister Zoe thought of it and before Jess, still in her coat, had even had time to have a restorative cup of tea and a bit of a think.

Jess took in the sight of Oliver's discarded clothes, unsorted laundry, strewn-about tapes, CDs and videos (how many were long-overdue rentals, she wondered). Any miss-you poignancy this vision might have had was diminished by the scale of clearing up that it would need. This was the biggest of the three first-floor bedrooms, overlooking the front garden and giving anyone with a penchant for serious nosiness a good view of the road and all the neighbours' comings and goings. Natasha had always said it was wasted on Oliver: boys were neither interested in the pursuit of gossip nor did they need the kind of clothes capacity that girls did.

'It would make sense,' Natasha persisted, walking into the room and spreading out her long skinny arms to spin round and glory in the space. 'I mean, what did Oliver ever want with a double built-in wardrobe? It was wasted on him, always mooching about in the same old stuff. I bet it's full of old unwashed football kit left over from school.' She opened the door and held her nose, pulling a face of exaggerated disgust. 'Boy-pong. BO and feet. I could fumigate it for you. And *Mu-umm*,' a familiar wheedling note came into Natasha's voice, 'think how much tidier I could be if I had room to put all my stuff away. I'd keep it really organized, I promise.'

Jess almost wavered. There was plenty of space to absorb the collecting of teenage clutter. Natasha was very good at that: filling those extra square metres wouldn't even begin to present a challenge. In no time, if she took over this room, there would be new mountains of magazines, a minefield of shoes, a jumble of school books, cosmetics and underwear – in other words, exactly what was in her own room right now only more, much more, all spread about, an invasion, a positive coup d'état, of clutter. The thought was too depressing, but not quite as depressing as the certainty that if she gave in, it would be like admitting that Oliver had really gone for good, would only join them from now on as a short-term visitor. She wasn't ready for that, not yet.

'No I don't think you can.' Jess was going to be firm. 'After all, he is coming back you know.'

Natasha frowned. 'Yeah but not for ages, and even then not for long. He'll only be here for a few weeks and then it'll be time for university.' But she could see the battle was being lost and the voice rose to a wail,

'You know I've been wanting this room the whole of my *life*.'

'But did he say you could? You can't just . . .'

'He didn't say I couldn't.' Natasha flashed back fast, sensing a loophole. 'If he didn't want me to have it he'd have locked the door, wouldn't he, and put a note on it saying "Hands off, especially Tash". I mean what are you going to do with it? Leave it exactly like he left it like some sort of shrine? Cos if you are that's just grisly.'

Jess laughed. 'What, leave it like this to gather even more dust? Are you mad? No I just thought I'd tidy it up a bit and, well . . .'

'Yeah like I said, just leave it for when the perfect prodigal deigns to come back.'

Natasha, furious at not getting her immediate own way, swept past Jess, crashing against the door frame as she hurtled out. She whizzed into her own room (second biggest, peaceful, overlooking the back garden and the railway line beyond) and slammed the door shut after her. Jess felt the house shake and made her way downstairs, holding on tight to the banister rail in case the whole building collapsed as one day it surely must beneath the accumulated force of so many years of door-slammings. Natasha would be looking into the mirror now and trying to force herself to cry. The bang on the shoulder from the door frame would help, for even drama-queen Natasha found it difficult, now that she was close to sixteen, to force a tear simply from a feeling of being slightly hard done by. She wouldn't come out now, Jess reckoned, until she'd worked up a good half-hour's calculated sobbing and her puffed-up, pinked-up face would later descend to the kitchen for supper, apparently subdued and miserably acquiescent, to give Jess an opportunity to reconsider, because for sure this wouldn't be the last they'd hear of it.

Down in the sitting room fourteen-year-old Zoe was apparently peacefully doing her homework at Jess's desk by the big front window. She looked like someone posing as Girl Being Studious, her long flat fair hair trailing prettily over her hand as she wrote fast in her book. The television wasn't on, and that, coupled with the fact that Zoe usually did her homework either sprawled across the conservatory table or upstairs on her bedroom floor with music drowning out most of her thought processes, made Jess suspicious. It exhausted her, this feeling of being on her guard the whole time, wary that The Girls were constantly up to something. They made a formidable team, capable of serious manipulations in the interests of getting what they wanted. Sometimes she suspected they crept out of the house in the dead of night, shimmied down to the hazel copse on the common to call up witches and devils and concoct spells.

'Sorry Mum, did you want to use your desk?' Zoe looked up and smiled at her. Such a sweet smile, so artless. The confidence of truly perfect teeth. Jess almost relaxed.

'No, don't worry for now. You're OK there. What's wrong with your own room?' Too late, Jess realized she'd walked into a trap. Zoe's smile broadened. Triumph, Jess assumed.

'Oh, it's a bit cramped up there, especially for this geography stuff. You have to spread out the maps and things and then there's all the pages of statistics. It kept falling off the bed and I kept treading on it. Just not enough space really.' Zoe's face turned back to her

14

books, the carefully nurtured seed planted. If Natasha had Oliver's room, she could move up to Tash's . . .

Matthew Nelson hadn't expected to feel so elated. He was pretty sure that wasn't the usual reaction to being made redundant. Instead he felt as if he'd been let out of prison early, without even having to go to the trouble of good behaviour. He should be feeling depressed. He should be thinking in terms of scrap heaps and hopelessness and hiring someone expensive and slick to make the grovelling best of his CV. Right now, driving west along the Cromwell Road, he felt an overwhelming delight at being alive. '*I'm free!*' he sang along to an old Who track on the radio. '. . . *freedom tastes of reality . . .*' He punched the air out through the Audi's open sun roof and laughed, loud and madly. A passenger in a cab that pulled up next to him at the lights stared at him nervously as if he might be nuts enough to leap out and make a grab for him. Matt could tell from an awkward shoulder-wriggle that the man was surreptitiously checking that the door was locked and he grinned at him, including the alarmed stranger in his all-embracing new-found love for his fellow humans. We are all one, he thought in his euphoria, brothers and sisters beneath our over-important clothes and our tender skin, grafting away our short lives with not enough time to stop and smell the roses. Well, he'd have time now. He'd have time to tend them and prune them and deadhead them and mulch, spray and propagate as well if he felt like it. Everyone should have that kind of time. And an allocation of gorgeous, full-bloom, metaphorical roses. It should be neither a privilege nor a surprise.

Matt watched his fellow drivers hurtling along the

busy road, cutting in where they could, overtaking pointlessly just to be slowed at the next junction. Too many looked miserable, too many were gabbling anxiously into silly little phones, making sure they kept in contact, convincing themselves they were essential. That had been him yesterday, this morning even, before The Meeting, before, as had been euphemistically stated, 'Options' (which were no such thing) had been 'Put'. Now he knew better. Those who were hired could always be fired. The truly tricky bit was going to be telling Jess.

The boy was out by the railway again. It was the third time she'd seen him this week. Natasha wiped the tears away quickly and stared out of the window. She knew he couldn't see as much of her as she could see of him, but she still didn't want to look like some snively little kid. He might have super-vision, might be able to see the spot that was building itself up like a disgusting pus-filled volcano just under the skin above her left eyebrow. Even as she knew she was thinking the ridiculous, she flicked her hair about so fronds hung down over where she was sure the spot was pushing its way to the surface.

From her window the boy looked more than interesting: for one thing he shouldn't be where he was, down there on the rail side of the fence. It was dangerous, there were notices up everywhere about keeping off. He looked mysterious, unsettled. He wasn't really doing anything, he never was, he was just being there, mooching about as if he was deciding something that really mattered but was going to take his time over it. He must have walked along from the level crossing up by the main road, past the allotments where her grandad dug his vegetables most days. There was nowhere else you could get through on to the embankment, unless he'd come through someone else's garden and found a gap in the fence. She didn't think it would be his own garden he'd walked through. She didn't exactly know all the neighbours, nobody did – even the parents just said hello and not much else unless it was Christmas – but she hadn't seen him around before this week and no-one had done any house-moving. He wasn't wearing anything like a school uniform: even up at Briar's Lane Comp you weren't allowed to wear jeans with holey knees. Natasha ducked behind her curtain as he looked towards her window. She wondered if he'd actually seen her and hoped he hadn't. If he ever did look right at her, she wanted to be ready. If she put her light on he could hardly miss seeing her now that it was getting dusk, but with the remains of the tears, and the spot . . .

'Tasha! Supper's ready!' Zoe's voice bellowed up the stairs. Natasha was hungry, she realized, though she minded Zoe breaking the spell. She liked it being just her and the railway boy. They shared, if it was possible, their solitude. They were both alone, both lonely, both, she was sure, with stuff on their minds. She could have stayed and watched him, made a point to her mother that principles were more important than mere food. The problem was that they weren't. She was ravenous. She switched off the light and wondered if the boy had noticed. Perhaps he was looking at her window and hoping she'd be there again tomorrow.

'So, Olly got off all right?' Matt didn't go in for hello-and-how-was-the-day, he just walked in through the

17

door and launched straight in as if he'd nipped out of the kitchen five minutes ago to fetch something. It was a trick that tended to wrong-foot visitors who would wonder if they'd missed an earlier entrance, or if they were invisible or if Matt just hadn't had the kind of mother who believed in teaching basic manners at a more formative age. Jess used to find it endearing, this eagerness to get on with conversation and bypass time-wasting pleasantries. Way back, in younger and more passionate times, he'd stride into the house and enquire loudly if she fancied a quickie without bothering to check if there was some stranger peering into the cellar to read a meter or Angie from across the road guzzling coffee in the kitchen. Just now, Jess was adding basil to a salad and wondering whether Natasha had stopped sulking yet. Matt reached over and picked a piece of lettuce out of the bowl.

'Fine. He just . . . sort of fled; in fact it wasn't very flattering, he could hardly wait.'

'No big farewells then?' Matt kissed the back of her neck. She caught a hint of Scotch, along with the warm smoky musk of pubs. 'You should have sent him off to the airport by himself on the bus. If you don't get the full-scale "Gonna miss you, Mom" scene, then what's the point of going with them?' He chuckled in a private-joke sort of way. Jess frowned. He was going to miss Oliver just as much as she was, he didn't need to pretend to be beyond that . . . what? girly? stuff.

'Have you been to the pub?' she asked. Matt was leaning against the sink, very much in her way, and looking strangely pleased with himself. He was a tall, broad man who enjoyed the fact that people assumed he was younger than his forty-eight years. He'd taken off his tie. Jess could see it trailing from his jacket

18

pocket, crammed in roughly the way a schoolboy embarrassed about his uniform would. As she watched, he took off the jacket and hurled it at the back door.

'What was that for?' she asked, mystified. 'It's fallen on the cat's bowl!'

He shrugged and laughed and went to sit at the table, ignoring the crumpled jacket 'Who cares? I don't intend ever to wear a suit again.' He reached across the table, pulled the opened bottle of wine towards him and poured himself a glass. Pausing suddenly, he looked anxious for a moment. 'You won't bury me in one, will you, Jess? People tend to, I've heard. Promise you won't?'

She laughed. 'Of course I won't! You can wear the full Manchester United strip if you want. What's all this about? You're being very peculiar.'

'It would have to be the away strip, I suppose. Going to meet God is hardly a home fixture,' he mused, then admitted, 'yes I have had a drink. I dropped in at the Leo for a quick sharpener just now.'

'So you left work early then.' He could have had a drink at home, with me, Jess thought. He could have used a bit of imagination, worked out that she'd like a bit of sympathetic company on the day their eldest child took off for Australia for several months. It was surely an important end to something, a start to a new stage.

'You could have . . .' she began, then stopped. No point nagging. It only made her sound like a control freak. 'So why no suits? Has the firm gone in for a dress-down policy? You'll have to spend a fortune at Paul Smith to get the look right.'

'No. I'm just not going back.'

19

'Not going back where, Dad?' Natasha breezed into the kitchen and joined her father at the table. 'What's for supper?' she asked, leaning back on her chair and looking as if she was expecting full-scale waitress service, an attitude guaranteed to get Jess steaming mad.

'Nothing if you don't get the plates out of the oven,' Jess snapped. Matt topped up his wine glass and poured one for her, though rather, she noticed, as an afterthought.

'Not going back to work?' she asked him. 'What do you mean?'

'Why aren't you?' Zoe, catching up quickly, joined them in the kitchen.

Matt surveyed his audience, whose attention he certainly had, and smiled. 'Because I've been made redundant, that's why. I have cleared my desk, brought home the metaphorical spider plant and I'm out of there. For good.'

Jess stared at him as if gazing on a stranger. Matt had worked at Cranbourne Communications for twenty-two years. Public relations, editorial advising and journalists' jollies were part of his identity. His was the face that had launched a thousand press parties for everyone from political apologists to minor royalty and TV moguls with excuses to sell.

'Why? What have you done?' Natasha's face was full of excitement, as if her dad was a schoolboy caught smoking dope behind the gym and heading for expulsion.

'Nothing. I've been downsized. Down-and-out-sized. It's that simple. The computer revolution has finally kicked in so less of us are needed. That and the fact that younger people are cheaper, of course.'

Jess bent down to take the jacket potatoes out of the

oven. Her hands were shaking. She wished he'd told her earlier, come home and taken her out (to the Leo maybe . . .) so there would be just the two of them discussing this, talking through it, getting themselves past the shock stage. Instead she felt he'd cheated more than a bit, picked his moment when she was occupied, diddling about with domestic stuff and her concentration was divided. The girls were there too, as he'd known they would be. Did they really need to be for this?

'Will we have to leave our school and go to Briar's Lane?' Natasha's eyes sparkled at the prospect. Jess waited with interest for the answer. Tucked away inside it was what they all wanted to know: the 'what the hell do we live on?' question.

To Jess's fury, Matt laughed. 'No. I get paid full whack for six months, then it's final goodbye with a lump sum, a good one, and on with the rest of life. We could come out of it quids in.' He reached out and patted Jess on the behind. She twitched away out of reach as he went on, talking to Natasha and Zoe, 'And your famous mother's working, so everything's fine.'

'Fine? What's so bloody fine?' Jess slammed the dish of potatoes down on the table. 'You'll only be "quids in" as you put it if you get another job pretty damn fast. What the hell are you going to do, where are you going to find another job like that one at your age?'

There, it was out. The A-word. Jess knew the score even if Matt didn't; the world was full of redundant men of his age – Jesus, there were even three here in the Grove – refugees from comfortable careers in midlife like stodgy complacent wives discarded for racy younger models. Matt could end up like Wandering Wilf who paced the south-west London streets all day, pretending he had a deep sense of purpose and telling anyone who asked that he was writing a whole novel in his head.

'I don't want another job "like that one" as you put it,' Matt said quietly as he reached across towards the steaming chicken casserole. 'Don't spoil it, Jess. This is the best day of my life.'

Two

. . . Tidying a teenager's room is like archaeology: over the years the chaos forms time-capsule layers beneath a crust of abandoned school work. At the top lie lager cans, surf magazines, long-lost videos and ticket stubs from recent gigs. Dig a little further (preferably in stout gloves) and you unearth an early Gameboy, a wheelless skateboard and . . .

Jess stopped typing and stared out of the window. The lupins by the front garden wall had the first signs of the blight that afflicted them every year. Someone had suggested it might be to do with living under the Heathrow flight path, it being a kind of unquestioned local assumption that excess fuel was jettisoned freely as the planes came in to land, though no-one had yet come up with a good explanation as to why this should affect only lupins. Surely they couldn't be the only kerosene-sensitive plants? If you took notice of the frantic headlines in the local paper, things fell off, or out of, planes fairly constantly. Frozen sewage had crashed through the windows of a primary school, a poor dead stowaway had once plummeted onto a building site and a bit of a wing (luckily, for the passengers, not a crucial bit) had demolished a greenhouse on the allotments. Eddy-up-the-road walked with his face permanently pointed at the sky so as not to miss the inevitable mid-air collision (and potentially profitable I-saw-it-happen statements to the press) that he was sure was imminent. Whatever was falling now, the lupins' leaves were starting to go that sad greyish colour. Soon they'd wilt and struggle, the flowers would be stunted and contorted and huge fat bugs would seize the vulnerable moment and move in for the kill. Jess wondered why she persevered with them. She should give up on the bloody things, she knew as she stared out at them; plant delphiniums instead and ring-fence them with slug pellets. Her father couldn't understand why she didn't turn over every bit of earth for organic vegetables but she was sticking with the lupins: she couldn't decide if it was simply because she was a hopeless optimist that she trailed home with a box full of them every spring from the garden centre, or because she was too stubborn to give in and admit defeat.

Across the road Angie, in her sleek baby-blue Ellesse tracksuit, hauled her DKNY gym bag out of her Discovery and unlocked her front door. Jess felt guilty; it should have been one of her own days for tone-and-groan (as Matt so sweetly put it) but she'd felt too vulnerable to face one of those jacuzzi tell-all sessions that she and Angie would inevitably have. Angie, divorced and with children boarding somewhere near Oxford, liked to think she was sensitive to her friends' inner tensions. She had time for them, she said, and enough of life's harsh experiences under her belt (and below her belt, rumour had it) to be both worldly-wise and impartial. She would persuade, with a light touch to the hand and an almost whispered, 'Come on, you know you can tell *me*' and it would all be out. The least Jess felt she should do was discuss Matt's redundancy with him before she confided in anyone else. From the collective household attitude so far, she was the only one who considered it something of a disaster. The girls seemed to think it was almost as thrilling as a large-scale lottery win. As he'd become more and more euphoric and expansive over dinner they'd ceremoniously recruited him as an honorary Idle Teenager in temporary replacement for Oliver and suggested he pop down to Tesco for a shelf-stacking job on the late shift. Matt had actually looked as if he might give it some serious thought. She could anticipate Oliver's e-mailed response when she got round to telling him: it would be 'Choice, cool'.

Jess read over what she'd written – a few hundred words of lightweight rambling on the delights of sorting the absent Oliver's bedroom, along with a hint of the poignancy of nest-flying. Five hundred or so words to go. There would be letters from readers after this one: some would tell her sad tales of teenagers who'd left at fifteen and never come back, others would tell her off for clearing up after someone who was legally a grown-up. One or two would rail about the pampering of boys and how mothers like her did not do their sons' future partners any favours by collecting up mould-encrusted coffee cups and giving them a wash. Only she would know that she hadn't actually had time to make a start on the room at all yet but, with the deadline only hours away, was making up her column as she went along; this was, after all, the entertainment end of journalism: you had to be part actor, part novelist, part sit-down comic.

Upstairs, as if to make up for the lack of Oliver's idle oversleeping presence, Matthew was huddled under the duvet snoring away the effects of too much of last night's red wine.

'No reason not to,' he'd said as he'd opened a second bottle. Natasha had smirked. 'What about your liver?' she'd said, saving Jess the trouble of mentioning it herself.

'Hey Tash, it's not every day you get your life back,' he'd replied, waving his glass around with cheery expansiveness and looking generally as if he'd discovered Santa was real.

Had the job really been that bad? Jess wondered now. Matt had never seemed unhappy, certainly never said he was, but then again it was something she couldn't recall that she'd actually asked him. You didn't watch someone come home from the same job every day for twenty-two years and expect to find new, fascinating things to say about it. Matthew only talked about work when there was something amusing to report. Occasionally he had mentioned tricky clients: the Oscar nominee who'd demanded a large-scale press briefing and then refused to discuss her film role but had plenty to say on veganism, or the clothes designer who'd assumed that public relations was something to do with Matthew procuring under-age boys for him. Out at parties or dinners, Matt didn't go into detail about his work. When asked he'd say he was in PR, in the kind of voice that made it sound too boring for further questions. He'd neatly deflect any remaining curiosity by asking what the questioner did

26

and then feign staggering fascination with whatever reply he got, whether it was accountancy, greengrocery or painting the scarlet noses on garden gnomes. Whatever his previous reticence, it would certainly have to be talked about now, along with the big question – What Next?

According to the clock in the top corner of Jess's i-Book it was coming up to eleven and there was still no sign that he intended to get up. Monica, coming in to clean, had been lied to and been asked to tiptoe around as Matt 'had a migraine'. Monica had given her a raised-eyebrow 'oh really?' look and Jess had felt a vague shame about not telling her the truth – after all, everyone would know soon enough that it would be for a hell of a lot more than just one day that Matt would be off work. But then there was the thought that Monica, the next morning, would be cleaning (and chatting) down the road at Clarissa Hamilton's. Jess needed a few more days to get used to the idea, work out some way of deciding Matt's jobless state wasn't so world-shattering, before she could fend off neighbourly nosiness disguised as sympathy.

Jess read yet again the first couple of paragraphs of her piece and tried to put herself back into the necessary light-hearted mood that identified her style. This was where the acting aspect came in, thinking herself into character before she could get on with the performance. . . . *And under the bed, half a plate of spaghetti bolognese, crusted over like lava on a long-dormant volcano . . .*

There wasn't really a plate of food under Oliver's bed, anything left over and edible would have gone straight into Donald the cat, but it was the kind of detail the readers liked. Domestically, she had to come

27

across as just that tiny bit more of a slattern than was strictly acceptable, give an impression of colourful barely-coping muddle. As in a TV sitcom, her children had to be just that bit more of a trial, though likeable if you dug deep enough, and her husband . . .

'God my head!' Matt's body slumped down onto the sofa. He was wearing his ancient navy blue towelling robe that had been pulled into long thready loops by Donald in his fond-kitten days.

'That wine must have been full of dodgy chemicals. I won't be buying any of that again.' He ran his hands through his fair hair. It stayed sticking up, making him look like a scruffy schoolboy from a bygone age. Jess smiled at him, just managing to stop herself from pointing out that without his income there wouldn't be much more in the way of wine-buying.

She'd thought about it in bed the night before as she lay awake wondering if, long term, Natasha had had a point: would the girls have to leave the Julia Perry school? At least her father would be thrilled about that: George had called Jess a traitor to her class for sending them to a private school – but then he'd said the same when she and Matt had got a mortgage to buy their first flat. 'A millstone' he'd called it, believing firmly then in the kind of state-owned rentable property, allocated according to need, that Soviet Russia went in for. Would they have to sell the house? Would Matt ever be employed again? He wasn't far off fifty, which, in terms of the dynamic young bods in charge of recruitment, was just on the edge of death. She'd gone over and over all those early-hours questions that hadn't, given the help of all that alcohol, lost Matt any sleep.

'Sorry, were you working?' Matt's head rose a little from his hands as he looked at her.

'Just doing my piece for Sunday after next. It's due in today,' she told him. 'Your eyes look terrible, all puffy and half shut.'

'That's the sun's fault. It's too bright. It should be more considerate.' He groaned and got up, heading for the kitchen. 'Any coffee on the go?' He held on tight to the doorpost, his face contorted into exaggerated angst and agony.

Jess laughed at him and he grimaced at her ruthlessness. 'Only for Monica and I think she's had it already. If you're making one I wouldn't mind, that's if you're up to it . . .'

'Not sure.' Matt tottered through the doorway. 'But for you I'll try.'

Jess grinned to herself as she added a couple more sentences. This was almost like having Oliver back, reminding her of the many Sunday mornings (or early afternoons) when he'd sworn himself off alcohol for life (maybe a day or two in reality) and tried to get away with doing nothing more useful than lying on the sofa like a Victorian consumptive, too fragile to clear a table or peel so much as a single carrot for lunch, and absolutely, definitely, *positively* not in a state to tackle any A-level physics revision. She wondered where he was – he'd still be travelling, she guessed. The flight to Singapore must have been about twelve hours, then on to Cairns for at least another six.

'When can we expect to hear from the wandering boy, do you think?' Matt had come back with the coffee and managed, with worryingly trembling hands, to get the slopped-over drops on the desk but not on Jess's keyboard. He settled himself on the sofa again.

'He promised to e-mail as soon as he could,' she told him. 'He seemed sure he'd find somewhere easily enough to do it from though he hasn't yet, I checked.'

'The whole place is probably covered with Internet cafés, full of backpackers calling home to plead for a cash top-up. I hope he leaves it a good few weeks before he starts on that one.'

'Mmm. Me too.' She swivelled the leather chair round and looked at him. 'Matt, we should talk about what's going to happen now, about you, and work and stuff.'

Matthew stood up abruptly and made for the door again, showing an amazing and instant recovery of agility. 'Fine, we will, but not just now, OK? Time for a shower.' He turned back then and grinned at her. 'We could go out to lunch though, chat then. I could be a feature you're writing, an interviewee, tax deductable.' He winked and left her alone. Jess heard him climbing the stairs, fast at first, presumably to get out of range of further questions, and then more slowly as he started on the next flight up to the big converted attic which had been their bedroom (plus bathroom) for the past four years. Perhaps she and Matt should move back down the stairs and take over Oliver's room themselves, get a lodger or two for the attic and help supplement the forthcoming lack of income. They could put an ad in *Loot*, 'Non-smoking professional with a busy off-premises social life and somewhere else to go at the weekends . . .'

She sighed and went back to her piece. Perhaps one day she'd be able to write about all this, in her light-hearted, joky, doesn't-really-matter kind of way, but somehow she doubted it. At the moment she seemed to be the only one who was taking this redundancy seriously.

*   *   *

Natasha and her friend Claire were perched on the cloakroom bench, their bodies woven among the coats for camouflage and their feet well up off the floor in case any of the staff felt like doing a quick check for lingerers. They were supposed to be outside playing netball, a game most girls of their age considered about as interesting as cabbage-growing. There were murmurings of other skivers from various corners of the room and a smoke-laden draught wafted in from the open window where someone had, at the risk of a term's worth of detentions, lit up a Marlborough.

'So what does he look like?' Claire was eager for details. Natasha thought for a moment before she answered. It had been a lot of truth-stretching to tell Claire that the boy definitely went to the railway line every evening just to look up at her window, and even more of a lie to say that he'd waved and tried to get her to come down. It was one thing to imagine the way you wanted the truth to be, another just to come out with those imaginings and hope that somehow they would work their way into being real. She hoped she hadn't pushed the fates too far – chances were now that she'd started talking to Claire about him he might just disappear and never come back.

'Well,' she hesitated, recalling what she'd actually seen of him in the dusky half-light. 'He's quite tall, though it's hard to tell when you're looking down at someone. He's got dark hair and it's a bit long, too long, like he used to have a good cut once but he's let it grow.'

'What was he wearing?' Claire cut to the all-important question. Natasha hesitated again. Claire was the sharpest-edged fashion-observer of their year. There were girls who wouldn't even go near Top Shop for a simple pair of trousers without feeling they should run the various options past Claire first for approval. 'Not *combats!*' she'd shrieked when Polly Mathers had talked about what she'd worn to a party a couple of weeks before. 'Combats are *so* dead!' Natasha might be pretty much up there with the knowledge about what *she* should be wearing but didn't really have much of a clue about what the coolest clothes were that blokes could select. Oliver had been no use as a guide – when he'd started saving up for Australia he'd got a job in the Gap and worn nothing but staff-discount sale stock. Claire had sneered that he looked like a keen, clean business studies student, quite beneath interest. Natasha hadn't dared tell her she'd liked (and borrowed) several of his sweaters.

'Er . . . well I couldn't really see too clearly. It's a long way down,' she said eventually.

'It's not that far. Shoes then . . . Nikes, Cats, what?' Claire twiddled the ends of her perfect striped-blond chin-length hair, checking for highly unlikely split ends.

'Definitely couldn't see shoes. And I don't care about shoes anyway.' Claire gasped at the near-sacrilege and Natasha laughed. 'Come on Claire, even you wouldn't reject the perfect boy just because his shoes were the wrong make!'

Claire wrinkled her freckled nose. 'Well he wouldn't *be* the perfect boy with the wrong shoes, would he? Beyond considering. So go on, when are you seeing him again? Tonight?'

'Possibly. Hope so anyway.' Natasha said it slowly, crossing her fingers with the wish that it might be true. 'He didn't actually say.' She felt more confident now that she was back on the truth-track. 'But I'll look out for him and, well, who knows.'

Claire's face screwed up in puzzlement. 'One thing though, what's he doing hanging about on the railway line? Is he suicidal but doesn't dare . . .'

'Jeez, I hope not. Romance shattered before it starts.'

' . . . Or has he got no home to go to? Where is he living, do you think?'

'I don't know. But I've got to find out. He's not like, well . . .'

'Yeah I know . . .' Claire laughed. 'The saddo tossers from St Dominic's who think they can impress their way into your knickers by waffling on about A-level options and their mummy's ski lodge in Verbier.'

'Exactly. This one's . . .'

'An exciting bit of forbidden rough.' Claire leaned forward and whispered it, sounding harsh and strangely lascivious – as well as deeply envious. The thought made Natasha shiver – whoever he was, the railway boy definitely had an air of being someone who was, well, off limits in all senses.

'OK, I'm ready for the interrogation now.' Matthew presented himself, showered and dressed, next to Jess's desk just as she was pressing the 'send' button to deliver Nelson's Column to the *Sunday Gazette*.

'Where do you fancy for lunch? Shall we see if there's room at the River Café? We could go mad, get a cab . . .'

Jess laughed. 'You are joking aren't you? I thought we could just have a sandwich, here. That's what I usually do. I had no idea your working day was quite so glamorous.'

Matt shrugged. 'It isn't, *wasn't*, I suppose I should say. Well not all the time. I just thought as it's the two of us, and you might need cheering up now Oliver's gone, well I thought we could treat ourselves. Still, if you'd rather not . . .'

'No, it's not that. It's just . . . anyway they've never got room, you have to book ages ahead. We could just walk up the road to the Leo, the food's not bad. Angie and I go there sometimes.'

Matt laughed. 'I'm surprised Angie comes out in daylight. Apart from going to the gym for a bit of pampering I always imagine she spends the days in a coffin waiting for nightfall. Does the woman have any kind of job?'

'Not really. She says that if David can still afford to run her as well as his new wife there's no point in taking employment from those who need it more. She does a bit of charity stuff.'

'Charity stuff! Ladies' lunches that nobody eats to raise a few quid for the starving millions.'

Jess frowned. 'Where's this new cynicism come from all of a sudden? You've never talked like this before.'

Matthew disappeared into the cloakroom and returned with his favourite crumpled navy linen jacket. 'I've never been out of work before,' he said.

The Leone Rosso (translated from the old Red Lion after much council wrangling and known locally as the Leo) was always busy at lunchtimes. Ben and Micky, subject to occasional speculation as to whether they shared more than the Leo, had been joint landlords for the two years since the Red Lion pub's frayed lino had finally been ripped away from the fine old floorboards beneath and the tattered beige anaglypta peeled from the walls and replaced by cerulean paint and flat plain mirror. The pair had done their best to select all the most useful bits of what the local clientele required in a place to eat and drink, and come up with a clever mixture of Italian restaurant, coffee shop, pub, wine bar and delicatessen. Those who worked in the area found it an excellent place to take clients – relaxed enough for friendly discussion but with food good enough for people to feel business was being taken seriously. This green and pleasant part of south-west London also teemed with self-employed creatives who liked to do their bit of mixing with humanity by popping out during the day for salami and melted Brie in a baguette with a glass of something red and fortifying. After a chat with Ben about the price of Parmesan, a browse through the *Daily Mail* (just to check on gossip) and a double espresso it didn't seem quite so lonely returning to a solitary desk to wrestle with a complex film treatment, a plot-sluggish novel or the dreaded VAT.

Matthew felt as if he was about to be debriefed. It was Jess who'd marched in first and chosen the table, at the back of the restaurant well away from the bar and remote enough from other occupied tables to put off casual acquaintances from drifting over to say hello.

'I don't want a stream of people coming up to you and saying "Don't often see you in here," and then expecting you to tell them why you are,' Jess said firmly as she perused the menu. Matt didn't need to be told that, and neither did Micky serving at the bar, who had merely nodded a brief greeting as Jess strode past, as if instinctively recognizing that this lunch had more purpose than the merely social.

Matthew had been tempted to put on a humble face, touch his forelock and say, 'No, Miss' but thought better of it. There was too much of an air of things waiting to be said, though only by Jess. He, being almost deliriously happy with life as a newly liberated, Job-Free Man, had nothing to say, nothing at all. It was all he could do to stop his face cracking up into grins and laughter.

'It's not as if I'm never in here,' he argued feebly, but then resigned himself to selecting food.

'OK, penne Amatriciana for me,' he said. 'And shall we have a bottle of something? Just something light?'

'After last night?' Jess's blue eyes were wide over the top of the menu. 'I've got to work this afternoon. Some of us have got a deadline.' He could see her wavering though, and beckoned to the waiter.

'But you've just sent the column in. Do they want the week after's as well?'

Jess sighed. 'No, this one's an extra. It's pretty tragic. A kid at a school up north jumped off the dormitory roof. It was in the papers, last week. The *Independent* rang up and asked for fifteen hundred words on parents who send their kids away to board and then lose track of the plot, haven't a clue who their friends are, what they get up to, all that.'

'I thought it was part of every teenager's master plan to make their parents lose the plot, boarding or not.'

She laughed. 'I'm sure you're right, the difference is I get paid to explain that to people.'

The words 'I get paid' stood out as if flashed up in neon. Matthew wondered if he was being ludicrously sensitive or if life from now on was going to be peppered with what felt like little digs. He didn't like it, he felt as if she was trying to puncture his balloon of euphoria.

'I still get paid too,' he reminded her. There was a

36

small silence while Ben brought Matthew's penne and Jess's fusilli carbonara and faffed about with Parmesan and pepper. He then fussed with the bottle, taking an age to draw the cork and pour the wine.

'I know you do,' she conceded eventually. 'But that's just for now. Six months goes so fast and, Matt,' she put down her fork and leaned forward, looking deep into his eyes as if to extract some extra truth, 'aren't you worried *at all*? Not the teeniest bit?'

'No' would be the strictly honest answer, but it didn't seem to be one that Jess would be able to deal with, not comfortably. Being free of his job had left Matthew with space for something wondrously selfish – the feeling of absolute non-responsibility. It wouldn't last, he knew, but for now – well he just wanted to hang onto that for a while, at least till he had to hand the Audi back and a bit of inconvenience kicked in.

'No I'm not really worried. Something will turn up,' he told her, recognizing even as he spoke that this was a limp and inadequate response.

Jess's eyes flashed fury. 'God, Matt! Be real for a minute! You're pushing fifty. Well-paid jobs don't just "turn up" for anyone these days, let alone people of . . .'

'Of my age. Yes I know. But, well, I've got a track record, and of course,' he added, assuming she'd appreciate a bit of humour, 'I did go to Cambridge.'

She didn't appreciate it. 'So what? So did thousands of others. Half of those are probably looking for work too. Can't you be serious? Just for once?'

Matt reached across and took hold of her hand. 'Look, we won't be destitute. Even after six months there's the lump sum, six scrumptious figures. With any luck we'll simply be able to stash that and I'll have something else to move on to. But in the meantime Jess, I really want to take some time to do a bit of thinking. I don't want to end my working life as a referee between fame-greedy celebs, power-drunk politicians and the scandal-chasing press. It's not a job for a grown-up.' He laughed for a moment. 'Which is probably why I'm not considered suitable to do it any more. I'm happy, really, leaving it all to eager young careerists called Prudence and Peregrine. And anyway,' he added with a grin, 'it's not as if you're not working, is it?'

Jess made her way slowly and thoughtfully through the generously portioned bowl of fusilli. She was working, it was true, though not earning anything like the amount it took to keep five bodies and souls, one cat, her car and a house together. Ever since her book *Teen Spirit: Potent Stuff*, a lively romp through what every parent would rather not know, had become a best-seller a couple of years before, she'd been in demand to write for every newspaper and magazine whenever there was a teenage crisis in the news. She'd written pieces on pregnant twelve-year-olds, shoplifting crazes, fat camps, body piercing and the pointless rip-off of work-experience placements. On radio she'd commented on sad suicides who'd hung themselves for being a grade short of Oxbridge, on the expulsion-for-drugs question and whether girls should still, in this new century, be banned from school for wearing trousers. All the while her *Gazette* column, light, frothy and snug-family based, came out every week and, over a year, just about covered Natasha's and Zoe's school fees.

'. . . so it's a matter of finding something different,

satisfying, inspiring, all that,' Matthew was saying.

'And that pays as well as your old job? You'll be lucky.' Jess laughed.

He shrugged. 'Or that doesn't.'

'Yo Matthew! What're you doing out here on a Wednesday? Taking a sickie?' Eddy-up-the-road, brandishing a bottle of Heineken, pulled up a chair and, uninvited, joined their table.

'You're on enemy territory, man. Weekdays this is self-employed skivers, old rockers like me and women only.'

Matt laughed. 'You got a category for unemployed?'

'Really? You out of work? Fired?' Matt nodded.

'Welcome to the club!' Eddy grinned at Jess and pointed at the wine bottle. 'Fancy another? Celebrate Matt's release from the daily grind?'

'What's to celebrate?' Jess asked.

Eddy nudged Matthew and winked at him. 'Plenty to celebrate, plenty! He can join our gang.'

'Gang?' Jess giggled. 'You sound like something out of *Just William*.'

'Oh we are.' Eddy leaned forward, his long, thinning dyed-brown hair dangling on the table. He smelled rather prettily of rose water. 'There's me and Micky and Ben and a couple of others, you know, we go round, have fun, make trouble. Sometimes we even get Wandering Wilf to stop his marching and sit with us for a bit. A new face is always welcome.'

Jess called Ben over for the bill, but he brought another bottle of wine instead. Matthew and Eddy looked at each other and at the bottle. Ben pulled up another chair and sat down with them.

There was an air of inevitability. Jess could see some kind of session looming. 'OK, I'll leave you to it, Matt.

39

I've got to get some work done so I'll see you later. Bye all of you. Have fun.'

'Oh we will,' Eddy called after her. As she neared the door she could hear the three of them giggling together and caught the words 'Out on the loose'. She didn't want to think about which one had said them.

Three

Natasha's school bag was too heavy and as she trudged home from the bus stop she imagined it must feel exactly like this to lug along a dead body in a sack. It was certainly almost as depressing a load. Julia Perry High School gave them far too much homework in her (and just about everyone in the school's) opinion. She was very much in envy of Mel, a former friend from primary school, who had gone at eleven to Briar's Lane comprehensive and now spent a lot of after-school leisure time hanging round in the square in front of the Leo, smoking and mucking about with her mates. It was the kind of aimless, can-kicking hanging about that the grown-up Grove residents disapproved of, as if the term Crime Wave was the definitive collective noun for more than three teenagers grouped together. Natasha would love to join in, just so she could some-times feel less as if she was on a schoolwork treadmill heading towards a string of A-grade GCSEs. It wasn't as if Mel's school did exams that were any different from hers either, and Mel had been clever enough, but Briar's Lane wasn't frantically keeping up a league-table position. She and Mel didn't really talk any more though, just nodded a shy hello like a pair of old lags acknowledging long-past shared crimes.

People from different schools didn't mix much, except on summer Saturday or Sunday nights down on the riverside where there'd be some intermingling. The boys, when it came to the question of who'd spilled whose drink, would occasionally intermingle to the extent of throwing a puny punch. A girl might get up enough social courage to ask a stranger either a) where she'd bought that skirt or b) what did she think she was looking at? Mel had a harsh bawdy laugh that Claire said was loud enough to shatter Kookai's shop window and sometimes on hot nights, when Natasha was battling with maths up in her bedroom, she was sure she could hear it above the high-street traffic.

There was music coming from Eddy-up-the-road's house. As she walked towards it she recognized the twangy, dated guitar sound of his one big hit. According to her mum he'd been famous in his time, a singer with some tired Seventies group called Spidercrunch that Natasha had never heard of. He was retired now, which she considered good news: his seemed to be one of the few wrinkly old bands that wasn't forever trying to relight a burned-out career, cluttering up the charts and making themselves look stupid trying to seem cool on *Top of the Pops*. Her dad had said Eddy existed on ever-decreasing royalties topped up by occasional revival concerts, Internet re-issues and once, cringe-makingly, she'd seen him on the Who-Did-He-Used-To-Be? line-up on *Never Mind the Buzzcocks* where he'd been dressed in a frilled pirate shirt, introduced as Never-Ready Eddy and looked as if he was about to weep. Eddy's windows didn't have any curtains at all, not even in winter, as a kind of anti-suburbia style statement. There wasn't a single resident of the Grove who didn't slow their pace to stare into the purple-walled, knocked-through sitting room with its scarlet piano and cowhide-and-chrome-trimmed bar, complete with a full range of spirits in proper optics. Now, as Natasha hauled her burden past Eddy's, she could see the back of her father's head through the window. He was sprawled on the pink paisley sofa and she could tell by the way his shoulders shook and his head went back that he was laughing. He didn't often laugh like that at home. Perhaps, she thought, it was something to do with not having a job any more. She could quite see that not having to go to work would make you very, very happy.

The boy from the railway was leaning against the gatepost outside number 46, almost opposite Natasha's own house. She felt a lurching pang of shock when she looked up and realized it was him. Did he, she wondered immediately, know that it was *her*? Had he ever actually noticed her? As she drew level she slowed down, keen to make contact of some sort but unsure how not to make a complete idiot of herself. He was taller than she'd thought he'd be, dressed completely in black (ancient-looking leather jacket that looked like he'd stolen it from a dead biker, scuffed combats, black Converse shoes, all noted to report to Claire).

'Hi.' His voice was so quiet that for a moment Natasha wondered if she'd imagined that he'd spoken. She stopped and turned to look at him. He wasn't smiling. He was still leaning on the gatepost, his hands in his pockets and his shoulders hunched as if it was cold, though it was a bright spring day with a lazy late-afternoon warmth.

'You live over there?' The boy's head indicated her own house across the road and she looked over at the vase of purple and white stocks that her mother had put on her desk in front of the window. The room would be full of their scent.

'Yeah.' Natasha could feel her face turning pink. He must have seen her looking at him. She stared down at her feet, willing the blush to disappear.

'I've seen you,' he said, 'up at your window. You were watching me.'

'Not really.' She felt offended by his conceit. 'I mean if you muck about on a busy railway line you can't expect people not to watch, can you?'

'What, in case I get run over by a train? You want to make sure you don't miss that.'

Natasha laughed. 'Too right. Not much happens round here. Don't want to miss the big event.'

He was smiling now, a crooked grin but perfect teeth. His hair didn't look very clean – it was too long, and a dull dark brown as if he'd spent a lot of time in a dusty room. He looked about nineteen. She didn't think he could be younger, he was too cocky.

'So is that your bedroom, round the back, where I see you?' The soft, low tone to his voice made the question sound mildly obscene and Natasha could feel the blush coming back.

'Yes. I do my homework up there too. That's why I see you – it's not like I'm looking out specially.' She felt confused, defensive. 'Anyway, where do you live, what are you doing out there?'

The boy shrugged. 'I live down by the allotments. Can't miss it, it's the blue Sierra.'

Natasha was puzzled for a second. 'You live in a *car*? No-one lives in a car!'

The boy shrugged again. 'They do. I do. Not all the time, but for now. It's a good car. Any chance of a cup of tea?' He flashed her a devastating smile, confident of a yes-answer.

'Er . . .' Natasha thought quickly. Was anyone home? Did she want them to be?

'It's OK, your mother's in. I saw her,' he said. 'I'm good at mothers.'

Jess flicked through her index cards and tried to remember the last time she'd written a piece about what the girls were currently wearing. It was a good old standby when she was running short on ideas, and the one that had started her off as a journalist. 'Shop Horror' had been the tag-line of the first piece she'd ever written: a fast, furious thousand words blending outrage with amusement sent on spec to the *Gazette*, all sparked off by catching sight of black lace hold-up stockings for six-year-olds, along with lurex bra-tops and miniature G-strings, in a nationwide high-street store. Who on earth, she'd thought, would dress their child up to be a paedophile's wet dream? Would a girl hardly out of babyhood really feel comfortable (in fact did anyone, really?) in cheese-wire knickers? The features editor had enjoyed her style, printed the piece only days later, invited her to send in occasional articles as and when she thought of them and then, after the success of *Teen Spirit,* offered her the column she was still writing.

Jess counted backwards, working out that over that time there wasn't much about her trio of adolescents she hadn't covered. She'd written about changing

45

schools, the deep traumas of broken friendships, first periods, exam pressure, dead pets, school trips – just about everything that the average broadsheet-reading family would recognize. It seemed a bit desperate to recycle old articles but the only new topic on her mind at the moment was Matt's redundancy. It didn't seem to be on his, though, and she felt as if she was thinking ahead (in the general direction of ruin and disaster) for the two of them.

It was getting late and Matt still hadn't returned from the Leo and the girls would be back any minute. Her afternoon had been busy – busy enough for her to push away the waves of panic about the future. She'd roughed out the piece for the *Independent*, taken chilli con carne out of the freezer for supper and put together a salad to go with it, phoned the plumber about the strange whining noise from the pipes in the loft, checked her e-mails for any word from Oliver (nothing yet) and scooped up the first heap of his abandoned laundry into the washing machine. A small moth of resentment was fluttering inside her. Matt was going to swan back home in his own time (for all time was his own now, wasn't it?), in a good mood, relaxed, pissed as a rat and looking for a snack to sponge up the alcohol. He'd open the fridge, forage around picking up the yoghourts and commenting on long-gone best-before dates, then he'd rummage in the bread bin, make a toasted honey sandwich and leave crumbs and three knives covered in butter and gloop scattered around on the worktop. After that he'd start on the crisps, which would make him thirsty again and she'd hear the swoosh of a can of beer being opened . . . She took a deep breath and reminded herself that although all this might be about to happen, there was no point getting herself worked up into a fury when it actually hadn't yet. And, more important, there was no point complaining when it did. Matt wasn't a child, he was entitled to live as he chose in his own home. He'd be pretty sure to point that out too.

'Mum? Are you in?' Natasha's head appeared round the door. Jess waited for the rest of Natasha to follow but she kept herself draped across the doorway, blocking the space, waiting.

'Oh hi Tash, good day?' The girl looked shifty and Jess took another large breath and waited to hear that she'd been expelled, got pregnant or robbed the post office. Might as well get all possible disasters out in the open in the same week, she thought, surrendering herself to the worst that fate could deal.

'Not bad, just usual. Er, Mum, I've got someone here. Can we go and make a cup of tea?'

'Well of course you can! Why do you think you need to ask all of a sudden? Oh and one for me while you're at it, please Tash.'

She heard the two pairs of footsteps thumping towards the kitchen. Mildly suspicious, for who was this mystery person? Jess got up to follow, to go – on the pretence of finding biscuits – and meet the friend whom she had not, and she was sure it was no oversight, been allowed to see. She retrieved her shoes from where she always kicked them off under the desk and wasted a few minutes shuffling papers around.

'There's a new pack of chocolate Hobnobs in the cupboard.' Jess loudly announced her impending arrival from halfway down the hall, recalling quite well that it was a teen law as unchallengeable as that of gravity that friends you didn't introduce to your mother had to be of the opposite sex. She was sure that neither of them would want her to catch them in a passionate clinch crushed against the fridge.

Natasha was leaning back against the sink, her arms folded across her front and her long caramel-coloured hair hiding much of her face. The boy, a lanky, dark-clad creature, was sprawled across two of the kitchen chairs. He had a sort of slender elegance about him, taking up a lot of space without looking awkward. There was a vague stale smell of cigarettes and the not-so-elegant hint of feet, a sharply remembered tang of Oliver.

'Oh hello,' Jess said brightly, grinning at the boy, 'I'm Jess, Natasha's mother. I'll just find those biscuits for you.' Natasha scowled but knew well enough the process for getting her mother out of the way.

'Er, Mum this is . . .'

'I'm Tom. Hello.' The boy didn't stand up (did any of them?) but held out his hand to shake hers. She felt quite touched by his formality – unheard of in youth, and he couldn't be much older than Natasha – and by his rather pitiful air of neglect. His hair could do with a wash and his hands looked as if they'd spent several months working on car engines in garages that didn't quite run to Swarfega. She guessed that he wasn't a St Dominic's pupil – the boys from there had that scrubbed, fresh-faced eager look as if they were all about to become those terribly young and vulnerable-looking policemen. This one, with a silver arrow pierced through his eyebrow (which wasn't allowed even at Briar's Lane), his general dustiness and shadowy eyes, looked . . . well dangerous, attractively dangerous. Jess busied herself putting biscuits onto a plate, adding more milk to her tea. She could feel

Natasha's tension beside her. 'So Tom, are you from round here?'

There was a suppressed groan from Natasha. 'Go ahead Mum, why don't you ask him for . . . what's it called when you go for a job? References?'

'I live round the corner, up the road. By the allotments,' Tom told her, ignoring Natasha. He gave Jess a lazy, catlike smile, his large dark eyes narrowing. 'Natasha told me her grandad's got an allotment. They're neat, up there, like all the owners really care.'

'They do,' Jess told him. 'My father has had his for forty years. The council keep threatening to sell the land off for housing but these old gardeners are tough opposition. Dad's declared his patch the People's Republic of SW14 and run a flag up on his shed.'

Tom laughed. 'The shed that's bright red? That's one cool shed. What's the flag?'

'Good old-fashioned hammer and sickle. Dad never quite got over the break-up of Soviet Russia. It depressed him no end. He's away in Cuba just now, having a look at the last bastion of true Communism while Fidel Castro's still in charge.'

'Tom doesn't want to know . . .' Natasha hissed the words at her.

'Oh I do!' he told her. 'People's families are interesting. Specially if you don't have one.'

'Don't you?' Jess sat down and looked at him. No wonder he looked so neglected. If he was a dog, Battersea would need to tidy him up a fair bit before he was put up for rehoming. Natasha was glaring at her, but Jess wasn't going to be sent away, not just yet.

'Oh, I've got foster people. Nice ones. It's OK.' Tom shrugged. Jess could see his face closing down as if he'd said too much. She could sense pain somewhere and hoped Natasha would be kind to him. Not too kind though. The girl was still only fifteen.

'Right, well I'll get back to work.' Jess took her tea and a couple of biscuits and left the two of them alone. She had the feeling that Natasha didn't really know this boy too well – she'd noticed that Tom had been swift to tell her his name himself as if Natasha didn't actually know it. She wondered where they'd have met. Girls from her school tended to team up with the St Dominic's lot, being socially and academically equivalent. Parents of children from both schools were comfortable with that. It was as if the schools had been paired off by a dating agency matching similar incomes, class and interests. If there was trouble to be got into everyone played by the same rules: parents could afford private abortions in case of sexual accidents. These teenage boys weren't about to have their path to the essential law degree hampered by an expensive scuffle over child maintenance. If school-work fell apart there was a good selection of nearby Kensington crammers for extra holiday courses and if it was a matter of drugs, well, most of the parents still went in for a spot of after-dinner dope themselves. For serious sorting out there was even the Priory nearby for some outpatient counselling or long-stay readjustment. Jess's father, George, felt that private education led to a form of social apartheid, reinforcing the separation of rich and poor. Sometimes, as when she noticed the gradual loss of contact between Mel and Natasha, she knew he had a point. He'd much approve of Natasha's new friend, Jess thought wryly. Probably invite him to look over his collection of Karl Marx memorabilia.

*   *   *

Zoe knew about this sort of thing. Her mum wrote about it all the time. She'd know what to do, which was obviously why she was the one Emily had chosen to tell. She only wished that, right now, she knew the right thing to say to Emily.

'You mustn't tell anyone. Promise, really promise,' Emily sobbed.

'Course I won't tell,' Zoe said, reassuring for the fifth time. The two girls sat on the allotment bench watching a woman in a big flouncy velvet skirt and purple boots hoeing between rows of vegetables. Zoe wondered what they were. Could be leeks, she thought, or they could be onions. Grandad would know and he probably grew better ones. He'd been way ahead of his time, growing everything organically, not just because it was better for the eater but because he was sure that spraying chemicals about rotted gardeners' brains. Emily was quite good at crying quietly so the hoeing woman took no notice of them. It was just as well it wasn't Natasha sitting next to her with this kind of problem, everyone would hear her wailing about it for miles around. Whatever she'd promised Emily, though, someone who could be more effective in the practical sense would have to know sooner or later. It would be best in the long run to tell Emily's mum, for one thing they'd need money – an abortion wasn't going to be within pocket-money range – but Angie wasn't used to having her mid-week afternoons interrupted by her own children. Emily was supposed to be seventy miles away, safe and cosy in her boarding school. Angie was probably up at the gym having an aromatherapy massage or her toenails revamped or something.

'Your mum should have let you stay at school here with us,' Zoe said, thinking aloud.

Emily looked confused. 'Why? Don't girls get pregnant at your school then?'

Zoe shrugged, 'Well, some I suppose. I mean, well, instead of getting pregnant you could have just gone down the road to Boots and bought condoms and stuff if you hadn't been shut away miles from the shops couldn't you?' She couldn't actually imagine, herself, shopping for that sort of thing, at fourteen you really didn't want to think about the embarrassment factor if you didn't have to: she'd only just got to the point of not blushing handing over money for Tampax at the checkout. Emily looked way too young as well. She was so thin, her legs looked like Bambi's and she often walked with her hands folded across her front as if she hadn't got used to having breasts. Her long brown hair was thin too and flopped miserably each side of her face. Zoe would bet she never got asked for ID when she requested a half fare on the bus.

Emily came up with half a grin. 'Yeah that's a good one. That means I can blame the school. I like that but I don't think my mum will go for it. And we'll both get expelled when they find out.'

'You're joking!' Zoe was outraged. 'I don't think that's an expellable thing at our school. And *both* of you? Why?'

'Betrayal of trust or something. No shagging is in the rules, written down. "Any boy and girl caught . . ." '

'They actually *caught* you at it?' Zoe giggled, 'How *embarrassing*!'

'No, course they didn't, but when I start to get fat, that'll be pretty obvious. And they'll know it was Giles. Giles and me, we've been together since last year. Everyone knows, even the teachers make jokes about

52

us. If we sit together in class they call us the Happy Couple.'

'You could lie.'

'What, to save him? Why should I? After he asked if it was really his? There's only been him, and only that once. He knows I'm no slapper, the bastard.'

Zoe shrugged. She didn't know what Emily got up to at school. She'd assumed it was all hockey and compulsory cross-country running and lashings of prep, like in Enid Blyton. Now she wondered if all they ever did was screw each other senseless behind the gym or whatever, out of sheer boredom. If that was it, then maybe it was the school's fault for not letting them just laze about watching telly. That was something that really sapped the energy.

This all felt unreal. It had been a shock just to have found Em waiting outside school for her. It was an even bigger shock to find that she, Zoe, was the only person Emily wanted to tell about her pregnancy. They'd been at the same playgroup, so if it was something to do with being her oldest friend, well she certainly qualified. But not her *closest* friend, surely. Since Emily had gone off to her Oxfordshire school they hadn't really had that much to do with each other. Angie liked the single life and in the holidays Emily and her brother Luke always seemed to be away at pony-club camps or skiing or spending time with their father in Italy. Matthew had said it was to keep them from scuffing Angie's elegant beechwood floor and lounging about making the primrose suede sofas untidy.

'Do you remember when you fell out of that tree?' Emily pointed to the low-branched oak on the railway side of the allotments, just beyond Zoe's grandfather's scarlet shed.

'I broke my arm.' Zoe smiled. 'I must have been about eight I suppose. I remember they called it a greenstick fracture and I kept saying that it wasn't, it was me that was broken not the tree branch.'

'Seems so long ago.' Emily sighed, hugging her arms round her thin little body.

'It was. We'll soon be fifteen, halfway through our teens. Halfway from ten to twenty.'

'Too young for babies.'

Zoe could hear the threat of tears in Emily's voice again, but could only agree, 'Yes. Definitely too young for babies.'

'I think I might take up tennis again,' Matt was saying as he stacked the dishwasher after supper. 'I think I'll join that gym you go to, get fit. We could go together.' He patted his stomach and Jess grinned at him.

'We could. And in the car you could listen to Angie talking about her latest love, or should I say lust, interest. She collects them you know, young builders and plumbers and what-have-you. It's what she means when she says she's "got the men in". And then she tells me all about it on the way to the gym.'

Matt looked doubtful. 'Blow by blow as it were? Does she have to? Perhaps she won't if I'm there.'

Jess laughed. 'But there goes my entertainment!'

'OK, I give in. You don't want me crowding you, I know. I'll mooch round the park, pick up a tennis part-ner there. Or drag Eddy out. He's OK. Should've got to know him better before. You don't get time, wasting all day in an office.'

'Tennis would probably kill him.'

'True. Listen, you didn't mind me staying in the Leo this afternoon did you?' Matt put the last of the glasses in the dishwasher and then put his arms round Jess. She snuggled against him, remembering how she'd thought she'd felt safe like that, all those years ago when she'd first met him. It was probably from reading too many drippy romances in which the heroines frequently leaned their pretty heads against hunky chests and felt secure and adored. This had been purely in the interests of research – Jess's earliest writing attempts had been romantic fiction, rather too cynically told to be acceptable. These days cuddled up to Matt she just felt comfortable – there was no such thing as secure – and thankful that with her ear against his shirt she could still make out a strong and regular heartbeat.

'Is that how you're going to spend your days? Hanging out in the pub with a clapped-out old rock star?' she asked, hoping it didn't sound as carping to him as it did to her.

Matt pulled away and looked at her coldly. 'No. Not every day. But when I do I'm not going to ask for permission.'

'But you just did! You just asked if I minded!'

'I asked if you'd minded about *this afternoon.* We didn't really have much of a discussion in the Leo, I thought you might have wanted to continue it at home, that's all.'

'Oh right. Well "at home" I had work to get on with so no, I wouldn't have been able to spend hours chatting to you about what you're going to do with the rest of your life. Anyway it looks as if you've already decided that one.'

'Course I haven't. We could try again tomorrow, a nice long boozy lunch, just the two of us, no interruptions.'

'Can't. I've got an editor lunch, Paula from the

Gazette. She wants to talk about the column and some other stuff.'

'Oh well, if that's more important . . .'

'Of course it is, especially now! Anyway I'm not cancelling – I like Paula.'

'I like Paula, I could come too. Or would that be crowding you as well?'

Jess almost relented. Matthew and Paula got on well: she'd been to the house several times, been sweet to the girls, flirted mildly with Oliver and laughed at Matt's jokes. But this wasn't social, this was work.

'Let's put it this way,' she said eventually. 'You didn't used to take *me* to *your* business lunches.'

Jess knew they were being juvenile. If she'd been listening to any of her children having this discussion she'd have told them quite firmly not to be so silly.

'Mum and Dad, you're shouting! We can't hear the telly and *Friends* is on!' Zoe stood in front of them like a cross referee. Jess wondered which of them would be awarded the yellow card.

'Sorry Zo. Just having a frank exchange of views,' Matthew told her.

'Is Natasha with you?' Jess asked suddenly.

'Yeah. Why?'

'Just wondered. She didn't say much over supper.'

But Zoe was already out of the door, back to her favourite spot on the sofa, curled up with the cat and with her bare feet tucked away under a cushion.

'What's that about Tash?' Matt asked. There seemed to be a truce, Jess thought, brought on simply by a change of subject.

'Nothing, really. She brought home a boy today.'

'She'll bring home dozens of those. She's a bit of a

56

stunner, our Natasha. I'll get the shotgun polished and ready, if you like.'

'No need for that, I hope! No, this one was strange. He looked like he'd been sort of abandoned, like a lost puppy. He doesn't seem to have a family.'

Matt reached into the fridge for another beer. 'Want one?' he asked. She shook her head, trying not to wonder how many alcohol units he'd packed away that day. 'So, not one of the usual posh boys,' he said. 'More the type old Angie would fancy?'

'I think he's a bit young even for her! I think he's been in care, something like that. He looks damaged.'

'A learning experience for Tash, then. Your dad would be pleased, having her exposed to someone who's done without the comforts of capitalist privilege.'

'You make the boy sound like something educational we've bought for her to play with. And that reminds me. Dad's back from his holiday on Thursday. He said he'd come over when he's checked over the allotment.'

'Better get him to bring something to eat with him,' Matthew suggested. 'After all, we can't afford to entertain now there's only one of us earning.'

Four

'Why do they put "pan-fried" on the menu? Is it supposed to make it sound posher than just "fried"? Or less fattening, do you think?' Jess was laughing as her lunch arrived. She looked down at the delicate arrangement of prawns perched precariously on top of a scaffolding of French beans and strips of celeriac and felt a childish urge to scatter the elaborate still life across the comically oversized plate on which it sat.

Paula Cheviot, editor of the *Sunday Gazette*'s Comfort Zone section, was opposite Jess at the inadequately small table in one of central London's currently hyper-smart restaurants. She didn't reply with an agreeing giggle as she normally would but looked a bit puzzled, as if Jess had questioned one of life's acknowledged truths – such as did moisturizer really make *that* much difference. Slowly, Paula picked up a rocket leaf and nibbled at it, a look of intense concentration on her face. She had something on her mind. Jess could tell by the small frown lines.

Paula never normally allowed such things to rumple her flat matt skin, for that would lead inevitably to the appointment at the clinic to have her forehead injected with botox into a paralysed (but smooth; divinely, age-defyingly smooth) expression of mild surprise.

Jess, in the process of loading her fork full of prawn, felt her appetite trickle away like chilled bathwater down a drain. Paula's phone call two days previously, the apparently spontaneous suggestion that it was high time they got together for lunch and a gossip, suddenly seemed like a carefully calculated ruse. It was a trap. Jess put her fork down, suddenly shaky with the fore-knowledge that she, like Matt, was about to be fired. His-and-hers dole cheques looked more than likely. After all, things went wrong in threes, didn't they? There'd be this, and then something would happen to Oliver in Australia, or the girls would be expelled from school.

'Oooh. This is *delicious*. Such a treat.' Paula's usual smile reappeared as she munched a delicate mouthful of duck with a coriander and lime dressing. 'How's yours?' she asked, her social skills back in place and the fleeting moment of seriousness gone.

'Fine.' Jess tried to rekindle her appetite, taking too large a mouthful of white wine and almost choking. She could have been wrong – Paula's mind might simply be full of which new-age diets to select for the next issue, or whether to commission someone to do a piece on Smart Cats.

'It's occurred to me lately,' Paula then began, playing nervously with her silver Tiffany bracelet, 'that per-haps the time has come for us to take a little trot down a different bridleway with your input at the *Gazette*, workwise.'

Here it comes, Jess thought, trying to maintain her breathing at a rate steady enough to keep her from faintness.

'You mean, change the format?' she prompted, praying that Paula didn't mean 'change the writer'.

'Mm.' With infuriating slowness, Paula worked her way through some more of her lunch. Jess was finding it hard to swallow a tiny piece of a French bean.

'Of course we love your column. Wouldn't be without it. Sweetly domestic chaos. Readers like that, makes them feel better about their own dysfunctional lives.'

'Glad to provide a service.'

'And you have, sweetie, you have, quite admirably. And for such a long time.' She reached out and gave Jess's wrist an electric little stroke. Her fingernails were perfectly manicured: evenly square-ended to look businesslike, but frosted candy pink for a hint of the girl within.

'Of course we absolutely don't want to lose you,' she went on. Jess's heart sank still further. The words sounded like a guillotine being jacked up ready for a long and vicious drop. 'We'd like to keep Nelson's Column going for at least another six months. There'd be sackfuls of letters to the Ed if we suddenly cut you out.' Paula giggled prettily. 'People look forward to your page, they need a kind of running-down phase, wean them off slowly.'

Jess pushed her food around with her fork, arranging the delicate pink of the prawns in a circle around the beans. Paula munched her way through her plate of warm duck salad and Jess watched fascinated: Paula had started with the lower left segment of the plate and was eating steadily across towards the top right. She reminded Jess of a termite, and she wondered if Paula approached other things in her life in the same way. She succumbed to the irresistible vision of her editor in bed with some gym-toned hunk, nuzzling her way down his body from right earlobe to left big toe, with a few savouring stops along the way.

About halfway across the plate Paula resumed her speech. 'I would like to run a few new ideas past you, Jess, see if you feel up to something a little more challenging. We had a meeting and thought it could be a good idea to send you out to do new things, and then you report back, the kind of thing which might strike the average reader in terms of, "Oh I've always fancied having a go at that." And if it works, well *super*. What do you think?'

'Sounds interesting. What kind of thing did you have in mind? Not abseiling down Canary Wharf, Paula, please.' Jess tried to sound perky and to look as if being 'challenged' was something that she was keen to rise to. The gnawing dread was still there though, along with a mild feeling of being cheated: if she'd suspected this lunch was more than just a jolly let's-catch-up chat session she'd have made more effort on the looks front. She'd have bought something new to wear, rather than making do with her much treasured but four-year-old Ghost jacket. She also wished she'd had Philip at *Hair We Are* trim her rather shaggy hair into the kind of short sassy cut that could hold its own here so close to Sloane Street. Her highlights needed a bit of toning down too. The last colourist couldn't quite believe that not everyone with mid-brown hair had a hidden craving to be blonde and had dabbed on chunks of pale gold with happy enthusiasm, radiantly confident of client satisfaction.

Around them, fellow diners looked as if they were having a much better time. Their feet beneath tables were surrounded by plenty of evidence of what Natasha called Big Bag shopping, plundered from the most delicious stores. Now, with Matt's career over and her own clearly on some kind of test drive, she'd be limited to the Small Bag variety, if any at all.

'We *could* have pudding,' Paula suggested as the waiter took their plates away. '*Shall* we?' Paula was leaning forward and sparkling her eyes at Jess as if the eating of a crème caramel was a huge and wicked temptation comparable with shoplifting at Harvey Nicks. The idea of something sweet was quite appealing, Jess thought, like a piece of chocolate when you're a child and you've hurt yourself.

'OK. I always love to have the kind of pudding I'd never be bothered to make at home. It's like cocktails. A home-made piña colada just doesn't have the same zing, does it?'

Paula's delicate fingers waved a little, as if she was just catching a thought. 'Now cocktails, that's one of the things I was thinking of.'

'You were?'

'We could send you out to do a course, learn how to make the perfect margarita, that kind of thing. And have you ever had a proper fitting for a bra? Or gone on one of those ghastly "flowers for the dinner party" courses?'

Jess laughed. 'No to all of them. Except the bra thing, and that was only because I was pregnant.'

'Well there you are then.' Paula leaned forward and smiled broadly. 'Lots to do, plus any ideas of your own you can come up with. It's more money of course, because it'll take up more time. And we send you out with a photographer. It'll be fun.'

That was an order. It probably would be fun. And the words 'more money' were very welcome. For a while, too, there would still be Nelson's Column as well, so she'd be earning quite a bit, enough to keep her from feeling like nagging at Matt quite so much anyway. Jess at last relaxed and plunged her spoon into her raspberry parfait. 'And so, Jess,' Paula began as Jess started to enjoy herself, 'how is that gorgeous husband of yours?'

Matthew was in the attic, still not dressed though midday had long since been and gone, sitting on the bed reading the Creative and Media vacancies in the *Guardian*. The paper was three days old but he assumed most of the jobs were still on offer, at least till the first wave of fast young things had had their e-mailed CVs downloaded and read. The problem was that he didn't want to apply for any of them – it was Jess who'd bought the paper, thinking she was being helpful and with a careful look on her face as if she was trying hard not to ask him why he hadn't rushed out first thing on Monday morning to buy it himself. He didn't want to waste any more of his life trying to pretend to people that they were exactly as wonderful as they thought they were, and that those aspects of their lives/work/reputations that they wished the world to know about were the most fascinating things on the planet. He'd spent twenty-two years being, well what had he been? Surely there had to be a better word to describe his working persona than *pleasant*. There wasn't. He'd spent all his working life buddying up to clients, colleagues and media reptiles to put other people's messages across. It was time he had a message of his own, something for those Out There to take notice of. His job had been the equivalent of a wall emulsioned in safe magnolia: simply a bland background for enhancement of someone else's artwork. Somewhere, deep inside, he could feel the long-dormant stirrings of a creative impulse. It was time for it to come out.

Matt folded the paper, shoved it in the bin and went to take a good appraising look at himself in the long mirror in the bathroom. The old working day hadn't really included much time for checking himself over properly. Last time he'd given his body a really good scrutiny he'd been sure he still didn't look his age. People were always surprised if he let slip a clue to the truth, such as recalling being on an A-level field trip the day Jimi Hendrix died. His body was still in good slim shape, but would soon miss the lunchtime gym sessions that he'd been treating it to for the past few years. He must be careful not to let himself go, as his late mother would have put it – it would be too easy to get beerily fat, pig out on crisps and biscuits and become jowly. He'd let his hair grow a bit, he decided, running his fingers through it and feeling the relieved satisfaction that all men have when only two rather than two hundred strands come out. He wouldn't let it get as long as Eddy's – which bordered on a sparse and stringy version of the Heavy Metal look (presumably in memory of starrier times) – but something with less city precision about it, less fierce control would be good.

Briskly, for soon Jess would be home, Matthew showered. Wandering back into the bedroom, he stopped to look out of the window to see who was coming and going in the Grove below. Opposite, Angie was climbing out of her Discovery wearing a silky blue ruffle-edged skirt that somehow got itself hiked up as she slid off the car seat, showing a lot of creamy upper thigh. Angie's shoulder-length blond hair bounced and fluttered as she fussed around, rearranging the skirt and leaning forward to reveal, from Matt's elevated point of view, the bonus of a good deal of breast pushing against a skimpy V-neck cardigan. As if she sixth-sensed an audience she looked around and then up, caught sight of him and waved, grinning. Matt waved back, distractedly dropping his towel. Angie's grin broadened and she turned to go into her house. Surely she couldn't see, from there, he trusted, that he'd been sporting a fine erection?

Claire and Natasha sat on the bench on the hockey-pitch side of the field. The school buildings looked pleasingly distant. Open space that big was rare in London schools and the field featured prominently in the prospectus, presenting an illusion of *rus in urbe.* It was therefore a source of constant disappointment to the staff that the pupils, collectively, tended to loathe any sport that required running about on grass and lost almost all their inter-school matches through sheer apathy. The grass was only really in full demand on summer break-times when the sight of five hundred girls with their skirts and shirts pulled up for maximum tan exposure caused many a local male to make a diversion for the chance to glance through the knot-holes in the fence.

'So when are you seeing him again?' Claire was ever-anxious for details and Natasha was delighted to be able to provide them. Claire was one of those girls you wanted to be *like.* It wasn't anything you could put your finger on but she just seemed comfortable with herself.

'He just said he'd be around, that I'd see him soon.' It was hard to make this sound like a definite arrangement. Put like that, actually spoken, it sounded dismally vague, as if he'd met her, been unimpressed and gone off to find better luck somewhere else.

'You could always go and see *him*, if he's living down the allotments!' Claire giggled. 'Do you think he really is? Has he run away from home or something?'

'He didn't actually say. He mostly wanted to talk about me. Ask me stuff, what I do and that.' It had been incredibly flattering, she recalled. He'd seemed really interested in her *as a person*. Boys from St Dominic's told you stuff about themselves, or more precisely about what they owned in terms of computers and CDs and things. Never, at any of the parties she'd been to or down the Costa coffee shop or anywhere, had she had anyone asking her what she liked doing most on Sunday mornings, or what was her idea of the perfect breakfast. She'd been so astounded, she'd almost spoilt it by asking why on earth he'd want to know those things. Just in time she'd thought about it, realized that if she was seeing somebody, properly, they were the kind of things she'd be wanting to know about him.

'Sounds like he's really interested.' Claire was gratifyingly encouraging, 'So he'll turn up again, bound to. He might hang about outside the school waiting for you then I can get a look at him.'

Natasha giggled. 'Yeah he might I suppose and that's OK but not knowing when or where I'll see him means it's a bit of an effort: I've got to keep the make-up on and my hair looking good *all the time*.'

'You're right.' Claire sighed. 'Whatever happened to

good old-fashioned dating: he stays home then phones you, you spend two hours getting ready and then you meet like in *Clueless* or *Sabrina*? Bit of a strain, but you can do it.'

Jess trailed home on the tube feeling sour and grumpy and tried to tell herself that she should, instead, simply be grateful. At least she'd still got her job. It seemed to be down to her to make sure she kept this new version of it, try to guess what was needed, find the right voice. At least Paula hadn't just fired her, said, with only mildly apologetic flippancy, 'Sorry darling, but you know how it is, *plus ça change* and all that! Younger readers to target!' A few Sundays from now, if the worst had happened, she could have opened the Comfort Zone magazine and found make-up tips from Britney Spears or 'Going for Broke: the toddlers' guide to dot.com investment' on the page where her column used to be. It might be fun doing this new stuff, she told herself as she turned off the main road into the Grove. At any other time it definitely would be fun, going out to sample a delicious (and possibly not so delicious) array of new activities. If only she wasn't feeling so much as if life was in a state of complete upheaval. It had never occurred to her before just how much she relied on the comforting security of routine. I am not a born adventurer, she thought as she reached her gate. I could no more take off to the unknown, all alone like Oliver has, than I could take up Formula One racing.

As she opened the door, Jess almost tripped over a sleeping baby in a buggy parked in the hall. The sound of deep male laughter erupted from the sitting room, but the baby stirred only faintly as if it was well used to such minor irritations. Inside, Matthew, Micky and Eddy were sprawled untidily over the conservatory sofas with Donald the cat, looking ludicrously thrilled to be allowed to join the Blokes, draped round Eddy's shoulders, kneading his paws into his long hair and drooling over his ear. In front of them on the low table was a selection of coffee mugs and empty Budweiser bottles. A packet of Natasha's favourite chocolate Hobnobs was tipped among the empties, leaving chunky crumbs among the debris. An overflowing ash-tray completed the mess and the air reeked of stale smoke, some of which smelled headily illegal. They were worse than Oliver, she thought crossly as they greeted her, waving and grinning guiltily like naughty schoolchildren caught skiving maths.

'Hello Jess!' Matt got up and hugged her exuberantly as if he hadn't seen her for a month. 'We've got a great plan! We're going to make all our fortunes!'

'And it's down to my new best mate here!' Eddy said, hauling the cat round to his lap and tickling his ears. 'We're going to make him a shareholder.'

Jess moved Micky's biker jacket from the back of a chair and sat down by her desk. 'I can't wait to hear, but whose is the baby? And is it all right out there in the hallway?' she asked.

'Oh that's Eddy's daughter's littlest. He's minding her while she fetches another one from the school. Go on, tell her the plan, Micky,' Matt said. 'I'll make her a cup of tea. It's what you do when the breadwinner comes home isn't it?'

'S'right, Matt,' Eddy slurred, clearly the one on the outside of all the Budweiser. 'You go and play the little house husband, put your pinny on.'

'What have you done, hacked into the lottery system

68

and fixed it so you win?' Jess was concerned about the sleeping baby, whether Eddy was fit to be in charge of her – could you be done for being drunk in charge of a child?

'We invented something.' Micky leaned forward and lowered his voice as if rival patentees were lurking outside the door. He looked so much smarter than the other two, in a sky blue linen shirt and elegant black trousers. Eddy wore a sweatshirt so ancient it was advertising a Cream concert. His jeans, inside which his plump thighs strained to get out, must have been bought in younger and leaner days too. Matt was heading the same unkempt way, she noticed, in a tee shirt that she was sure she'd given to Monica for the duster bag.

'It's a cat tracking system,' Micky told her. 'You know people are always losing their cats. And cats are always losing their collars. So what you want . . .' Eddy leaned forward and cut in. 'What you want is like you get in posh cars for when they're nicked. You need a satellite tracking system. A sort of moggy GPS.'

Matt came back in slopping a mug of tea which dripped on Jess's jacket as he handed it to her. 'Guess what we're going to call it,' he said eagerly. 'Just guess. You'll like this.'

'It's going to be called . . .' Eddy started and the others joined in, 'the Cat Sat!' They laughed like children who'd just heard their first real joke.

'The Cat Sat?' Jess said. 'As in . . .'

'Yeah, you've got it, as in The Cat Sat on the Mat!' The fact they seemed to find this so screamingly hilarious confirmed it was definitely more than tobacco they'd been inhaling. So they were spending the day smoking dope like students. No wonder all the biscuits had gone, they'd got post-spliff munchies.

'Everyone will want one. They'll be really expensive so everyone will think they're *the* thing to have.'

'And for lions too. Or have they already got them?' Micky looked solemn.

'Lions have.' Eddy nodded his head too hard and the cat clung on tight looking alarmed. 'I saw it on that vet thing with the Norwegian woman, the fanciable one.'

'Yeah I like her,' Micky agreed. 'But she was scared of the lions, a real wuss about the puss. We just need smaller ones than the lions have got. Kitten size.'

'Lions?' They'd completely lost Jess. She didn't want to put a downer on things but it was obviously one of those situations where you'd had to be *there*. All she longed to do was to go upstairs, put on some shoes that were more comfortable, brush an irritating shard of prawn from between a couple of top molars and let the end of the day creep quietly closer. Matt was leaning back with his hands behind his head, grinning as if he'd completed more work in this one short day than in the previous twenty years. He couldn't be serious, she thought, surely to God he couldn't think there was real mileage in this.

On her way home from school Zoe hesitated outside Angie's house. It would be a huge betrayal to go in and inform her that her daughter was pregnant. Not that she'd do it quite like that, of course she wouldn't. She couldn't just march up the path, rat-tat-tat on the dragon's-head knocker and come out with it the second Angie opened the door. Emily would never forgive her. But then why had Emily told her in the first place if she didn't want her to take over doing something about it? As she dithered by the hedge, pulling leaves off and

70

shredding them as she tried to think what to do, her own front door across the road opened and a dishevelled-looking Eddy tottered out, pushing a baby in a buggy. Micky from the Leo followed him and together the two men ambled down the path and off up the road towards Eddy's place. She could hear them laughing, kind of silly and loud like her parents and their friends towards the end of a long boozy Sunday lunch.

'I suppose they think they represent fine upstanding examples of the male of the species!' Angie's rather little-girly voice, coming from far too close to the hedge, startled Zoe. There wasn't time to make a run for it. 'And what are you doing, hovering among the leaves? Are you waiting for the coast to be clear?' Angie appeared, wearing one of those special multi-pocketed gardener's overalls that Zoe had seen advertised in the *Gazette*'s magazine. There was always a picture of some smiling clean woman in a straw hat with a trug-thing full of roses. Angie was clearly making full use of her purchase: Zoe could see at least five implement handles as well as a ball of string and some pink suede gloves festooned about her body.

'Don't you have to be careful when you bend?' Zoe pointed to a fork sticking upwards from close to Angie's waist, aiming dangerously towards her left breast.

Angie looked down at the prongs. 'Oh I do. One wrong move and all my silicone will leak out!' she giggled. 'Listen, do you fancy a glass of orange or something? I do miss Emily and Luke when they're off at school – I could do with some young company to make up for it.'

Zoe felt trapped. In Angie's maple and mint-green

71

kitchen she felt as if the only words that could form themselves in her head were 'Emily' and 'Baby'. It was always the way when there was something you really didn't want to say. It was like when her mum had confided to her, a couple of years back, that she was going to buy Natasha the suede boots she'd been craving for her birthday. The word 'boots' had seemed to be everywhere. It was in things like the computer, needing to be rebooted when it crashed, in the bootleg Stones album that Eddy-up-the-road had given her dad, in her mum asking her to get the shopping from the boot of the car. She'd almost gone faint with the effort of not telling. She felt just the same now, perched nervously on the edge of one of Angie's chrome and pale wood chairs, tracing her name on the glass table-top in drops of orange juice that she'd spilled because her hands were trembly. She bit her lip as the finger and the drop of juice started forming the word 'baby' on the glass and she hurriedly smudged her hand over it before Angie, who was opening a packet of Sainsbury's scones, could see.

'They'll be back for the Easter holidays soon. I can hardly wait!' Angie bustled around with plates and strawberry jam and found a pot of clotted cream in the fridge.

'Why can't they go to school here like me and Natasha?' Zoe asked as if she'd just thought of it.

'Here? But where?' Angie looked puzzled.

'Emily could be with us, at Julia Perry's.'

Angie laughed. 'I don't suppose you remember, but there was an entrance exam! Emily took it but didn't pass. Simple as that.'

'But there's . . .'

'Yes. Briar's Lane comprehensive.' Angie gave her a

look that was obviously supposed to imply something. Zoe immediately got the gist but made herself look as if she didn't understand, just for the meagre delight of seeing Angie wriggle about trying not to admit to snobbery.

'I mean, I'm sure some people do awfully well there,' Angie stammered as she poured herself a cup of tea from a tiny silver pot. 'It's just, that, we felt Emily might need a bit of extra help to achieve her potential, you know, and well, we could afford it. And you must have noticed,' she lowered her voice as if the kitchen had filled up with people who'd disagree. 'Some of the behaviour, and the things some of the girls wear, and so young . . .'

Zoe smiled, no longer worried that she'd blurt out anything about Emily's pregnancy. Angie lived in a total fantasy land. Zoe would rather slit her wrists than tell her what really went on. But it did mean she and Emily would have to deal with things by themselves.

Five

'. . . and sometimes the friends they bring home resemble strayed pets: slightly lost-looking, underfed
and a bit grubby round the edges. Always they're in
need of a good meal. If you offer one the answer will be
a decided 'no' as if they'd prefer starvation to the terri-
fying prospect of sitting at your table and being
cross-examined about their GCSE options, but later
when you're looking in the fridge and there's no sign of
the last bit of Cheddar and all the yoghurts . . .'

But there were always exceptions.

'Mum! I'm back and . . .' Natasha crashed into the
house, pulling with her the boy who'd been in the
house a few days before '. . . what's for supper and is
there enough for Tom?' Feeling almost guilty, for it had
been this strange boy Tom she'd had in mind as she
wrote, Jess quickly closed down the computer. Even
so, she could feel her face going pink, as if his un-
fathomable blue eyes could read behind the darkened
screen.

'Hello Tom,' she said. 'You're very welcome to stay. It's only a sort of posh sausage thing but there's plenty of it.' Tom grinned at her. He had, she thought, one of those smiles that looks as if it's been worked on. At some stage in his young life he must have spent time gazing in the mirror and perfecting the 'guaranteed to charm' version. She hoped it wasn't so calculated when he used it on Natasha.

'Great, oh and Tom that's my dad,' Natasha said, hauling Tom out of the room before Matthew, whose steps she could hear approaching from the kitchen, got the chance to say or do anything dad-like and embarrassing.

'Where are you off to?' Jess heard them clattering up the stairs and called after them.

'Only my room!' Natasha yelled back. 'Got CDs to play!'

' "Only my room!" ' Matthew looked at Jess. 'Is that OK do you think?'

She shrugged. 'Well, we let her go up there with her female friends.'

'Isn't that different?'

'It depends on whether you trust her or not.'

'It's not her . . .'

'No, I know, I know. Well, they won't do anything with us around the house. Though we could suddenly find there are things we need from upstairs, that should unsettle them.'

'I do need to phone Micky about tomorrow, I'll do it from the bedroom.'

'Tomorrow?' Jess queried, but Matt was already halfway up the stairs.

In the kitchen Jess hunted through her shelf of cookery books, took the sausages out of the fridge and poured olive oil into a pan. Even with Tom there would be more than enough: she was still catering, mentally, for Oliver. She missed having him around. He enjoyed cooking and ever since he was old enough to be trusted with a knife he'd been a comfortable kitchen-companion, never getting in the way and being happy to do the boring, mundane necessities like peeling potatoes and grating cheese. She smiled to herself as she remembered his confusion over the term '*sous-chef*' as Matthew had nicknamed him when he was about eight. He'd interpreted it as 'Sioux-chef' and asked her if she'd get him a full Indian brave headdress (or *native American*, she reprimanded herself, in these PC days).

Matt came back into the kitchen, grinning as if Micky had told him a joke too filthy to share. She'd ask him about the progress of the Cat Sat once she could trust herself to try and take it seriously. Angie had been cross with her that morning at the gym for treating it as a joke. 'It's important not to undermine their confidence, even if they're living in complete fantasy,' she'd said, as if she had experience of nothing but suddenly redundant men. Besides, the change in her own career was still very much on Jess's mind. Since the meeting with Paula before the weekend she'd woken in the middle of each night, convinced she too no longer had a job.

'In fact,' Jess now said to Matthew as she splashed cider onto the page telling her how to achieve Delia Smith's perfect braised sausages, 'I'll probably end up a good bit worse off if you think of it on a rate-per-hour basis, once the column is defunct.' The cider had smudged the recipe where it told you how many apples were needed and Delia did like to be so precise.

Jess took four large Bramleys from the fruit rack and started on the peeling and coring.

'Yeah, but,' Matthew reasoned, 'it's not as if you were spending the free time doing something else that earned money, is it? So can't you think of it more as a pay rise, pure and simple?'

Jess laughed. ' "Free time!" What do you think I do all day? Loll about on the sofa scoffing booze and biscuits and smoking spliffs like you and your pals? Some of us are keeping the ol' homestead running! The entire contents of Sainsbury's don't get here by themselves.'

Matthew opened the fridge and took out a pint of milk. He looked at it for a second and then at Jess and then went to the dresser cupboard and took out a glass to pour some into.

'You'd have drunk that out of the carton if I hadn't been here, wouldn't you?' She pointed the apple corer at him. 'Doesn't take long for a man to descend into yobbery.'

Matthew's upper lip now had a slender moustache of milk, just like, she thought, Oliver when he guzzled his drink too fast when he was little. She must check the e-mails again, see if he felt like telling them what he was up to.

'Would I do that?' He dodged the corer and slapped a milky kiss on her cheek. 'And Sainsbury's could get here by itself. You should try on-line shopping. I'll do it for you if you like. All you have to do is make the list and leave it to me.'

'Huh! "All you have to do . . . !"' she spluttered, searching in a cupboard and wondering if Delia's spirit would appear in a puff of furious smoke if she left out the tablespoonful of cider vinegar. There didn't seem to be any. There were balsamic, red wine, tarragon, malt, rice, white wine and Jerez vinegars but none with 'cider' on the label and a cute design of beaming, ruddy-faced farmer and lush, fat apples. Typical. Jess scribbled 'cider vinegar' on a purple Post-it note and slapped it onto the fridge door where it joined several other memory joggers that had mostly not been heeded. Theirs was not a kitchen that ran on hyper-organized lines: at any given time there might well be four loaves of bread gathering mould in the bread crock, but quite possibly no butter to put on them.

She put the casserole in the oven, stacked the ludicrously large number of knives and spoons she'd used into the dishwasher and went to switch on her computer again. The girls had started mocking, gleefully saying that the Perfect Son wasn't so perfect now, was he? Never called, never wrote. But at last he had.

'G'day folks! Cairns rocks and is cute place, but strangely no beach. The hostel is full of Canadians and smells of socks. Say hi to the girls. Ol.'

Well it wasn't much but it was something, she thought. Brief, to the point and at least he was alive and presumably well. She wondered about a reply, whether she should tell him that they were all OK too, if you didn't count his father being suddenly unemployed and having a career change to 'inventor', her own job about to change course and his little sister entertaining a strange boy in her bedroom.

The doorbell went just as they were all sitting down for supper. 'I'll get it!' Zoe yelled from the hallway. 'Hey it's Grandad! I bet he's all tanned. Wish I was.'

Quickly, Jess totted up the sausages. There'd just be enough, and there was plenty of mashed potato and a big salad.

'Lay an extra place for him, Tash,' she said. 'You

know he never says no to food.' He also made sure that if he was going to turn up 'unexpectedly' it would be uncannily close to a mealtime. Jess didn't mind: her father lived alone and since her mother had died three years before had been at the mercy of a determined widow three flats along from his, who he swore was fattening him up for a kill. He preferred, at home, to hide from his predator and eat alone listening to *The Archers*, who he considered a bunch of capitalist incompetents who should be turning Ambridge into a massive collective farm with profits quite literally ploughed back into the land.

'It's OK, let me.' Tom opened the drawer beside the sink and rummaged for cutlery. Jess hoped he'd washed his hands. There was a vague staleness about him today that should, she thought, have made whoever took care of him at home suggest he had a shower. She was surprised Natasha didn't seem to notice or to mind, for she was a girl who took her own personal hygiene to new levels of high art.

George Colville was dragged into the kitchen by Zoe. Jess hugged him. 'Hi Dad, how was the holiday?'

'Less of the holiday, it was a pilgrimage. The last true bastion of Communism in the West.'

'I thought Cuba was the plebs' new Caribbean all-sand-and-sangria venue,' Matthew teased.

George grunted. 'Only for the culturally bankrupt with no sense of history,' he said, pulling out a chair and sitting down at the table. 'Just about to have supper were you? You carry on. Don't let me interrupt.'

Natasha laughed and handed him a cold beer from the fridge. 'You always do that, Grandad. Like we're going to sit and eat round you?'

'Just so long as I'm not in the way. And who's this?'

He looked at Tom. 'I've seen you before. Are you a friend of Oliver's?'

Jess, beating the last of the cream into the potatoes, watched from the corner of her eye as Tom put out his hand to shake George's.

'I don't know Oliver. I've only just met Natasha,' Tom said, shrugging and slouching his hands back into the pockets of his jacket.

George had narrowed his eyes, Jess noticed, and the fan of pale lines that spread far into his temples creased with the effort of thought. He was looking suspicious, as if in the effort to recall the boy his mind was only choosing to run through mildly unpleasant recent encounters with various people. Jess remembered when she was a teenager herself, trying to get away with pretending to be staying over at a friend's house when there was a party to go to that didn't start till the time she was normally expected to come home. At that time, when the words she most often spoke to her parents were 'It's not fair!' she'd dreaded her father's staggering perspicacity: it had been accurate almost to the point of clairvoyance. Tom's confident grin faltered a fraction as he waited for George to recall where he'd seen him before.

'No good, son. Can't place you. You kids all look the same, but it'll come to me.' George laughed, letting Tom off the hook for now. 'Good grief, Jess, what are you doing buying salad? I've got lettuces by the dozen running to seed down on the patch. You should've sent one of the girls round.'

'We like them without holes, Grandad,' Zoe said solemnly. 'Sorry, but it's true. Some of yours look like fishnet tights.'

'Cheeky brat! That's good organic stuff. It's what

80

idiots are paying twice over the odds for down at that fancy deli by the square. Do you know, I was thinking on the plane on the way home, you could keep half this borough in properly grown veg if everyone dug up their back gardens in these smart roads round here. In Varadero there wasn't a patch of land that didn't have a dozen tomato plants and a couple of rows of sweet-corn on it. You could have a community shop, or a farmers' market. Cut out all that flying in of out-of-season stuff from thousands of miles away. No-one needs fresh broad beans in February.'

'We could dig up the school field and plant cab-bages. Everyone hates hockey. I'd rather do weeding,' Zoe said.

'You shouldn't have to buy food at all,' Tom sud-denly said. 'It should be free, like water, like it's a right.'

'Eh lad, nice thinking but you've a lot to learn.' George shook his head. 'Water's not free. And if governments could think of a way to charge you for the bloody air that you breathe they would. So, tell me what I've missed, what's been happening while I've been away?'

Zoe's bedroom window looked out over the Grove. It was late and there was no-one in across the road at Angie's, all the windows were dark, even though the woman who ran Neighbourhood Watch had been round and said they should always leave a light on to make burglars think there was someone in. She won-dered where Angie was, and if one of the reasons she'd sent Emily and Luke away to school was so that she could just go out whenever she felt like it. Perhaps she'd thought it would be cheaper than an au pair and better than having kids around who kept asking her which bloke she'd been out with this time.

Zoe was bored. She sat on the old wicker rocking chair picking bits of ginger fur off her old toy cat and wished Natasha hadn't found the boy. He was weird. He didn't say much, as if he thought being mysterious made him interesting. He and Tash were still out in the back garden, down by the shed, probably snogging and groping and pretending they were being really daring. Zoe had done all her homework apart from writing about the dead-pig poem and she really, honestly, didn't think there was anything she could do about that. Ted Hughes had said everything there was to say about the poor animal, and there didn't seem anything she could add. It was a strange thing for anyone to write about, a pig lying dead on a barrow. What was the point of analysing the *way* he'd written it, like they were supposed to. He just *had*: enough said. Surely poetry was something spontaneous, just an inspired passing thought, not written so that generations of fourteen-year-olds could come up with guessed-at meanings that the poet might or might not have thought of. He must have been really, really fascinated by the pig and then just written about it straight off, from the top of his thoughts. It was a bit of a cheek of them even to mess about with analysis, though Mrs Gibbs might not have the same opinion when she didn't hand anything in. Perhaps she should write about why she hadn't written anything, though you could only get away with that once. There was nothing on television. She'd even had to watch *Goodness Gracious Me* by herself because of Natasha being with Tom. It wasn't the same laughing all on your own.

Downstairs the front door slammed and then Zoe

heard Natasha's footsteps thumping on the stairs. Just for a moment she was sure her door would open, that Tash would rush in, sprawl on the bed and tell her all about what she and Tom had been doing in the garden. Zoe had already decided she would pretend she found the whole thing very boring, even though really she'd be zinging with excitement, knowing that one day it would be her sneaking out to make a start on all the sex stuff, just as it must have been Emily with the Giles person. Natasha would have a go at her for not listening but would work out that Zoe had things of her own on her mind and drag out the Emily-thing from her. Then they could sort it out together. Natasha would tell her there was nothing to worry about, there'd been a girl in her year, that she knew a number they could ring, a doctor who wouldn't say anything, no problem. Zoe waited, staring down at the dark, empty Grove below, but the door didn't open. Instead she heard Natasha come out of the bathroom and go into her room, heard her flinging her shoes at her wardrobe as she did every night. She might as well go to sleep.

Below, on the pavement opposite, someone looked up at Zoe's window. Zoe only caught sight of a shadow in the lamplight, a shadow that went behind Angie's hedge. Angie was coming home quite early really, Zoe thought as she closed her curtains and went and lay on her bed.

'So what are you doing today?' Jess, fresh from the shower and feeling an early-day briskness, realized she'd asked the wrong question as soon as it was out, for Matthew let out a long and anguished groan and turned over in bed, pulling the duvet up over his ears.

'Oh come on, Matt, don't be so dramatic! I only

wondered. You ask me often enough.' She leaned over, pushed a hand under the quilt and tickled his ribs. He squirmed and pulled away but then turned back to her, grinning. 'Actually, I suppose I could just stay in bed all day, couldn't I, making use of room service and a willing wife.'

'Whose wife would that be then?' she asked, towelling water from her hair. She was dripping on him and he sat up and yawned, rubbing the cold drops off his head. 'Oh anyone's, I'm not fussy. Just don't . . .' He looked suddenly serious and she felt vaguely foolish, now awkwardly fastening her bra while he frowned at her. Even after all these years it would be nice to have your husband at least pretend to be mildly appreciative at watching a woman dress.

'Don't what?'

'Don't question me. Stuff will happen. Give it time.'

'I'm giving it time.' Jess pulled her cream linen sweater over her head. 'Did I sound like I wasn't?'

'In a way.'

'Well why don't you check out that on-line shopping thing you were talking about, that would be useful.'

Matthew flung himself out of bed and slammed into the bathroom. 'And don't do that either!'

'Jesus, what now?'

'Don't find me things to do! Stop CONTROLLING!'

Down on his allotment, George checked his purple sprouting broccoli and picked a few of the shoots. The problem with growing vegetables was the glut-or-famine thing. Somehow things were either ready all at once or there was nothing whatever to harvest. He didn't go in for show vegetables like Dave on the next plot, who pared down his broad beans to the last perfect pods so that there were none grown on for eating and all the earth's goodness went into the few cherished samples all plumped and perfected to competition standard. What was the point of that? Only in a nation of affluent careless plenty could anyone who grew food waste half their crop for the sake of the prize specimen. It was almost fascist, somehow vaguely Nazi-like, jettisoning less than perfect (and that was subjective) produce. It defied nature and all common sense. He pulled a snail off one of his own French bean stems, picked off one of the succulent but immature pods and crunched it into his mouth.

'Nothing like it,' he muttered to himself.

'You always talk to yourself?' George whirled round, flustered at having a private moment of delight observed. The boy, Natasha's friend Tom, was by the shed, leaning on the side (the dodgy side with the bottom planks going rotten) with his hands in his pockets. He looked impudent, grinning that strange sideways grin and giving him the direct challenging stare of someone who might not be up to any good.

'I talk to myself whenever I feel there's something interesting to say,' George told him. 'What are you up to here? Natasha's not around, she'll be on her way to school by now.'

'I'm living here,' Tom said simply. 'Down there.' His left shoulder shrugged in the direction of the railway line. 'Do you want a radio? For the shed?'

George picked half a dozen more of the French bean pods and held them out to Tom. 'Try these. And no thanks, I don't want a dodgy radio.'

'Why do you think it's dodgy?' Tom took the beans, broke them all into two and ate them all at once. He was a bit skinny, George thought, and scruffy too, as if home wasn't a place he liked to hang about in too long. And where was home? The boy's accent was a rural one, not local. George would guess at Devon, though a while ago probably.

'It's dodgy because you're a shifty teenager. You are not a branch of Comet with a nice tempting offer pasted up on your huge out-of-town warehouse window, now are you? Do you want a cup of tea? I was about to make a brew before I get going on all this weeding. I've been away three weeks and it's like leaving your cat to be fed by someone else – it's never done quite the way you like it. Cats and plants can tell.'

'OK. Thanks,' Tom said. 'And the radio, well I haven't nicked one. I haven't got one at all, but I can get you one if you want. I just thought I'd offer.'

George unlocked the shed and opened the door. A warm woody scent filled the air, tinged with the scent of dried earth and the oil he used to clean his tools. He loved that smell. It reminded him of his own father and of being a child in a garden, learning the mysteries of how the earth worked, how plants grew and fruited and were reborn simply following the seasons. Nature took and gave no more than was essential for survival and he'd often wondered if that was where his interest in what he thought was the simpler version of politics came from: no-one needed more than enough, greed was an evil that killed off man's purity. Animals only required food, water and shelter: so why did humans strive for so much more in terms of rubbishy wealth and possessions at each other's expense?

'Last night, when you said you'd seen me . . .' Tom began as he sipped at the mug of strong tea George had handed him.

'I wondered when we'd get to that.' George grinned

at him. 'I knew someone was living in that old Sierra. I noticed yesterday morning, there's a blanket on the back seat that wasn't there before I went to Cuba. And you were on the railway line in the early afternoon, walking across like it was just a country lane.'

'Quickest way across.'

'You'll still get yourself killed. And haven't you got a home to go to or shouldn't I ask?'

Tom grinned again. He was keeping his teeth in good nick at least, George thought. He must have got this living-rough business well sorted out.

'You can ask,' Tom said.

The table in the left corner next to the bar of the Leo was becoming Matthew's own. At eleven thirty each morning he felt perfectly content to take his seat there facing the window where he could watch the local to-ings and fro-ings and pick up one of the tabloid papers to read. He was well ahead with the plots of all the TV soaps (though he never watched them), knew which movie stars were sleeping with each other and which outfits had been approved of at the latest batch of awards ceremonies. He was up to date with which members of the royal family had forsworn cocaine and which ones had yet to be tempted to experiment, and he could hold his own in any conversation that involved the selection of decent midfield players for the England team.

'Usual?' Micky was polishing glasses behind the bar, wearing a large white apron and looking immaculate and sober.

'Mm. Please. And have you got some of that chocolate cake? I didn't bother with breakfast.'

Micky tutted. 'You should. It sets you up. Men

without work get fat, lolling around all day. You'll end up at Shape Sorters lining up for a weigh-in, a bollocking and a cabbage-only diet.'

'Can't wait,' Matt grunted. 'Where's the papers?' He looked around. Usually there was a tidy heap of them on the table by the door. Micky had long since given up trying to hang them up on the smart wooden holders that chic cafés used: too much crockery had been swept dramatically and noisily to the floor by people trying to wield the batons and turn the pages at the same time.

'Nicked. People think each one is provided *just for them.*'

'That's because you make each customer feel so special, Micky.'

'Bloody cheek,' Micky laughed, handing him an extra large café latte.

'There's a local rag on the seat behind you.'

Matthew picked up the newspaper and read, without much interest, about plans to close Richmond Park to through traffic. It was a debate that seemed to have been going on for years, from what he could gather, and he felt there must be a lot of missing information that would give him the right clues to the real state of play.

'May I sit here?' Matthew looked up, startled. Angie's blond hair swung in front of him, inches, it seemed, from his face.

'Course you can.' He felt ridiculously flustered, recalling that he'd just about flashed his dick at her only the week before. 'How are you?'

Angie ordered a hot chocolate from Micky and sat down opposite Matthew, who marvelled at the performance she made of arranging her bag on the seat beside her, her jacket on the back of her chair and the sugar bowl at the ready directly in front of her. Eventually, satisfied, she answered him. 'I'm OK, not as OK as I'd like to be though.' She leaned closer. 'I think there's someone watching me. I even thought, one night when I came home, that someone had actually been in. I think it was only imagination, but since then it's like, when I'm in the house at night, or sometimes when I'm gardening, that I'm not exactly alone. Do you ever get that? Or Jess?'

Matthew pulled a face that was supposed to show he was considering this seriously. 'No, I haven't noticed and Jess hasn't said anything. Who do you think it could be, any ideas?'

She had very pretty nails, he thought, looking at the perfect squared-off ends which were improbably white for someone who claimed to do their own weeding. They sparkled with glimmering polish, which was, he'd say, purely nail-coloured and probably desperately expensive.

'Not sure. But the bloke next door keeps wandering about in his front garden and measuring. I'm sure he mentioned ages ago that he wanted to build an extension. I don't fancy the idea of him getting any closer to my place.'

'Check it out in the paper,' Micky leaned over the bar and suggested as he handed Angie her chocolate. 'Planning applications are near the back before the sport.'

'Would he need planning permission?'

'Sure,' Micky said. 'The houses might be only Victorian but it's a conservation area. And he's an architect, isn't he? He'd know. Check the list.'

Matthew found the page and looked through the list of applications. They were mostly shop-owners applying for change of use or to put up a bigger and brighter sign over their premises.

'There's quite a lot. Number 12 in the Grove is after a conservatory.' Angie moved herself into the seat next to him and read over his shoulder. 'And, look, there it is, number 45, a two-storey extension!'

'Who's got a two-storey extension, lucky sod?' Eddy came into the Leo and joined Matthew and Angie, laughing dirtily. 'Some of us can only manage a bungalow these days. Catch my drift?' He winked at Angie, who giggled.

'House next to me,' she explained. 'He's creeping closer and I don't like it.'

'Well we can't have that,' Micky said. 'You'll have to object. We'll all write to the council saying you've got, oh I don't know, a right to light or something. Also, shouldn't he have told you about it? I mean don't the council send you the info in case you want to challenge the plans?'

Angie wrinkled her nose. 'I might have had something,' she admitted. 'There *was* a council letter but I always throw them away because it's usually just a survey or a complaint about the hedge growing over the path.'

'Someone in the Grove's always got builders in, faffing about with roof extensions and flash decking where perfectly good stone used to be. I can't remember when the road had less than two skips parked in it,' Matthew said. 'And do the council take any notice of objectors?'

'Worth a shot.' Angie smiled shining rays of gratitude at Micky.

'Does anyone think we need any more conservatories as well?' Eddy said, looking down the list.

'Well I've got one. I can hardly grumble about other people wanting them.'

'Course you can. Where's your miserable-old-git quotient?'

Matthew grinned. 'Jess would tell you it's alive and flourishing.'

'Well then.' Eddy lit a scraggy hand-rolled cigarette. Flakes of tobacco shed themselves across the table. 'No more building then, not in the Grove, not for anyone. Agreed?' Angie hesitated for a brief moment, thinking regretfully, Matt assumed, of the pool of boyfriend material the builders had provided. She sighed, prettily, and gave in.

'Agreed,' came the chorus.

Six

Jess knew it was ridiculous to be dithering over what to wear when the point of this outing was to sample the services of a personal shopper in a major department store who would pick out something wonderful and new. She could be coming home only a few hours from now with an entirely altered wardrobe philosophy: an aversion to her customary shade-range of blue to grey perhaps, or a new-found need to wear hats. It shouldn't matter if she turned up in her oldest Saturday-mornings-at-the-garden-centre jeans or a jacket so old it was eagerly awaiting the return of the house-brick shoulder pad. Knowing this didn't stop her from getting up at the same time as the sun and flicking through the hangers along the rail in her wardrobe, feeling increasing hopelessness as she considered and rejected each item. She didn't want to let herself in for even the tiniest flicker of disdain from someone super-attuned to the nuances of fashion. It was bad enough having woken up in a depression feeling middle-aged, middle-sized and with legs that were long past their best-before date. Just now every skirt she owned seemed to be the wrong length and she certainly didn't want any possible 'before' photos of her wearing trousers, if the camera was the sort that added an instant ten pounds. Nothing, she thought as she stared into the cupboard, seemed to go with anything else, or if it did it was for the wrong kind of weather.

'Difficult time of year, spring,' she muttered to herself, cursing Paula Cheviot and her bright ideas. Paula had been positively gushing on the phone, as if this assignment was so good she could hardly bear to delegate someone else to do it.

'It's one of those things the average reader wouldn't *dream* of doing,' she'd trilled. 'But they all could. Everyone should try it. So much fun having someone else dress you up like a dolly. Selfridge's at 10.30, photographer Robin will meet you there. You'll *love* it.' That, Jess gathered, was an order.

'What on earth are you doing?' Matthew was still in bed, and as he was currently still filling the In-House Teenager gap so recently vacated by Oliver, he probably would be for several hours to come. To Jess, his voice sounded exaggeratedly growly, the way Oliver's used to when she suggested he might care to get up at some stage and consider dropping into college for his double maths class.

'I'm looking for something to wear,' she told him.

'Are you mad? Even God hasn't woken up yet,' he grumbled. 'Does it really matter that much what you wear? Isn't that what they're supposed to be telling you?'

Jess pulled out a navy blue Jigsaw jacket and draped

93

it on the bed across the fidgeting little heap that was Matthew's feet. The jacket was a trusty standby, a well-shaped old friend with a flattering Nehru collar. 'Well, they're going to get some kind of impression of me the second I walk in. I don't want to have a "near-menopausal suburban frump" sign flashing over my head. The person in charge would be pointing me at the mid-calf box-pleat skirts and gold-button blazers.'

'Selfridge's don't have that kind of thing any more. You should take me with you. See what they can come up with for a man of newly acquired endless leisure.' He hauled himself up from the depths of the duvet and yawned. 'Any chance of a cup of tea?'

Jess laughed. 'Ask one of the girls. They should be up by now.'

As if she'd been waiting outside for her cue, Natasha slid into the room. She had her purple satin dressing gown wrapped tightly round her and her body was contorted in an attitude of exaggerated agony.

'It's not fair! We've got an inset day and I feel terrible!'

'Insect day?' Matthew looked at her with his head on one side like an appealingly dim budgie.

'You know, teachers catching up with their own curriculum, that kind of thing,' Jess explained. To Natasha she said, 'Nobody told me you had a day off. What's the matter? Do you feel feverish?' She put her hand on Natasha's forehead. It felt cool enough, though her skin was a bit clammy.

'Nah, just a period, just the usual,' Natasha groaned and sat down heavily on the bed, bending forward so her head was on her knee.

'Oh women's stuff.' Matthew waved a dismissal at

her. 'Imagine if all we men went wobbly once a month.'

Natasha looked up and stared at him, then at Jess, and the two of them laughed. 'Imagine!' they said together.

'Mum, if I take some paracetamol and if I feel better, can I come out with you? Please? I really can't face doing maths.'

Jess hesitated. Natasha was looking particularly vulnerable. If she said no, the poor girl would probably burst into tears. On the other hand, a teenager, especially one of changeable and hormonally unstable mood, might not be the best companion for her first proper assignment as a roving journalist.

'OK,' she agreed eventually. 'But on condition you are quiet and polite and remember that this is my job, not just a jolly outing. You have to promise not to strop and absolutely definitely not to show me up.'

'OK I promise. And if I'm really good will you buy me something? Please? Just something little, and really really cheap?' Natasha was doing her best to look her most persuasive.

Jess looked at the heart-shaped little face, the huge eyes that silently pleaded 'pamper me'. She remembered period pains; at her school they not only didn't get you off games but earned you an extra run round the hockey pitch. Her mother had told her they were a trial run for childbirth and there'd been times, when she was about fourteen and whimpering on her bedroom floor clutching a hot-water bottle to her middle, when she'd wondered why anyone had children at all if this was only the half of it.

'Maybe,' she conceded to Natasha. 'It depends.' Too late, Jess realized she'd given the answer that any

95

teenage girl would translate as a 'yes' so definite it rated on the same level as a sworn affidavit.

Matthew groaned from the depths of the duvet. 'You'll regret saying that,' he predicted. 'She'll scorch your credit card.' Natasha, triumphant, padded out of the room and down the stairs to get ready. Jess turned back to the wardrobe. Somewhere in there must be the skirt that went perfectly with the blue Jigsaw jacket.

'What did she say?' Zoe was already up and dressed and in the kitchen raiding the fridge and the cupboard for food supplies to get her through the day. Emily's school out in the Oxfordshire sticks might be pretty easy-going in some ways but they might draw the line at letting a stranger in for lunch. Boarding schools might be really weird, like prisons or something. They probably had a head-count every hour or two to make sure people hadn't sneaked in from the town to get a free meal or join in a quick game of lacrosse or raid the trophy cupboard.

'It's fine. I should be able to keep Mum out for hours, long enough to keep her mind off what you might be up to anyway. Are you sure about this? You've never been there before. You might get lost. Why can't Emily just come back up here and see you?'

'She doesn't want to go to the clinic by herself. I *told* you. I said I'd meet her at the school and then we'll hitch into Oxford and I'll get the coach home from there. Apparently it's general studies afternoon, whatever that is and they more or less do what they like.'

Natasha laughed. 'Well we all know what Emily likes. Stupid little slapper.'

Zoe looked at her, fearful. 'Tash, you promised you wouldn't tell anyone. Emily would kill me if she knew

96

I'd told you. You won't say anything will you? Promise again?'

'Course I won't,' Natasha reassured her. 'But if you're not back by six and if anything happens to you . . . well I don't think you should hitch, that's all.'

'You're starting to sound like Mum. Nothing will happen. I owe you one.'

Natasha looked at her for a long moment, weighing up whether this was a good moment to strike a deal on the payback. She heard her mother's feet on the stairs, clumping awkwardly in unusually high shoes. There wasn't time just now. The return favour she needed would have to keep for later.

Jess had assumed Robin the photographer would be a woman, someone she wouldn't mind having alongside her in the changing room, someone who would understand that at her age there were bits of her that were completely off limits for photos. Instead, waiting by the Personal Shopping area and festooned with the equipment of his trade, was a pale, twitchy young man whose hair had clearly turned prematurely grey. It stuck up in untidy silver clumps and as she and Natasha approached he prodded at it in a way that suggested a nervous habit. He didn't look like the sort who would understand if she pointed to her neck and asked him to keep that bit in the shadows.

'Robin? Hi, I'm Jess Nelson and this is Natasha, my daughter. I brought her along for a bit of moral support.' Robin's eyes widened with what looked like terror at the sight of Natasha.

'Are they doing both of you then?' he asked, sneaking a quick glance at his watch.

'No, it's supposed to be just me. But don't worry, I

don't expect it will take too long.' She might be new to this, but Jess wasn't going to have him rushing her.

'But if they offer . . .' Natasha cut in.

'Well yes, of course, if they offer . . .' Jess teased.

'Where are all the celebs?' Natasha whispered as she and Jess sipped their coffee in the waiting area. 'I thought there'd be at least Madonna and Posh Spice.' Jess had privately thought there would be too, but the other customers, settled into deep armchairs and quietly flicking through magazines, looked surprisingly ordinary – very much along the lines of up-for-the-day from Surrey.

'Perhaps celebrities get appointments out of opening hours,' Jess suggested, looking at her watch. Robin was taking a long time to set up his equipment. He seemed to be struggling with an endless supply of diffusers, reflectors, deflectors and tripods, all pulled out of a couple of bags that looked far too small to have held everything, like magicians' props. The woman beside Jess, too well-mannered to ask directly what he thought he was up to, glanced up now and then as he made experimental light-meter readings on Jess's face. Marilyn, a cheery thirty-something Scot who was to do the clothes selecting and who looked as if this job kept her in better muscle condition than all Jess's efforts at the gym, had already taken a Polaroid of Jess as well as one of the 'cute wee girl' for good measure. Jess had gritted her teeth at the description of Natasha. That was the kind of thing that would normally have the 'wee girl' glaring and glowering but Natasha simply smiled with her maximum radiance and asked if it was all right if she too filled in a form about her clothing preferences, just for fun.

'Of course, my pet! Let's see what we can find for

you too!' Jess gave Natasha a look but it was too late. 'We're not actually buying anything,' she hissed at her.

'That's not very fair to Marilyn is it?' Natasha countered. 'That's just wasting her time. We should buy *something*, the *Gazette* should pay.' She looked down at her questionnaire. 'It says here which designers do I prefer? What shall I put?'

'Just put Miss Selfridge and Top Shop. Don't go getting fancy ideas,' Jess told her crossly, wondering, rather guiltily, if she'd spelled Nicole Farhi's name right. It seemed vaguely sinful, somehow, chewing over the merits of Donna Karan and Jasper Conran when the once-bountiful well that was Matthew's income was about to run dry. This is just my job, not real life, she reminded herself, as one of Marilyn's colleagues hurtled in towing a rail crammed with new-season delights.

Zoe got off the coach in the middle of the small town. With its old market hall in the centre of the square and so many half-timbered shops it reminded her of a film set for something Jane Austen-ish. There was no sign of Emily and she stood nervously at the bus stop feeling awkward, shifting her bag to her left shoulder and wondering what she was supposed to do now. Emily had said she'd try to meet her, but she hadn't actually promised and Zoe wished she'd listened more carefully when Emily had been giving her the directions to the school. At least it wasn't raining and miserable. It was warm enough now to take off her sweater and tie it round her middle. She waited for what seemed like endless minutes and then went into a small, scruffy supermarket.

'Mansfield School? Just behind the library and

across the rec,' the assistant, pricing up tins of peas and too bored even to look up from her work, told her as if Zoe was likely to be familiar with these landmarks already.

'Thanks,' Zoe muttered, too disheartened to pursue the matter and hoping she'd have better luck with the next person she asked. At least it seemed to be within walking distance. That meant Emily and Giles must have been too lazy to wander as far as the local chemist for contraceptive supplies. Perhaps they spent all their spare cash on drugs and booze instead. Her mum had been writing about that not long ago, about how some boarding-school kids competed at being bad. She wished she hadn't come. Emily must surely have someone at school she could have told, someone who could help her sort this problem out. Didn't they have matrons who were motherly and forgiving and could be counted on to give them a big hug, a cup of cocoa and the number of the nearest abortion clinic?

'Zoe! You came!' Emily was bounding over the rec-reation ground, expertly sidestepping dollops of dog mess.

'Course I did. Said I would didn't I?' Zoe put her bag down and allowed herself to be hugged. Emily felt horribly bony. Maybe she'd been sick a lot in the mornings and got thinner.

Emily's delight evaporated. 'You're not cross are you? What's wrong?'

'Nothing. It's OK.' Zoe shrugged. She didn't want to give Emily any reason to dissolve into the kind of tears she'd gushed the week before at the allotment. Her eyes already looked huge and troubled and ready to pour all over her big broad cheekbones. They could be hours mopping up if that happened.

'Come and see everyone.' Emily linked her arm through Zoe's. 'I'd really like you to meet Giles.'

He was the last person Zoe wanted to see: she wouldn't be able to do anything but picture him having sex with Emily and even if he looked like Leonardo DiCaprio she'd rather not think about that, but she was curious to get a look at the inside of the school.

'Do you sleep in dormitories?' she asked as they pushed through a tatty green door into a disappointingly modern addition to a grim Victorian building just like the old hospital near home that was being pulled down. Zoe had hoped for something that looked grand and important, like Winchester College which she'd seen on the *Antiques Roadshow* on television.

'No of course we don't. We share rooms in twos and you can't choose who with because you're supposed to love everyone here in a kind of, what is it, *democratic* way. Being best friends isn't encouraged. I'm in with this complete spoon called Louisa who practises the bloody clarinet all the time.'

Zoe laughed. 'If you loved everyone *democratically* wouldn't that mean you'd have slept with more than just Giles?'

Emily frowned. 'Ssh! Someone might hear. That was against the rules, *completely*. I told you. We can do anything except sex, drugs and watch the kind of telly that we really like. Oh and we can't run in the corridors.'

'Sounds fun. *Not*.' They'd reached the end of the building. Zoe could hear music behind the double doors facing them and identified Travis's 'Driftwood' which Natasha had played to death for the three days after she'd bought it.

Zoe felt horribly shy. Walking into the crowded

common room reminded her of crossing the square by the Leo when Tash's old primary-school friend Mel and all her mates were sprawled on the benches smoking. You didn't want to be unfriendly because they might say something horrible that you'd just about hear after you'd walked past, but if you smiled and got blanked it felt worse. Here, though, she needn't have worried.

'Everyone, this is my very best friend Zoe from home!' Zoe didn't catch any of the names, there were too many. The girls all looked similar, as if living together for so long they'd evolved a look of their own. They blurred into a type: remarkably clear complexions, long straight hyper-clean hair, trousers in varying shades of beige balanced on slim hips and tight pastel cardigans. They were smiling (perfect teeth), friendly and delighted to see her, as if a visit from the outside was an exciting novelty.

'And Zoe, this is Giles.' Emily pulled her down the room to where a lank-haired boy was slouched across a tatty blue armchair. She felt quite disappointed, almost cheated. She'd assumed that any bloke who could charm the knickers off someone as young as Emily must be the school stud: an irresistible mixture of Michael Owen, Brad Pitt and Dylan the guitarist from Simplicity. This boy, shortish, running to soft plumpness around the neck and with a prize-winning outcrop of very busy acne, was someone she and her mates wouldn't waste the effort turning to look at even if he yelled at them from a passing Ferrari. He glanced up briefly, grunted something unidentifiable in a tone that suggested it was a huge effort to be even basically polite and went back to reading the sports pages in the *Sun*.

'We'd better get going.' Emily tugged at her arm. 'We'll miss the bus.'

'Bus? I thought we were going to hitch.' Zoe had been looking forward to that. It would have added even more to the ridiculous drama of the day.

'You don't wanna hitch,' Giles grunted. 'Getta cab.' Zoe glared at him, but he hadn't looked up from the paper.

'Maybe you should give us the fare,' she hissed at him. The room quietened.

'No, Zo, come on. Let's just go.' Emily pulled her out into the corridor. 'What did you say that for?' she yelled into Zoe's face as soon as they were a few safe steps from the door.

'Well, he doesn't exactly seem to care much about where you're going, does he? Is he always getting girls pregnant? Has he got an account at the clinic?'

'It's nothing to do with him! Not now! Oh let's just get out of here.' Emily stumped off out of the building and strode ahead towards the town centre.

'Yeah,' Zoe growled to herself. 'Let's go.'

'It's happened again: there's definitely been someone in. Don't tell me I'm imagining it, the house smells different.' Angie leaned forward so that her breasts seemed to be propped up on the table like a presentation pair of George's firmest allotment cabbages. It crossed Matthew's mind that she could have worn something that covered her front rather more adequately. She was a bit long in the tooth (though not *that* long), to be honest, for those cute little cardigans that Natasha and Zoe favoured and which reminded him of babies' matinee jackets. This powder-blue one was undoubtedly cashmere, threaded through at the

edges with lavender satin ribbon that was supposed to
tie the top edges together. It seemed to have given up
under the strain of Angie's anatomy and the loose
ends dangled helplessly. Matthew wasn't used to eyeing up women in a sexually questing way. At work he
had had to be scrupulously non-interested to the
point where he'd no longer dared to think about it:
the sharp-edged females in the PR business prided
themselves on being able to read a grubby male mind
from the far side of an armour-plated door. But now he
was free from office life it was as if some long-lost
primitive urges were filing back into the brain space
vacated by conferences on media might, clients' flow
charts and the phone number for *Question Time*'s
researcher.

'Did this mystery intruder take anything?' Matthew
asked.

Angie frowned, then just as quickly stopped as if
remembering not to furrow her brow and make lines.
'No. Nothing. That's the thing. I mean you can't complain to the police when there's nothing to complain
about, can you? I'd even left jewellery lying about in
the bedroom. I couldn't see anything missing.'

'No, well you wouldn't,' Matthew commented.

'Wouldn't what?'

'See it. If it was missing. Sorry, just that in PR you
use words carefully. It's in case you're misinterpreted.'
He laughed. 'You can stretch the truth till you can
make balloon animals out of it, but you have to choose
words that won't leave you floundering to explain
yourself.'

'Oh.' She wasn't interested. 'But you don't do that
any more,' she pointed out.

'No.' Despair threatened, to his surprise. 'No, and

that's good,' he rallied. 'So why do you think some-one's been in?'

'I told you, it smells different. And the towels were wet in the spare-room shower.'

Matthew could feel his face breaking into an unat-tractive smirk. 'Have you had someone in that you've, er, invited?'

'What and forgotten about?' Angie snapped. 'Look, it was probably the cleaning lady or something, or a stray cat got in and sprayed. Forget it.'

After she'd gone, Matthew wandered round the house wishing Jess would come home and cheer him up. They could go down to the travel agents and book themselves a last-minute weekend in Barcelona or something. Or check out some Internet bargains. It would do them both good to get away, blow some of the golden payout on a bit of foreign fun.

The new and unwelcome feeling of despair lingered at the back of his mind, getting in the way of the won-derful buoyed-up excitement at life's possibilities that he'd had since the great redundancy day. He wasn't the only one who'd left the company that day, but he was the only one who had no intention of ever going back there, not even for a visit. One or two had made tenta-tive plans to meet up every second Thursday in the month for a drink but he didn't want any of that. It was too much like clinging to the wreckage of a career. And besides, without that career what on earth would they find to talk about? If they'd wanted to discuss their gardens or their families or their passion for scuba-diving off the remotest coasts of Scotland surely they'd have done it before now.

He grabbed his jacket from the newel post at the bot-tom of the stairs, checked that his keys were in his pocket and went out. He'd go and talk to Ben and Micky, have some lunch and put more thought into some kind of future career plans. Maybe the Cat Sat, as a concept, hadn't really got legs, so to speak, but something else would come up, it was only a matter of time.

Jess calculated that she was already about three hundred pounds down and it would have been a lot more if Natasha had had her way. There wasn't any point working like this: at this rate she'd end up spending far more than she was being paid. Marilyn had hurtled round the store with Jess, Natasha and Robin in hot pursuit, barely stopping to grab clothes from the rails. 'You like Donna Karan don't you Jess, we'll try this in both colours, oh and you'd love Colette Dinnigan and this Elspeth Gibson. Now Natasha, Anna Sui is just your sort of thing, and what about Press & Bastyan?'

It was probably because of the camera: everyone in the Personal Shopping area seemed to be joining in freely in a most un-English sort of way. Natasha, of course, had taken over as the star turn. Being 5'8", long-limbed and slim, and with a small cute face like a naughty elf she was a dream to dress. All the Home Counties ladies cooed and smiled at her and told her she looked gorgeous each time she emerged from the changing room and sashayed about in front of the mirrors while Robin's camera snapped away. Unnoticed, and quite relieved that this was the case, Jess picked out a pair of black linen Nicole Farhi trousers for herself.

'Everything looks just lovely on you, dear,' Marilyn told Natasha. 'Though I don't think pale pink is your colour.' Mid-rose was though, it was finally agreed, and Natasha, gazing at her reflection, put on her most persuasive, begging, '*please* Mum' expression. The dress did look wonderful. It was two layers, one deep pink, one purple, high-waisted with a drawstring under the bust, short and with little puffed frill-edged sleeves that reminded Jess of toddlers' outfits. There was absolutely no chance she would get away with saying no to Natasha. Jess looked round at their audience's eager faces challenging her to deny her daughter, sighed, and gave in, fishing in her bag for her credit card.

'Thanks Mum.' Natasha was so thrilled she linked her arm through her mother's as they left the store. 'Shall we get some lunch now?'

'I can't afford lunch,' Jess grouched. 'What had you in mind? The Ivy? The Savoy?'

Natasha giggled. 'Mm, either would be nice.'

'We should get home. I need to write this up while it's still fresh in my mind.'

Natasha tugged at her arm. 'Can't we just grab something fast? I'm starving. I really need something with chips. Let's just go into . . . look, there's a Café Rouge over there.'

Natasha was halfway through her steak when she suddenly went silent and looked strangely sad.

'What's wrong, Tash? Has the pain come back?' Jess asked.

'No. It's just, all that money.'

'I know. Still, according to your dad he shouldn't have any trouble getting himself some kind of job again soon.' If only, she thought, saying it made it true.

'No, it's not that.' Natasha pushed the rest of her food to the side of her plate and started picking through her salad with her fingers. 'I was thinking about Tom. He's probably never even seen that kind of money, and we

107

just bought a dress and a pair of trousers with it. Just one dress, not even loads of dresses. Just one.'

Jess wasn't sure which way to feel. On the one hand she was delighted that her daughter was showing signs of growing a social conscience, but on the other she didn't want her not to enjoy a bit of personal luck.

'We don't do this every day, Tasha, this was just a treat, a one-off.'

'Some people just don't get treats. Tom doesn't.'

'I take it you really like him?' Jess knew this was a risky question. Natasha might immediately clam up. One of Nelson's columns had been about exactly that: the delicate business of extracting romance information from a teenager. She'd likened it to trying to twiddle out the meat from inside the tiniest of a lobster's claws: it required gentle persistence, steady concentration and light-handedness, otherwise you were left with something that wasn't whole, was messed-about-with and not particularly satisfying. So it was with adolescents. Natasha clearly had something to say but would need delicate handling if she was to be persuaded to come out with it.

'It's like, well Tom hasn't got a proper home.' Natasha hadn't answered Jess's question. Jess wasn't sure she minded that: how much of a fifteen-year-old's love life did anyone really feel like finding out?

'He said he's all right though, living with foster people.' Jess reached across the table and helped herself to a piece of Natasha's tomato. 'Do they give him a hard time?'

Natasha grinned, looking down at her plate as if the grin wasn't meant to be shared. 'No, not any more,' she said.

'Well that's good, isn't it? And he can come and see

us whenever you want him to, you know. The way he wolfed down that dinner last week, he certainly seemed to be in need of a square meal.'

Natasha's face brightened. 'Can he? Can he live with us for a bit? He could have Oliver's room, especially as you wouldn't let me have it.'

Jess laughed. 'You're fifteen and you want your boyfriend, who you've known less than a fortnight, to move in with us! Are you mad? Suppose you go off him in another week, what happens then? We can't send him off to a rejected boys' rehoming centre, you know!' Natasha wasn't laughing and Jess put on a more serious face. 'Sorry love, let's just see how things go, shall we? Invite him for supper again, whenever you like.'

Natasha looked at the floor and muttered, 'So you can see if he's really *suitable*.'

'No. So that *you* can. Shall we go home now?'

Natasha looked up, flustered. 'Er, do we have to? Can't we do something else?'

'No! No more shopping!' Jess counted out coins for the tip and put her jacket back on.

'But Mum, it's early . . . I know, you really need a haircut. Let's go and do that somewhere. I'll tell them what to do and then I'll just sit and read magazines. *Please* Mum, let's not go home yet.'

Seven

'. . . scuba-diving the Barrier Reef – totally awesome, water colour the most spectacular blue ever. Moored up at a little island, no trees just a sand mound in middle of the reef, with beautiful turquoise sea with darker patches marking out the reef as far as you could see. The mountains of Cairns in the background and a few high cirrus clouds. Stunner . . .'

She was glad he was having a good time, she was delighted for him but it was impossible not to be hugely envious. Oliver sounded so blissfully free of worries, as if, with no more exams to think about, no work to get up for, he was gradually emptying his head of everything except the joy of the moment. It must be like being a small child again. Jess imagined him lying on the sand, staring up at the sky, watching the high thin clouds scudding past. She remembered doing that when she was a teenager, she and her friends losing themselves to the mildly trippy feeling of the sky's movement till they felt the earth turning fast with them perched precariously on top of it, like being on a slightly nerve-wracking fairground ride.

She reread Oliver's e-mail and printed out a copy to show Matthew, who was in the garden reading the paper. She could just see the back of his head, beyond the conservatory window. His body was very still, as it always was when he was concentrating thoroughly, and she concluded he was reading something riveting about football rather than checking the job vacancies. Like Oliver, he seemed to have no cares in the world. Unlike Oliver, he was wrong.

She went through the kitchen and out to join him. The day was going to be hot in that unexpected, catching-you-out way that early April often was, and the rhododendron outgrowing its massive pot was drooping and desperate for water. Matthew didn't seem to have noticed, or if he had he'd chosen not to do anything about it. She would reel out the hose later: it needed unwinding all the way back to sort out a kink close to the tap that was holding back the flow because someone had been careless rewinding it last time. That was the downside of delegation: you too often had to allocate the job to someone who frankly didn't give a damn, and the resulting cock-up made you cross. On the other hand if you didn't delegate you ended up doing everything yourself, which also made you cross. All in all, she thought, if you didn't lighten up a bit it made for a pretty bad-tempered life.

'Look at this.' Jess held the e-mail out to Matthew. 'Oliver's having the best time, sunning himself on a yacht round the Whitsunday Islands.'

Matthew grinned. 'Maybe that's what I should do with all this spare time, go off backpacking like a

111

student and then come back full of the joys of youth again.'

'It would be a second childhood in your case,' she laughed. 'Or should I say an extended adolescence?' She sat down beside him on the bench and picked a few weeds out of the pot of thyme beside the conservatory window. The garden desperately needed attention. It was something Matthew used to deal with on Sunday mornings, usually as a way of coping with a mild hangover. The worse his headache was, the more energetically he'd pushed the lawnmower. Without the routine of daily work, without the contrast between work-days and other days, other routines had vanished too. Matthew had never exactly been one for the unbreakable ritual of Sunday morning car-cleaning (unlike Angie's ex-husband who had woken the Grove shortly after every Sunday dawn with the whine of his mini-vac sucking dust from his precious Audi's carpets), but there had been the chores that had got done simply because of the urgency of cramming them into what little free time there was. Now, with the weeks of non-occupation stretching ahead (Jess slapped down the thought that it might well be years), Matthew was becoming distinctly lazier. The grass had got to the waving-in-the-wind length and was sprouting a fine crop of dandelions. The surge in spring growth showed that in the race to the top of the trellis the bindweed was easily outstripping the clematis. The honeysuckle, wondrous though it would smell in a few weeks when it flowered, was now so rampant that it was clogging the conservatory guttering and causing cascades of water to overflow onto the terrace whenever fierce spring rain fell.

'There's an awful lot of moss on this terrace,' she

commented, scraping at the stones with her foot. A sticky greeny-brown wodge of it collected on the end of her shoe. She scuffed it off on the edge of the bench leg where it stayed in a solid lump that resembled dog mess.

'Hmm.' Matthew had gone back to Manchester United's chances in next Wednesday's match against Real Madrid. Oliver's e-mail lay face down on the bench between them.

'Any chance you could give it some attention before it gets out of hand?' she ventured.

Matthew folded the paper with exaggerated care and placed it neatly down on the bench beside him.

'Do you want to make a list?'

'Of what?'

'You're doing that thing again. Finding things for me to do. Things to fill my time that will keep me out of trouble.' He wasn't smiling. His eyes were cold and humourless.

'You usually do the garden stuff, that's all. What's the problem?' Jess asked.

'Do I? I thought we both did it, on a casual as-and-when basis. Or is it what men with nothing better to do fill their days with? Do you want me to join the bowls club and get a slow old dog so we can waddle off for walkies on the common?'

Jess stood up. 'You're overreacting. The new equation is, I'm really busy and you're not. The garden needs attention: at the moment you have time for it and I don't. But if you frankly can't be arsed, well just let it grow, I don't much care any more than you do.'

Jess slammed back into the house and straight out again through the front door, pausing only briefly to collect her gym bag and car keys. The childish phrase 'it's not fair' seemed relevant, she thought, as she started her Golf and pulled out into the Grove. It was nearly a month now since Matthew's working life had so abruptly ended. For all that time he had done nothing except stay in bed late, then get up and mooch down to the Leo to hang about with all the other work-free men in the area. From what she could gather, they sat around giggling through the tabloid papers, telling each other jokes and working out ways to make them-selves instantly and immensely rich.

Ben and Micky were the only ones actually making any money, running the bar and craftily encouraging the long hours of idle boozing and schmoozing. Eddy was still convinced the Cat Sat invention was likely to take off and had got as far, according to Matthew, of drafting an advert to place in a magazine he swore was called *Pussy Pals* to entice fond owners of precious pedigree breeds to invest in its development. It never bloody would get developed, Jess thought angrily as she crashed through the gears and pulled away too fast from the traffic lights at the square, not while its inven-tors spent 95 per cent of their time planning the spending of their mythical profits and the rest of their time playing daft jokes like ringing up the local paper to report that the people at number 17 had sold their dustbin area to a mobile phone company so they could put up a mast.

Jess turned into the gym car park and almost im-mediately changed her mind. It was mid-morning now, one of the busiest times. The changing room would be full of post-school-run mothers wittering on to each other about whether it was worth little Sebastian going in for a St Dominic's scholarship, when, after all the expense of extra coaching, it was only worth a 20 per cent reduction in the fees. Week after week she heard the same conversations repeated. Probably in their time she and Angie had gone over the same topics about Zoe and Emily. Not once had she heard anyone mention anything that didn't involve proof of being majorly well off. There were debates about the merits of beech flooring over oak, of St Lucia over Tobago for holidays or Swiss over Slovenian for au pairs.

Once, she and Angie had listened with delighted amazement as a woman with a massive house on the corner of the common had shamelessly patronized her companion, saying, 'Oh I do so envy you your garden; I'd love to have one that small, so much more manageable. The gardener does put in eight hours a week, but still . . .' and so on. The gym changing room was a fantasy never-never land for the communal solving of non-problems. Not once had she heard anyone compare the tricky downside of sudden unemployment with, say, the collapsing of a twenty-year marriage or the realization that a child was actually severely thick and not acceptably dyslexic at all.

Jess turned the car round and headed out of the car park again. 'I'll go and see if Dad's at the allotment,' she said to herself. And then, she thought, she'd go and map out a few chapter headings on the computer. If she had only six months left of writing Nelson's Column, perhaps there was scope for collecting together the work of the last couple of years and putting them out as a book. It had worked for Jilly Cooper.

'I can't believe Emily could be that stupid,' Zoe said again. She was sitting cross-legged on Natasha's desk in her bedroom, picking at some loose threads at the hem of the curtain.

115

'I can. She was always a track short of the full CD,' Natasha told her. 'Don't you remember that time when she came round and said that her rabbit was lying down and had gone all hard and she thought it was because it had stuffed itself with too much food and would get up again after a sleep?'

'It probably *did* die of overeating. She was always giving it bunny-munch sugary snacks. Maybe if she'd given herself a few bunny-munches, then she wouldn't be bloody anorexic. I can't believe she thought she was pregnant. She probably hasn't even *done it*. God it was so embarrassing!' Zoe put her hands over her face as if she was still in danger of blushing scarlet. 'When the woman came in and asked Emily, in that oh-so-gentle way, why she had thought she was pregnant! I could've killed her! The woman looked sort of *pitying* as if she'd never met anyone this ignorant.'

'Probably hadn't,' Natasha agreed. 'But Zo, didn't you ask her if she'd done a pregnancy test? Hadn't Giles asked her? Hadn't anyone?'

'No. I just assumed. I mean if someone says they're pregnant and drags you with them to a clinic you imagine they know what they're about. I don't think Giles gives a toss either way.'

'She's still got a problem though,' Natasha pointed out. 'She's got too thin for periods and that's dangerous. The school must have noticed.'

Zoe shrugged. 'All the girls there were thin, like *really* thin, the ones I saw anyway. They all wore really low beige trousers and you could see their hip bones, all jutting out and pointy. Funny, because all the boys I saw were really pudgy. Perhaps they grab all the food, like pigs at a trough.' She glanced out of the window. 'Hey look,' she pointed to the end of the garden.

'There's Tom, down by the railway. Are you supposed to go out and meet him?'

Natasha hurtled across the room and peered out of the window. 'Where is he? Oh yeah I can see. No we hadn't fixed anything but I think I'll go down anyway. Actually Zoe, there's something I wanted to ask you . . .'

Matthew felt bad about Jess and about the garden. On his way back from the Leo that afternoon he thought, though not too deeply, about cutting the grass. He wouldn't make a thing about it, none of that 'OK, look at me, I'm doing this for you' attitude. He'd just get on with it and be cheerful. He'd cut back the honeysuckle a bit and hack out the scraggy remains of last year's perennials as well so the new stuff could get going properly. It wouldn't take long and he could do with the exercise. As he walked down the road he patted his stomach. It wobbled alarmingly and felt like an unfamiliar thing, an addition like a small bag. He'd only had one pint, too, along with the baguette with Brie and salami and all those squishy semi-sun-dried tomatoes. He'd always been slim, slim but solid. He'd taken it for granted that the outside edges of his body would remain the same, holding everything inside together in the same shape for more or less ever. The front part had now broken away just a little to hang over his chinos in the style of a gossiping neighbour leaning forward slightly over a fence to pass on a discreet confidence.

He slowed as he approached Eddy's house. There was a police car parked outside and he wondered if some miserable Grove-ite had noticed that Eddy's sturdy pot-plants lined up on his kitchen window sill were exactly that: pot. It would be a shame to see Eddy carted away to be done for possession, and tragic if it was 'with intent to supply'; he'd got used to the reminiscences of his fame days and rather envied him his stock of tales of disgraceful behaviour. It must have been fun to have a working life that involved, and so very profitably, the kind of seriously bad conduct that would have got you expelled from even the worst sink school.

It wasn't Eddy's house that the police were visiting, Matthew realized as he slowed his pace even more out of sheer curiosity, but the one next to it. Matthew could see the front door standing open in the manner of all premises where there is disaster. Eddy was just inside the door, ushering out an infantile constable. Eddy's arm, Matthew noticed as he grinned at him over the gate, was firmly round the slim shoulders of the householder, an attractive, divorced red-headed woman he'd spoken to only once, at the kind of Christmas drinks party where everyone's apologetically brought along a lost-looking house-guest and no-one gets past the 'Oh number 34! I've always admired your stained-glass porch' stage.

'Eh Matt, Clarissa here's been burgled,' Eddy called as the constable returned to his car. Eddy and Clarissa emerged from her house and she turned to double-lock the door with great care.

'Burgled? Bloody hell,' Matthew said as the two came down the path.

'I'm just taking her into my place for a quick medicinal one.' Eddy winked at Matthew. Clarissa seemed quite content to be snuggled into Eddy's chest as if she still needed protection from the thief, either that, Matthew thought, or she was in such a state of shock that she was oblivious to the tatty condition of his ancient Eric Clapton Live at the Budokan tee shirt.

'Did they take much?' Matthew asked.

'Small things. The radio, CD player, the kids' PlayStation, stuff like that.' Clarissa's voice was whispery. She looked up at Matthew and gave him a weak smile. She was terribly pale, more as if she'd discovered a body than a burglary. She'd clearly been crying – her fierce, angry green eyes were damp and her lightly freckled skin had livid pink patches on her cheekbones. Eddy was obviously looking forward to doing further comforting.

'What did the police say? Are they likely to catch them?' Matt asked. He was enjoying stalling Eddy, who was by now almost hauling Clarissa in the direction of his own front gate.

Clarissa shrugged. 'They said there was a lot of it about and to call up my insurers.'

'Did you see that young bloke they sent?' Eddy commented as the police car drove away. 'Practically a sodding teenager. Probably on work experience. Bloody burglars, they're not big enough fish for them. But if I get my hands on whoever did it . . .' He clenched his available fist and punched at the air, a disconcerting few inches from Matt's nose.

'Er right, I'll leave you to it. See you tomorrow?' he said to Eddy.

'Yeah man, tomorrow, usual place.' Over Clarissa's bent head he turned and leered at Matthew before guiding his prey up his garden path. Matthew headed on towards home, looking forward to opening a beer and telling Jess the news. The garden could wait awhile.

*　　*　　*

119

The garlic was going to be ready early this year. The leaves were thick and strong and George was terribly tempted to pull up a bulb and see how it was coming along. When he'd been a child, he had found it impossible to resist, following his father round the garden and tweaking out a carrot here and there to see if it was ready. Then, and it must have been over sixty years back, he'd said the rabbits must have done it and his father had been kind and pretended he was right. Looking back all those years, George marvelled at the patience of the man: those had been years of hardship. Growing food then hadn't been a hobby like it was now. Every wasted carrot would have meant just a few less mouthfuls of nourishment for someone who really needed it. The people who worked these allotments now mostly did it for exercise and to escape from the confines of home, not because of the sheer need for food. The woman a couple of plots down the row grew fancy lettuces, red ones and green ones all laid out like a chessboard, and then complained about spoiling the pattern when she picked a few leaves to eat. And Dave, who was easily ten years older than him and must remember the days when the difference between feeling full and going without was the number of potatoes you could scavenge from the earth, well he only grew competition stuff now. He had a weird thing about mammoth vegetables too, which George suspected were all but inedible. How much flavour could there be in a five-pound onion?

'I've got the weeds out from the radishes. Anything else you want me to do?' George grinned at the boy. He wasn't a bad worker, this Tom, not considering how young he was.

'No, you're all right for now lad, thanks.' George

fished about in his pocket for spare cash. 'Here y'are. Don't go spending it on those alcopops!'

Tom laughed. 'No-one drinks those, well not blokes anyway.'

'Girlie drinks, are they? They always like the sweet stuff, nothing's changed there since I was a boy. Some things never do.' He gave Tom a long hard look. 'Kids have always run away from home. I bet one of Adam's brothers did a runner from the Garden of Eden.'

Tom shrugged. 'I haven't run away from home.'

'You've run away from something though, haven't you?'

'Dad! Hallo!' Jess pushed open the main allotment gate and picked her way along the narrow grassy path towards her father's scarlet shed. 'Oh and hello Tom, what are you doing here?'

'He's been helping me. He's not a bad worker, for a teenager.'

'No school?'

'Not everyone stays on to eighteen, you know Jessica, even in these days of NVQs and the like,' George teased. 'Some of them like to get on with the real doings of life.'

'Er, yeah. I've gotta go. Gotta see someone.' Tom scurried away so fast that he left Jess with only the fleeting impression of his dazzling smile, fading slowly after him like the Cheshire cat's.

'He's still seeing Natasha,' she said. 'But they keep to themselves. I just see them sliding in and out of the house now and then. All I'm getting is a back view. She sort of asked if he could move in, have Oliver's room but I said no. Now she's giving me the polite-but-non-communicative routine.'

'Do you want her to tell you everything she's up to?

121

You never did at her age, especially when there was a boy on the go.'

'I suppose not. Though how are you supposed to know if there's something to know if there's nothing you are being told?'

George laughed. 'Oh you know all right. With girls anyway. I thought you were the expert on all this stuff. You're the one who's always writing about the kids.'

'Only in a superficial way. For the column I write about jolly things like the impossibility of agreeing on paint colours for their rooms or about how you never get four teenagers together who'll agree to eat the same things. I've used little bits of them for entertainment, that's all.'

'You could call it exploitation.'

'No you couldn't. I've never written about anything that really matters.'

George gave her a long look. 'Perhaps you should,' he said.

'What matters right now, and don't ask me to write about it,' she said, 'is that Matt is the one who is behaving most like an adolescent pain in the neck. I feel, oh I don't know, like I'm the only one in the house who can see further than the end of next week. It's not a pretty view either.'

'All you're seeing is doom and despair, I suppose.' George, annoyingly, chuckled.

'What's there to laugh at? You should see the collection of direct debits that goes out of our bank each month. I spent a ridiculous amount of money when Tash and I went out the other day, almost as if I was convincing myself it was still all OK. I'd have taken everything back to the shop but they'd only give me a credit note and that's no use down at Sainsbury's.

122

Since then I've seen nothing but hopelessness. Not far on from now I can see everything being cut off, bit by bit. Electricity, gas, prosecutions for non-payment of council tax . . .'

George cut in, teasing. 'You blackballed from the gym, your *Vogue* sub cancelled, no more manicures . . .'

Jess laughed. 'OK so we've got a few non-necessities, but not many. And I know there are millions worse off than us. It's not just that. Matt just doesn't take anything seriously any more, so I end up being the worry-villain all by myself. It's turning me into a nagging dragon and I hate it.'

'So don't do it. Refuse to play.'

'Easier said.'

'No it isn't. Hell, girl, don't be so defeatist.'

'I've been waiting for you! Guess what!' Matt appeared from the kitchen as soon as Jess came through the front door.

Just in time, she managed to stop herself saying, 'You've got a job.' She hoped it would be that, but she could tell by the gleeful expression on his face that this wasn't going to involve something as dull as the world of the Occupied Adult.

'Go on then, surprise me.'

'Eddy's seducing his next-door neighbour. She's been burgled and he's taken her back to his for a spot of "comforting".' He came out with a thoroughly dirty snigger. 'Nice going, Eddy,' he chuckled. 'Don't you think?'

'You remind me of a couple of fifth-formers discussing who they've pulled at the school disco!' she laughed. 'Anyway tell me about the burglary. I take it it was Clarissa. I can't see Eddy snuggling up to the

VAT inspector from number 27.'

'Probably some kids got in. I don't think Clarissa's up to speed with intruder alarms.' Jess filled the kettle. Matt went silent for a moment and she could almost hear the cogs of thought clunking along in his brain. 'There's a lot of companies selling security systems. But I wonder if any of them do it on a purely advisory, just-between-friends basis, you know, without any hard sales pitch for one particular company. Of course, I'd have to know absolutely everything that's available . . . must be on the Net somewhere . . .'

'Surely if it was a just-friendly-advice thing, there wouldn't be any money in it.' She could have kicked herself for putting a downer on things, but somehow she was beginning to wonder if Matthew's former career had involved any contact with the Planet Real at all.

'Ah. Yes, you spotted the fatal catch. Back to the Cat Sat, I suppose. In the meantime my love, my bread-winner, I'm off to cut the grass.' He gave her a hefty, beer-scented hug. 'You see? I may be mostly useless but I'm not all bad. I'll have a cup of tea when that kettle's boiled.'

Eight

Eddy's bedroom was a big surprise. Natasha, though she'd never given it any previous thought, would have expected it to be a seedier version of Oliver's room: all discarded socks, CDs strewn around, beer cans, open cupboards showing clothes chucked in carelessly and a musty smell you didn't want to spend any time with in case you caught it on your clothes. That was the style of ungracious living that she somehow expected of all men who lived alone, as if even when they got to Eddy's age there would still be a fond regression towards teenagerhood. Instead there was no sign of any abandoned clothes and not so much as a used wine glass in sight. He must have had his cleaner in just that morning, she decided, imagining an oldish lady with rigid cauliflower curls, a floral apron and pink Marigolds, picking up underwear at arm's length and dropping it into a laundry basket with a slight shudder. The room smelled faintly of new paint too, which she assumed was why there wasn't even the hint of a mark on the walls and door which were the colour of Flora margarine.

Eddy had a vast pale wooden bed, the smart low sort with no twiddly details, as featured in her mum's *Elle Decoration*, covered with a snowy duvet and a lot of plump square pillows. The edges of the pillowcases were lacy, like the tops of little girls' socks. A massive ginger cat dozed on a small blanket on a moss green silky chaise longue under the window, cuddled up to a well-worn honey-coloured teddy bear. The cat yawned and stretched its fat paws towards Natasha as she leaned across it to look out of the window.

'You wouldn't dare go on that bed would you?' she said to the cat as she fondled its ear. 'Neither would I.' Nervously, she glanced down at the fat-looped cream carpet, checking her path from door to window, dreading finding the prints of her trainers ingrained in the pile. There was no trace of her. There must be no trace of Tom either.

She wished he'd be quick. Natasha could still hear the shower running from along the corridor. Tom would use up all the hot water at this rate and fill the house with steam. That would be such a stupid give-away. 'Wouldn't it make more sense,' she'd suggested, 'just to come to our house and use the shower there? Mum wouldn't mind.' But he hadn't wanted to. This was what Tom was used to: wandering in and out of houses big enough to have spare, barely used guest bathrooms and making free use of the facilities. The trick was doing it so that people didn't even notice anyone had been in. He'd told her he didn't want to get out of practice.

Eddy's own bathroom must be somewhere through one of the long row of mirrored doors on the far side of the bed. She really wanted to look, to see if it matched her idea of an ancient rock star's vanity salon. She'd been well wrong about the bedroom, but surely his personal en suite should have mirrors surrounded by lights, a sound system of its own and acres of rhinestone-encrusted marble? By rights he ought to have a huge black oval jacuzzi and one of those mega shower rooms that had millions of water jets and doubled as a steam room and sauna. She couldn't look though, couldn't risk even one of her fingerprints on those mirror doors. Even if she polished marks off with the sleeve of her sweatshirt, she'd never get it to look as perfectly smearless as the cauli-head cleaner could. Anyway, she had to stay by the window, check that Eddy wasn't coming back. Tom had been sure he wouldn't, but you never knew. He knew Eddy's routine: he did the same things every day. He got up about ten, went to the Leo for a late breakfast, read all the papers, chatted to Natasha's dad and a few other lounging-around blokes, came home for a while and then went off out again. Right now, according to Tom, he should be halfway through a cheese and ham croissant and on his second cappuccino.

'Stonking bed. We should test it.' Tom, wearing only a dark blue towel, sarong-style, flung himself into the middle of the immaculate duvet which fluffed up around him like a cloud, then resettled slowly. Natasha gave a tiny frightened scream. 'No! Quick get up! He'll notice!'

Tom laughed and lay back on the pillows. His hair was damp, he was making wet patches.

'No he won't. Half the time he doesn't even know what day it is. Come on Tash, come and lie down, just for a minute.' She moved out of reach.

'Not a chance! I know what "just for a minute" means. No way am I doing anything in a house I've broken into when the owner could come back and find me any moment.'

'We didn't break in,' Tom pointed out, as if it made all the difference. 'You'd think a man who lives next door to someone who's just been burgled would bother to lock his kitchen window.'

'It was a very small window. I don't suppose he thought anyone could get in through it.'

Tom sat up and turned the damp pillow over, plumping it back into place. 'No, well, people never do. But some of us are like cats; get one bit through a gap and the rest follows, no problem. You're born with it, or you're not.'

'You make it sound like some kind of real talent, like being able to draw or play the violin.'

Tom looked angry suddenly. 'Don't diss it. It gets me a living. How many people who can draw a bit can say that?' He got off the bed and stalked out of the room.

Natasha fluffed the bed back into its former neatness and looked out of the window again. She couldn't quite see all the way to the square – there was a horse chestnut tree in full flower in the way. If Eddy really did change his routine and suddenly sauntered into the Grove they wouldn't have long to get out of there. It had been exciting getting in. She'd felt adrenalin whizzing through her as she tiptoed across the kitchen floor, looking around her too fast to take in what was there and what wasn't. She'd gone into the sitting room, seen that stupid bar thing Eddy had but couldn't tell anyone who asked her now whether the front of it was covered in zebra fabric or a cowhide pattern. She'd make a lousy burglar. She'd be the type who'd struggle

128

out of a house, staggering under the weight of an ancient worthless video machine, not having noticed the £5,000 in cash that someone had left lying on a table.

'OK, let's go.' Tom was back in the room, this time with his clothes on. 'Next time I'll get in a bit earlier. His washing machine's got a quick economy cycle. Very useful.'

Natasha pulled the door closed behind her, wishing she could remember whether it had been open or not. Tom smiled, reached behind and pushed it slightly ajar, adjusting the angle. 'He wouldn't have left the cat shut in.'

'I didn't think of that. I'm rubbish at this.' Natasha giggled, relieved to be on her way off the premises. 'You didn't . . . it wasn't you who did the house next door, was it?' she queried, suddenly anxious. 'Sorry, I shouldn't ask.'

Tom stopped halfway down the stairs, just behind her. He pulled her back against his body and whispered into her hair, 'Hey, look at me. Am I taking anything from this place? Have I got Eddy's guitars stashed up my tee shirt? Any of his whisky supply? And it would be so easy.'

Natasha's heart was thumping again. She couldn't look at him, couldn't let him see that somewhere in the back of her mind she was wondering about stray credit cards, a watch maybe. It wasn't as if she'd say anything to anyone, she just wanted to know. Or maybe she didn't. 'No. Sorry. Come on, let's get out of here.'

'You've got to stop thinking of it as your problem,' Angie told Jess. At the table next to them, in the health club's café, a pair of women with newly extended nails delicately wielded forks to tackle their lunchtime salads. They reminded Jess of small children, concentrating hard on the unfamiliar skill of dealing with cutlery.

'But it *is* my problem. It's a problem for the whole family. It's just that Matthew doesn't see it as one at all. He's happier than he's ever been, going out to play like a little boy and not a care in the world.' She sighed and pushed away her half-eaten low-fat, no-flavour carrot cake.

Angie giggled and reached across to help herself to the abandoned cake. 'Well I hope that's reflected in the bedroom department. A happy man is a sexy man, I've always found. It's certainly true with workmen; you can really bank on the ones who whistle on the job, as it were.'

By Angie's reckoning then, Jess worked out, Matthew was practically singing full-scale opera. She laughed. 'Oh yes, I'll admit the unemployment situation hasn't got as far as his dick.' That was all she was willing to divulge. She wasn't going to tell Angie that Matt had taken to sneaking up on her in the shower for a spot of mutual lathering-up, or how he'd woken her a few nights before from a deep and satisfyingly dreamy sleep in the early hours and said, 'Do you fancy doing it in the garden? Under the stars?' She'd pointed out that as the nights were still cold enough to shrivel a brass monkey's balls, his own might get severely frost-nipped. 'OK,' he'd said, snuggling down quite contentedly to go immediately to sleep, leaving Jess with her brain revving up into pre-dawn deep worry-mode. From the back of her mind she could sense her mother's dire warnings about All Men. 'Never say no to your husband,' had been more or less the extent of Jess's sex education. 'If you let them go wanting, they'll go and do their wanting with someone else.' It hadn't meant much to Jess at the blasé know-it-all age of fourteen. The very idea of a 'husband' had been enough to make her grimace with scorn and flounce out of range of any further embarrassing admonitions. Now, from the position of vulnerable middle age, it was all too easy to imagine Matt, in his current state of hyper-excitement and new glee at life in general, discovering that a spot of sexual diversion would be a fun way to fill in some of this extra free time.

'Of course your Matthew wouldn't go off the straight and narrow,' Angie said, making Jess sure she was reading her thoughts.

'Wouldn't he? Why wouldn't he?' Jess asked. Angie's eyes were glittery, the way they always were when sex was the subject.

'Well . . . he loves you. He's got you and the children and well . . . I don't know, he looks like a man who's happy with his life as it is.'

'I thought he was before the day he got sacked. I'm beginning to think I was reading him all wrong all those years. I do that. I take things too literally. It's like when it says on the menu "coffee will be served at your convenience" I immediately imagine them carrying a tray into the Ladies. Just now I feel as if I didn't know anything. And my own job's all up in the air. Tomorrow I've got to go and have a proper bra fitting so I can write about it and I'm bound to go and buy one as well. It'll be the Selfridge's overspend all over again. I have no discipline. It's as if I'm pretending nothing's changed.'

'Oh I know, I mean once you've tried things on . . .'

Angie giggled. 'Shall I come with you? Then you can sort of buy one by proxy instead.' She shoved the last of the carrot cake into her mouth and said, spitting crumbs, 'I can at least help you get used to being poor.'

The Leo was pretty quiet. Matt could see Ben eyeing the door and wondering where the punters were. Wednesday didn't seem to be a good day for going out for lunch. Only a few couples occupied the tables, along with a scattering of office singles who were bolting down plates of pasta while reading the newspaper.

'It's competing with the cheap hamburger joints that's impossible,' Micky was saying as he gathered up the empty lager bottles from Matthew and Eddy's table. 'You don't get the women with kids in if you don't provide the tacky sort of garbage the little brats want to eat.'

'And there's plenty of them out there, every one a potential paying punter. It's affluent breeding country round here and they're all going off to Pizza Express instead of in here.'

Eddy commented, 'The park's full of gorgeous young nannies. I see them when I'm out with Lola's kids. You can't walk down the path to the pond without getting mown down by a three-wheeled jogger-buggy. And they cost.'

'Well Burger King are putting mozzarella on their Whoppers,' Matthew said. 'And if they can get away with that, why don't you try making something that will appeal to all these mothers *and* their children? There's got to be some mileage in trying it.'

'It would give us some crumpet to look at while we're gracing the premises as well,' Eddy chortled.

'It could take off. You could have a chain of bars.'

Matthew was in full enthusiastic flight now. 'All you have to do is think up daft names for the menu that would appeal to children, like, oh I don't know, a "Pokémon patty" or a vampire sausage or something, but make sure you list what's in it in full-on Chelsea-mummy terms. Stick in plenty of extra-virgin-drizzled sun-caressed tomatoes and a ton of basil. That always gets them going.'

'And we'd have to do some sort of chicken nuggety thing.' Ben leaned over the counter and joined in. 'But make sure Mr & Ms Picky-Parent know it's free-range, pan-fried in peanut-free oil, with organic, wholewheat-floured batter and hand-chopped herbs. We could do them a bit of rocket salad, or at least a garnish.'

'They'd want chips. The kids, anyway.' Eddy rubbed his portly stomach. 'Well, and me too. I like chips.'

'We can do chips. Those skinny French things would go down well, like the ones you get at *Le Caprice*,' Matthew said.

'*We?*' Ben and Micky said together. 'You buying in then, Matt?' Ben asked.

'Er, no, slip of the tongue. Anyway, are you selling?' Micky and Ben looked at each other and then at Matt. 'No,' Ben said, though Matthew thought he detected a hint of uncertainty.

'Definitely not,' Micky added.

'I can hear something. Matt, wake up, there's someone in the garden.' Jess sat up in bed and turned her left ear, the one that was more acute, towards the door.

'Hmm?' The sound from Matt was almost like a purr. He was smiling in his sleep, as if he wasn't going to wake up till his thoroughly enjoyable dream was over. Jess prodded him again, harder this time, jabbing him on the shoulder. If there was someone trying to get into the house, she didn't want to have to face him or her alone. 'Matt, I heard someone outside. It could be a burglar.' At last Matthew sat up, albeit reluctantly and Jess couldn't blame him for that: however much women had achieved over the last century, no matter how far they'd come in the workplace, running their own lives, their homes, their finances, when it came to things that went bump in the night it still seemed to be more suitable to send a person well-equipped with muscle and testosterone to do the investigating and challenging.

'What did it sound like?' Matt whispered as he climbed out of bed and groped on the floor for his jeans. Jess didn't hurry him. She fully sympathized with the need to face a ruthless intruder clothed rather than vulnerably dressing-gown-clad.

'A sort of scraping noise. Rustling. Coming from the back, near the conservatory or even on it. *Could* someone get in, do you think?'

'Not very likely, everything's locked. I checked after Clarissa got done over.'

'What about Natasha!' Jess leapt out of bed and wrenched the door open. 'She must be scared stiff!' There was no way of seeing out from the attic into the back garden: on that side there were Velux windows set high in the sloping roof and only of use for counting the stars and the passing planes.

Matt laughed softly. 'She'll be asleep. A herd of wildebeest could race through her room and she wouldn't stir.'

They were both at the top of the stairs now, squinting down into the darkness. Jess shivered and wrapped her arms across her front to stop herself trembling, as if her bones could be heard crashing around in her body.

Matt, silent with bare feet, walked slowly down the stairs. At the bottom, he flung the bathroom door wide open and switched the light on fast. She almost giggled: Matt had flattened himself back against the wall, reminding Jess of TV cop shows when they're searching for the armed villain.

'Woss goin' on?' A bleary-eyed Natasha appeared on the landing next to Matt, scratching at her tangled hair.

'Your mother thought she heard something, down in the garden.'

'Oh thanks Matt,' Jess said. '"*Your mother thought.*" I *did* hear something. I'm not losing my mind.'

''S just the cat.' Natasha yawned. 'He's on my bed. He jumped on the window ledge and I let him in. Can we all go back to bed now?' Without waiting for a reply she went back into her room and shut the door on them. Jess heard a bad-tempered grunt as she got back into bed. Natasha had never liked having her sleep disturbed. But in the morning, Jess knew, Natasha probably wouldn't even remember waking up.

'That was close,' Tom whispered into the soft downy back of Natasha's neck. 'Suppose they'd come in?'

'Jeez. Dad would've killed you. And me too, I expect. Still, he didn't though.'

'Nah, not this time.'

Robin was already there. Angie and Jess could see him as they walked down from the car park. He was photographing the shopfront from the far side of the road, stopping much too often, Jess thought, to adjust his lens settings. A pair of women walking past hesitated and turned back to look at him, then across at the window display full of highly titillating underwear that he was focusing on, after which they picked up speed and practically scurried down the road.

Angie giggled. 'You can guess what they're thinking,' she said, smirking. 'Mucky perv. He really shouldn't have worn that mack. He's practically in dirty-old-man costume – do you think he hired it?'

'Paula said she'd try to send a woman photographer,' Jess said. 'There's no way he's snapping at me wearing the goods.' In fact there was no way any photo of her in any state other than fully clothed was going to appear in the magazine. 'Oh, but sweetie . . .' Paula had protested when she'd called about the arrangements, though she'd given in unflatteringly quickly when Jess had mentioned the dreaded C-word: cellulite.

Robin crossed the road as they arrived and Jess introduced Angie. He nodded perfunctorily at her and then turned to Jess. 'I don't know what the brief is . . .' he began. Angie snorted a giggle and he glared at her, turning pink. 'Brief, *briefs*!' she explained, pointing at the shop window full of beribboned lace knickers.

Jess tried hard to keep her face composed. 'Angie's got a . . . a sense of humour,' she explained, pretty certain he hadn't had much experience of one of those. 'Come on then, let's get in and get on with it.'

'I've already met the owner.' Robin's gloomy tone suggested it hadn't been a happy encounter. 'She's let me set up just inside the door but she won't let me go any further in, not with a camera anyway,' he said. He sounded sulky, as if he'd been denied a treat. He probably had, Jess thought, smiling to herself.

The manager of the shop was a small, chic, well-upholstered woman who was making a careful and largely successful effort to look as if she wasn't on the far side of retirement age. 'Hello, I'm Olive Cutler,' she beamed at Jess, holding out a hand that supported a diamond ring Liz Taylor wouldn't have scorned to show off, and a pair of ornate gold bangles so heavy Jess wondered how the narrow wrist could support them.

'Hallo. I see you've already met Robin, and this is Angie. I brought her along because . . .' Suddenly Jess couldn't think of a reason.

'Because I adore underwear,' Angie gushed. 'It's my absolute *favourite thing.*' Olive Cutler beamed approval at Angie and then looked Jess up and down quickly and not quite so approvingly, as if measuring with her practised eyes.

'I take it you haven't had a proper bra fitting before?' she said, which Jess thought was possibly rather rude of her. After all, was it that obvious? She pulled her shoulders back, and her tummy and bottom in, trying to recall the rules of perfect posture as practised by her ballet teacher so very long ago. All she could remember was something about tucking her tail in, which had made her think of putting her dollies to bed.

'Well, not since I was pregnant,' she conceded. The inside of the shop was like being inside a child's jewel box. The walls were lined with deep scarlet velvet and thick curtains, with fat-fringed gold pelmets separating the sales area from the fitting rooms. The other sales assistants, a couple of black-clad young girls, looked as if they'd taken full advantage of the stock and, with shoulders back and heads erect, seemed to glory in their high, pert bosoms.

Olive Cutler led the way behind the curtains like a diva flouncing from an unsatisfactory stage. 'Tch!

Pregnant! Completely the wrong time to be fitted! With your body changing from one day to the next!'

Angie and Jess looked at each other, trying not to break into giggles. Olive held open the door of a large fitting room and they filed in.

'Right. Let's have a look at what you're wearing and we'll see what can be improved on,' she ordered.

Obediently, Angie and Jess stripped to their bras. Angie, Jess noted, was wearing a purple and pink polka-dot satin balcony number for the occasion, causing her breasts to loom up over the fabric in a challenging manner.

'So you don't mind if they escape then!' Olive commented, at last allowing herself a wry smile. Angie, daunted, flipped up her hands to protect her vulnerable body. Jess had gone for the sensible approach, wearing her plainest and most comfortable bra, a pristine white one that hadn't yet met with a colour-run accident.

'Well that doesn't fit, does it dear?' Olive's experienced fingers tweaked at the front of Jess's bra, pulling it free of the flesh. 'They're staring at the floor, aren't they?' Jess looked down at her front, feeling as if she'd certainly failed. 'I'm a 34B, have been for years,' she rallied.

Olive Cutler laughed. 'Oh I don't think so,' she said. 'Never mind, we'll sort you out. Just wait there.'

'Aren't you going to measure us?' Angie suggested, with commendable bravery, Jess thought.

'*Measure?*' Olive looked as outraged as if Angie had asked for a view of her knickers. 'We don't measure! No need!' And she swished out of the room and back through the curtain.

'I hope Robin isn't up to no good out there,' Jess

138

whispered – anything louder couldn't be risked, head-mistressy Mrs Cutler might rush back in and tell them off.

'Oh sure, he's probably dancing about with a leopard-print thong on his head,' Angie giggled.

Mrs Cutler returned with her arms full of multi-coloured frills and lace. 'Right, you first, seeing as you're the reporter,' she said to Jess. Speedily she fastened her into a primrose yellow bra that was almost entirely soft, intricate lace. 'Gorgeous!' was Angie's verdict. 'Expensive,' Jess mouthed at her behind Olive Cutler's back, having caught sight of a pallor-inducing price tag.

'Too tight,' Olive decreed. 'Digs in across here.' She pointed to the tiniest irregularity in the diagonal line across the front.

It took a long time: Jess and Angie were wearying of taking bras off and on. Several times Jess had been certain they'd arrived at the perfect fit only to be told, with unarguable firmness, that she was completely wrong.

'I don't know what they'd say in M&S if we took the entire stock into the changing room like this,' Jess commented as the pile of underwear surrounding them on the floor grew and grew.

'Oh you soon get the hang of what to look for, with practice.' Olive stood back and smiled; Jess stared at her reflection in the mirror. She looked OK, she thought, more than OK in the wispy scarlet item.

'Now that's perfect.' Olive tweaked at the straps and showed her how the back of the bra should be straight, not pulled out of place by them.

'You'll have to buy it now,' Angie prompted, taking her turn at being fitted and making a face at being strapped into something more demure than her own purple satin.

'I know,' Jess agreed.

'We do matching panties.' Olive scented a full-set sale. 'High cut or mini or perhaps you veer towards a string?'

'Er high cut for me.'

'Oh I'm a thong girl myself,' Angie giggled. Olive Cutler gave her a look as if any doubt about that hadn't even crossed her mind.

Robin was blushing scarlet by the time they emerged from the changing room. Olive's two assistants were talking him through the stock, suggesting he might like to buy something 'for a friend' or for a 'special occasion sir?' With great speed and hands trembling, he photographed Jess browsing through the racks of knickers as if she was a genuine customer.

'Psst, got anything to fit my friend here?' Jess spun round. Matt was in the shop, accompanied by Eddy who had fluffed his hair out and was pouting, in an attempt, with no great effect, to look girly.

'Matt, get out, will you!'

'Interrupting your work, my precious?' Matt leaned across a rack of sumptuous bridal basques and kissed her cheek. 'Me and Eddy are looking for some special pulling-knickers for him, what do you think? These pink fluffy ones?' Matt plucked them off the hanger and held them up to the over-strained crotch of Eddy's faded jeans.

'Oooh! Gorgeous! Do you think they're me?' Eddy minced round the shop, squealing and holding the marabou-edged knickers against him.

'Er excuse me! Do you intend to buy those?' Olive Cutler's voice cleaved the air like a whistling axe.

'Would you mind either purchasing or *buggering orf*?' she hissed at Matt, with no decline in dignity. 'You're disturbing my customers.'

'Sorry.' Matt and Eddy stood side by side with their heads hanging, looking like naughty ten-year-olds.

'Jesus, Matt, haven't you got anything better to do?' Jess asked as Olive went to ring up her purchases (well she had to buy them now, hadn't she?) at the till.

Matthew looked up at her, puzzled. 'Anything better? Well . . .' He scratched his head. 'Well no. I haven't, actually.'

'You're completely impossible! I could get fired over this if Mrs Cutler complains to Paula!' Jess told both men off as they left the shop and walked back to the car.

'Yes but you love us don't you?' Eddy put his arm round her and crushed her against him.

'One for me too.' Angie snuggled up to Eddy, demanding her share of the hugs.

'I suppose so,' Jess admitted, squeezing Matt's hand. In spite of him messing about she felt pretty pleased with life just for the moment: with neither the effort of a diet nor the expense and pain of surgery, she had, according to Olive Cutler's practised eye and professional judgement, lost two inches and gained two cup sizes. Not a bad morning's work.

Nine

Zoe felt burdened by other people's secrets. She wished she could just sick them up and flush them away like a bulimic with a chicken sandwich. She wondered if this was how Emily felt about food, that when it got inside her it was a sort of contamination that had to be got rid of as soon as possible. It was as if she was carrying round in her head more than just her own life, but had had the nastier bits of other people's dumped on her as well. She needed to get on with having fun and mucking about with her mates at school. She wanted to get into her own trouble over forgotten homework and for wearing her uniform in a messed-about way and doing text messages on her mobile in Physics. Instead she felt she had to be good, just in case if one thing went wrong, everyone else's badnesses that she was carrying would all tumble out too. It was like hearing the 'call waiting' message all the time when you were trying to get connected, completely frustrating and time-wasting.

She hadn't wanted to know about Emily and the baby (the baby that *wasn't*) in the first place, and now she knew something even worse about her. Babies got themselves born or miscarried or whatever given time, but the anorexia thing wouldn't go away, not without a lot of other people being involved and years of awfulness. Emily had phoned a couple of times from school and said she was fine, everything really, really was fine. There was nothing to worry about. For a second or two Zoe had relaxed, thought, well maybe that woman at the clinic had frightened her into eating properly again. Maybe they could just get back to seeing each other a bit in the holidays, with no big deal and none of that new-best-friend stuff, but then Emily had admitted she was ringing from the school medical wing: she'd fainted in Maths. 'I faked it, I was just messing about. I hate geometry,' she'd giggled. Zoe had gone cold.

There'd been a girl at her school who'd nearly died of starving. She used to sit with everyone else and eat lunch because the staff had been warned to keep an eye on her, but she'd always raced straight off to the bogs after and smelled of sick all afternoon. No-one had wanted to be her partner in Chemistry when it was experiments. That girl had fainted all the time, and she'd had to stay indoors on games afternoons because she was just too shivery and feeble to be allowed to get chilled. She'd gone to be locked up somewhere in the end, everyone said. Her mother had come to the school and cried and shouted at the Head. You could hear her all down the corridor. She'd screamed about why had no-one said anything, why had she been the last to know, which they all had thought was stupid, how was everyone else supposed to see what was happening if her own mother couldn't?

Zoe thought about Angie, thought about going round and telling her that her little girl was a way-off nutter fast heading for death, but it would come out sounding as if it was Zoe herself who'd lost the plot. Anyway, surely Angie, even flaky, smiley, happy-as-a-sunflower Angie would notice that Emily was just bloody ill? Emily would be back for the holidays soon. From then on, Zoe decided, she wasn't going to take on any more of her problems.

Zoe lay in her bed with her hands over her ears, wishing she was one of those sleepers that even bombs don't disturb. She didn't want to hear Natasha's window sliding open. She didn't want to hear the secret giggles and whisperings that were none of her business. She was having to sleep with her head under the pillow because Tom and Tash talked all the time. They thought they were being really quiet and she couldn't hear any actual words (or anything else, thank God), but it was a bit like having a mad moth in the room. It just drove you crazy. They'd get caught one day, she was certain. The thought made her tremble and sweat. One day Tom would sleep through Tash's alarm and Mum or Dad would come in to wake her for school and find him there in bed with her. She scrunched up her knees and waggled her toes in horror at what would happen then. It would be her fault. Somehow she'd get the blame, she was sure. If no-one had told her anything, there'd be nothing for her to know. Nothing to stress about.

'Love the new pieces, darling. You're tremendously good at this, you know.' Jess was amazed: Paula rarely

144

commented on anything she'd written these days unless she'd gone over length and she wanted to check if Jess had any preference for which bits were cut. Even that, Matt had once pointed out when Jess was just beginning, was a privilege.

'That's what the subs are for. There's never usually time to consult the writer. Once the copy is in it's theirs and writers aren't supposed to be precious about their works.'

'You make it sound like I'm selling tea bags or something,' she'd smiled, back in the days when she'd seriously agonized about which adjective, which participle, only to find that her careful infinitives were as often as not split by some trainee sub-editor on work experience.

'Tea bags would be about right,' Matthew had agreed, dispiritingly. 'If you want creative agony you should go into fiction. Don't look for it in journalism.'

Looking back, now, on that conversation, she should have picked up the hint that he was pretty jaded about his own job. All that contact with the fickle sensation-seeking press, the effort of trying to get them to put into print the gist of what his clients were trying to sell, only to know deep down that the world wasn't going to give any idea, any product more than its few minutes of fame and none of it really mattered anyway.

Jess, feeling buoyed up by Paula's praise, said to Matthew as they were clearing up from breakfast, 'We haven't had Paula here for supper for a long time. She likes coming here, she told me she enjoys getting a dose of family life without having to produce one of her own.'

'It probably puts her off, that's why. I bet she gets into her taxi and breathes a big "thank goodness" sigh.'

145

Matt laughed. 'But OK, I'm up for it.'

'What about this weekend?'

'Sure, but just Paula? Can't we dilute her with a few others?' Matt pulled a face. He wasn't sure about her, Jess knew. She was one of those women who couldn't talk to a man without touching him, making little claiming dabs with her fingers all over his arm. She was a strong woman too, seriously keen on skiing and sailing: the dabs on the arm could be quite hard. The last time he'd met her, at the *Gazette*'s Christmas drinks party, he'd said he felt as if she'd left dents all over his skin.

'No, not just Paula. She'd feel like an aunt being given duty food.' Jess thought for a minute. 'She's between men, as it were, at the moment.'

'I'm not surprised. She's probably put them all in traction.' Matt laughed. 'I'd be happier if we have a sort of walkabout party, then I wouldn't have to sit next to her and get injured.'

Jess considered for a few moments. The word 'party', sounding so jolly and spontaneous, always involved more expense than you thought it was going to. You started off with a list that said 'booze and food' and the next thing you knew you were looking up Delia's canapés, wondering about hiring more plates and ordering crates of the sparkling stuff from Oddbins.

Matthew must have been thinking along the same lines. 'What about a barbecue?' he suggested. 'I know it's a long way to midsummer but the weather forecast's good for the weekend. We could do Friday, early evening with the kids, have Eddy and maybe Wandering Wilf and a couple of the blokes round as well. I quite fancy that.' He was looking thoroughly enthusiastic now. 'I'll shop. I'll cook,' he volunteered.

'You can just get on with work and not have any reason to have a go at me for doing nothing.'

Jess didn't honestly think Paula would much enjoy a barbecue, unless it was on a kind of irony level. Although she thought it was fun to sit in their kitchen and listen in to the mild family bickering that passed for conversation in the Nelson household, she was a woman of decidedly urban pursuits and preferred the sort of social gatherings at which she could wear very high-heeled shoes with bejewelled and minimal straps. Jess was quite well aware that Paula's idea of an alfresco feast would be having coffee and a Danish beneath the chic heat lamps outside the Bluebird café on the Kings Road. Nor was she sure about Eddy, who still was of the belief that as he'd been a rock star he must therefore be irresistible to any woman he set his sights on. Paula, being still under forty (just), would probably never have heard of him and might well cut him dead with an icy sneer. On the other hand, Matthew was showing more enthusiasm for a slice of home life than he had since the Redundancy Day and besides, she thought, Paula knew a lot of people in the newspaper business. Loosened up by plenty of wine and with Matthew at his most hospitable and charming, Paula might just have heard of some freelance work going . . .

'OK, let's do that then. And we'll have Angie over as well if she wants to come. Luke and Emily will be just back from school and I know she likes them to see our lot. For some reason she has them down under "suitable".'

'That's only because they don't go to Briar's Lane. She's a typical first-generation snob,' Matt chuckled. 'She wouldn't care if they mugged old ladies and had the Grove franchise for cocaine dealing as long as they speak nicely and say please and thank you.'

Matthew ripped a page out of one of Zoe's abandoned maths books and started making a list. Jess looked over his shoulder at what he'd written. 'Booze, more booze and food.'

'Mmm, that should just about cover it.' She grinned at him.

The lad, Tom, was taking boxes out of the old Sierra's boot and transferring them to a scruffy white Nissan Micra parked on the edge of the allotments. From the way he was carrying them it was obvious they were on the heavy side. George carried on with the weeding and pretended he wasn't watching him. They seemed to be ordinary cardboard supermarket boxes, labelled for things like bananas and baked beans. He'd have worried if the labels had been for new hi-fi equipment, mobile phones, anything like that. So far he hadn't had to know anything *tricky* about the boy and he wanted to keep it that way. If Tom was in the business of liberating goods from the rich to redistribute to his impoverished self then it was best not to know. He felt he understood him, understood that some people don't want to live with their families, just couldn't face it. You read about the reasons for that every day in the papers. With young boys it so often tended to be about stepfathers, men who wouldn't share their woman with her son and mothers who feared a lonely, near-destitute time of it if they took their boy's side – for after all, a teenager would be moving on soon anyway, wouldn't he?

Living in the old car, with George keeping an eye on him, had to be better than living with the old winos under the bridge by the railway and the kid seemed to be able to cope without whinging, without unduly suffering and without spending his days hanging round Leicester Square either busking or begging or risking his life as a rent boy.

'Begging's degrading,' Tom had said when George had brought up the subject, in a roundabout and generalized sort of way, while the two of them were taking a break from planting out the carrots. 'Busking's OK, at least you're offering a service. People can take it or leave it. I'm not musical though.'

'Me neither,' George had agreed, though he'd wondered if it was true. He liked music, he could sing well enough and remembered, note-perfect, pieces he'd heard from years back. Tom might be the same, just another kid who hadn't come across the opportunity to take it up, or any other skill that might give him a respected place in the world. Zoe and Natasha and Oliver, they'd been given opportunities by the dozen, everything on a plate like a sort of activity cheese-board: ballet and gymnastics, swimming, riding and sailing. Oliver had joined the London Scottish juniors for rugby training and Zoe, after a flu-ridden afternoon spent on the sofa idly watching the Olympics on TV, had briefly taken up fencing. By the time they were ten they'd tried out piano, violin, guitar and flute, giving all of them up in a petulant strop when they found they weren't instant experts. Oliver kept the guitar up for a while, getting the hang of it sufficiently to enable him to strum it therapeutically when he wanted to do the lone-teenager thing of skulking in his room. The way music education was these days, there might be a thousand potential Jacqueline du Prés out there wasting their talent for the sake of a couple of recorder lessons and the presence of an old piano in the corner of the home to thump out a few first notes on. It was the same with cricket, he thought as he watched Tom cramming the boot lid of the Micra down on the last of the boxes. If just the few rich prep-school kids got to learn the game, and the state-educated lot only got to have a go if the school field hadn't been sold for executive housing or to put up a mobile phone mast, it didn't provide much of a pool of choice for the next decade's England eleven. No wonder the current middle-order batting was rubbish.

'You moving house?' he called out as Tom wandered back towards the Sierra.

'Just got some things to take somewhere,' Tom replied. He didn't look old enough to drive, George thought. He looked a good couple of years younger than Oliver. And where did he get the car?

'The car's my brother's in case you were wondering.' Tom sidestepped the suspicion before George could voice it.

'But does he know you've got it?' George asked.

'He will when he gets home.' Tom grinned cheekily. 'But he'll get it back.'

'I won't ask about a driving licence.' George turned back to the weeds that hid among the spinach.

'You can if you want.' Tom shrugged, then said, 'You've missed a few over there. Give us the hoe, I'll get them.'

Matthew, ambling across the square in the direction of the High Street and the friendly Italian greengrocer, almost didn't recognize Natasha coming towards him with one of her friends. He'd certainly noticed her, the long slim legs were quite unmissable, leading in one direction to a skirt that was surely short enough to merit detention at school and in the other to incongruously clumpy shoes that gave her a childlike fragility. She hadn't seen him; she had her arm linked through her friend's (Cathy? Carla?) and they were leaning in towards each other, laughing at some private joke, oblivious to everyone on the street. It was one of those shock moments that children land on you, he realized, as if they do a sneaky extra amount of maturing in the night and you're suddenly faced with an image for whom you had to fast-forward the mental picture from someone five years younger. Oliver had done that all the time, he remembered, but then boys did — they grew so frighteningly fast which, he thought, perhaps accounted for the frequent look of bewilderment on the adolescent male face.

'Hi Dad!' Natasha detached herself from her friend and dashed over the last few yards of pavement to kiss Matt. He felt deeply touched that she wasn't too embarrassed to do that. 'You remember Claire, don't you?' she said.

'Hello love. Yes of course I do. How are you, Claire?'

'Fine thanks Mr Nelson.'

'Call me Matt, please. Otherwise I feel old.'

'OK.' Claire smiled, a long, slow, perfect-toothed smile. She was going to be a stunner, Matthew recognized; they both were. For a second or two he imagined the pair of them out at night, in a pub, in full pulling-power make-up and wearing little string-strapped dresses and the kind of silly gorgeous shoes that had to be kept on with will power. It wasn't a comfortable picture. This was his daughter and the best friend he'd known since she was eleven and submerged in a school uniform bought for several years of growing into. He had one of those blood-rushing moments, where he could feel the swift approach of the day he had to realize that some other male being had permanent priority in Natasha's affections. It was surely still a long way off, but the day wasn't as distant as he'd have liked.

'Gotta go. Ring me.' Claire and Natasha kissed each other like lunching ladies and Claire moved away. 'Bye *Matt*!' she called, looking back and he wondered if he was imagining a bit of flirting impertinence in her voice.

'So Dad, where were you going?' Natasha put her arm through his and they walked on along the broad pavement in front of the shops.

'Buying supplies. We're having a barbecue on Friday night. Mum's boss Paula's coming and I'm doing the cooking.'

'How typically male!' she mocked. 'What are we having, charred dinosaur?'

'I can cook. You know I can. I thought we'd have some little chicken kebabs marinaded in a sort of pineapple and chilli thing and then . . . well down at the Leo the other day the lads and I came up with this upmarket fast-food idea. I've just had a word with them and we thought we'd try out a few recipes, see if anyone thinks the idea's marketable.'

'What, like McDonald's? Mum won't want that.' Natasha's face was a vision of scepticism.

'No. Well yes, I suppose so in a way. Though appealing to a different client base, let's say.'

'Everyone likes McDonald's though. Even posh people.'

'Posh *children*, you mean. I'm thinking of something aimed at the parents, the organic free-range sort. Well, wait till Friday, you'll see.'

'What does Mum think?'

'Ah, well, I haven't actually mentioned it, not as such. It might be just as well to sort of . . .'

'Keep quiet?'

'Yes. If she asks about food I'll just say I'm going to surprise her and she's not to get involved.'

'OK, I'll keep out of it. Can Tom come?'

Another blood-rushing moment threatened, then subsided. There was no need to feel like that *yet*, surely? She wasn't even sixteen . . .

'Yes of course he can. Any friend of yours, all that.'

'. . . mistake to think it's a way to get teenagers to join in a social event. Barbecues bring out the worst: Zoe won't eat anything with a crumb of a charred edge – black bits being carcinogenic and she wants to survive past A levels. Natasha thinks it's all too primitive and . . .'

Jess stopped typing and thought about Oliver and barbecues. He was just like his father with them: happy to battle with the blazing coals, to prod at slabs of meat, cheery enough about getting crushed garlic all over his fingers, slooshing out the olive oil for a marinade and completely oblivious of the fact that the meal required more than just the stuff you cook on the fire. If it was just for the family she would more or less trust Matt to get it right and buy enough salad, potatoes, rice and vegetables to put together an entire meal. Anything he'd forgotten, well there was plenty of last-minute stuff in the cupboards. But there now seemed to be quite a lot of people coming, and he was up to something in the kitchen, something that involved the food processor and a lot of herbs. She could smell coriander and basil and coconut and there was something that reminded her of a Thai chicken dish they'd had in a restaurant and tried unsuccessfully to re-create at home. She hoped, as she worked, that whatever exciting new taste sensation he was concocting he'd also remember that you needed something else to go with it.

'Do you want any help?' She ventured into the kitchen and filled the kettle, having a swift look round to see what he was up to.

Matt, poring over a notebook with a frown of concentration and a biro between his teeth, looked up at her with an expression of worrying alarm.

'No!' he said rather too quickly. 'It's fine. You just carry on working and I'll take care of everything. It's all in hand.'

She laughed. 'Now why does that make me feel . . .' then she stopped and continued making the tea. She'd been about to say 'redundant', but stopped herself just in time.

'Feel what?' he asked.

'Nothing. Makes me feel wonderful. Really. I'll leave you to it then.'

'Hmm. Good. Off you go and get your nails painted or something,' he murmured, back into the depths of his notebook. And *I* was trying so hard not to be patronizing, she thought.

'OK, so what have we got?' Ben and Micky, leaving the Leo for a few hours in the hands of grumbling and resentful Friday-night bar staff, peered at the trayful of uneven and unmatched burgers on Matt's worktop. Matt looked at them thoughtfully, trying to recall which were which. He'd made three different sorts, one lot according to a combination of his and Jamie Oliver's imaginations, one with a choice of spices plagiarized from Ken Hom and the third following instructions from Micky.

'I think these are chilli,' he said eventually, pointing to the selection that had a distinctly orange look about them.

'And which are my sun-dried tomato ones? These pink things?'

'Yep. Only – well I used those oily half-grilled ones instead. I thought they'd go better in the processor, no sharp-edged bits.'

'Good thinking,' Ben said. 'We'll have you sweating on the early shift in our kitchen yet. How was it on costings?'

Matt scrabbled through a pile of bills and mail on the dresser. 'It's all here, written down. Obviously unit-price-wise it would come down a lot if we bulk-bought and did some freezing . . .'

'Mmm. Freshness is rather the point . . .' Micky murmured, studying the figures.

'Yes of course it is.' Matt felt weary suddenly. What the hell did he think he was doing, diddling about with recipes for a suburban bistro? Did any of them really, truly, deep down believe even in their wackiest flights of fantasy that they could come up with anything that would eventually rival Burger King? And suppose they did, what would his role be? Inevitably he pictured himself back at a desk, trawling through the lists in his Psion, organizing mailshots for magazines, setting up launch events, toadying to the press again, ever the obliging PR. The very thought made him feel depressed.

Micky and Ben weren't stupid. They might let him

loose trying a few prototype recipes on his own guests and giving him their patiently non-critical opinions, but when it came to major catering know-how, they were the ones who'd done the courses and knew what was what. It was their bar, for heaven's sake. They were only letting him in on this because of his connections, his address book and his usefulness. It reminded him of when he was small and the big boys on the rec had let him play cricket with them because, he one day realized, he was the one who owned a halfway decent bat. His joblessness seemed, at that moment, a miserable burden. The freedom feeling had gone missing. He hoped it intended to come back soon.

'Cooee! Anyone in here?' Paula appeared in the kitchen clutching a huge bunch of tulips lavishly wrapped in tissue paper in several shades of orange. Yellow ribbons trailed from the package, curling down over her hand like a Victorian child's blond ringlets.

'Matt darling! Wonderful to see you!' She pressed her entire body against him (rather unnecessarily hard, in his opinion, though he wished he was feeling more up to enjoying the moment) and slapped a sticky lipstick kiss on the corner of his mouth. Over her shoulder he caught Ben and Micky smirking and blowing camp mock kisses at him.

'The front door was wide open so I just came right in! You should keep it shut you know, Jess told me all about the burglary along the road.' Paula ripped the tulips from their pretty packaging and started opening cupboards looking for a vase.

'Here, I'll get it,' Matt said, taking a plain oblong glass vase from the dresser cupboard. Paula picked it up and inspected it for suitability.

'Haven't you got anything more, *round*?' she asked.

'With square ones they tend to go all droopy.'

'Ooh I know the feeling,' Ben cut in. Paula smiled at him, looking uncertain.

'I'm sure we have, somewhere.' Matt glared past her at Ben. 'But let's just leave them in this for now. I'll sort it later. Come on outside, Jess is there with the girls.' Jess hadn't seen the flowers arrive, it occurred to him. Surely they were meant for her?

Jess, listening with Clarissa to Eddy's tale of how a makeshift barbecue in a dustbin lid on the hard shoulder of the M1 had set fire to his band's first van back in '68, saw his face change like someone who'd just caught sight of Madonna shopping in Sainsbury's. She turned and saw Paula approaching in cream leather trousers so tight that anyone with iffy eyesight could have been given the impression of naked skin.

'And who is this?' Eddy muttered to Jess, keeping his eye on the vision picking her high-heeled way across the terrace towards them.

'Paula, lovely to see you!' The two women kissed briefly and Jess could almost feel Eddy's hot breath on the back of her neck.

'Paula, this is Eddy Valera. He lives just along the road. And Clarissa who lives next door to him.' Clarissa, knowing her time was up, grinned briefly at Paula and strode off towards the bench for some 'aren't men bastards' solidarity with Angie. Paula's delicately extended, perfectly manicured hand was grabbed in both of Eddy's and he hauled her back in the direction of the conservatory. 'Let me get you a drink. I don't suppose you ever went to any Spidercrunch gigs a few years ago . . . ?'

*   *   *

157

'Dad did all the food,' Natasha said to Tom. 'So I suppose we should go and eat some of it.' She disentangled herself from him and leaned back against the shed door.

'Sure. I'm starving,' he agreed, shoving his arms back into his jacket. Natasha fastened the buttons on her shirt and pulled her sweatshirt over her head, then cuddled up close to him again and breathed in the scent of the battered and oily old leather. 'Whenever I smell leather, whatever happens when I'm old or at university or married or something, I'll always think of you,' she said.

He held her tight against him and kissed her hair. 'And whenever I smell burning sausages on a barbie, I'll think of you too!' he teased, opening the shed door and making a run for the food before she could hit him.

'You've got to try one of these,' Zoe told Emily, handing her a plate from which a steaming fat burger hung out over the side of its bun. 'Dad's got a master plan to set up a smart burger chain and make us all mega-rich. They're at the experimental stage but it smells all right.'

Emily screwed her nose up and looked at it with suspicion, then turned to Matt who was waiting for an opinion. 'You need to make them a bit smaller, for a start,' she commented. 'Or you'll go broke.'

'I'll keep it in mind. We haven't got round to portion control yet. Just try it. Zoe's got one of the other sorts, a tomato and herb one.'

'What's mine?'

'See what you think, guess the flavourings.'

Emily nibbled cautiously round the edge of the food. Then Zoe watched as she reached across the table for ketchup. She took the top off the bun and carefully squirted a letter E over the burger's surface. Then she very slowly arranged two slivers of raw onion in a cross, added four small circles of dill pickle, placing them meticulously in the four arms made by the crossed onion, and replaced the bun lid.

Zoe wished Angie was watching, but Angie was now swapping horror stories about Things Bin-Men Leave on Your Drive with Clarissa and wasn't interested in her skinny daughter's meal rituals.

'It'll get cold,' Matt prompted, exchanging a glance with Zoe.

'OK, OK.' Emily eventually lifted the burger and bit a neat piece out of it. She chewed it slowly, reminding Zoe of a programme about wine tasters.

'What do you think?' Ben joined them, eager to see what the youth market made of his idea.

'You're all looking at me! Don't watch me!' Emily wailed, showing an unattractive chewed mass of food. She bolted from the garden, running through the conservatory and kitchen towards the downstairs loo.

'Back to the drawing board Matt, do you think?' Ben poured himself and Matt generous glasses of wine.

'Probably, very bloody probably,' Matt agreed, gloomily.

Ten

Jess's head was hurting and she didn't want to hear any more about hamburger flavourings. If Matt couldn't cope with everyone laughing then it was his problem – she didn't want to know. Matt was lying on the bed, snug in his blue towelling robe. He'd propped up the big square pillows and was comfortably reclined with his arms wrapped across his chest, reminding Jess of a child snuggled safe beneath a scruffy but treasured security blanket. Jess was taking her time getting ready for bed: the headache made her move slowly. Even brushing her teeth had been a tentative operation for fear of the buzz from the electric toothbrush pushing the pain up another notch of intensity. She opened her underwear drawer and rustled around looking for a forgotten packet of aspirins. 'I don't want Anadin Extra because of the caffeine. Any of that and I'll never get to sleep,' she murmured.

'I don't understand what went wrong with the chilli,' Matt was saying.

Jess grinned at him. 'You nearly killed poor Angie. How much did you put in?'

'Only a couple of tablespoons. It's what it said in the recipe, two or three tablespoons. If anything it was a bit less.'

Jess finally unearthed a torn-off bit of foil bubble containing a couple of Nurofen and swallowed them down with the last of a large glass of water. Probably she was simply dehydrated – too much wine, too much talking and then too much taking Angie across the road to home and dealing with her panic attack brought on by the unexpectedly savage chilli-flavoured burger. This had involved full-scale gasping, clutching at throat and chest, breathing dramatically into a Sainsbury bag due to lack of recommended brown paper ones and then another glass of wine, on Jess's part just to be neighbourly and on Angie's as a calmer. Emily and Luke had ignored their mother's choking and gasping, becoming immediately absorbed in a TV programme about wolves.

Right now, something occurred to Jess. 'How was tablespoon written?'

'Tsp of course. How else?' He was giving her that look, the one where he was telling her she was quite obviously the idiot of the two of them and not even to consider that *he* might be.

Jess laughed. 'Ah well that's it then. That means teaspoons. You must have put in about four times the amount you were supposed to.'

Matt slumped further down on the bed, folding his arms even tighter and frowning.

'Jesus I can't do a fucking thing right. I wasn't supposed to nick anyone else's recipe in the first place. The whole idea was to be original. Ben and Micky will think I'm a right case.'

'Of course you're not. Anyway don't tell them, just say you were experimenting.' Jess lay down next to him, slid her hand under his robe and stroked his warm chest. Matt sighed but still looked miserable so she moved her hand further down and slithered across to nuzzle at his neck. He surely couldn't, she thought, really care that much: it was a mistake anyone could make.

'No don't.' Matt took hold of her marauding hand and pushed it back at her, like a petulant infant refusing a placatory toy. 'I'll probably only do that wrong as well.'

'You never have before.' Jess stood up and headed for the bathroom for more water. 'Come on Matt, stop sulking. Really the burgers didn't matter. It was funny, everyone coughing and trying to be polite. Didn't you think so? Just a little bit? Where's your sense of humour?'

'I'm saving it for something funny. That OK with you?'

Sarcasm didn't really merit a reply, Jess considered as she ran water into the glass. She leaned back against the warm towel on the rail and looked at herself in the long mirror. She was wearing her favourite nightwear – a pale purple silk nightdress, quite short, strappy like the kind of summer dresses that only suited slender women under thirty-five. After that, something seemed to go wrong with the upper arms. Perhaps she shouldn't be wearing this now, not even just for sleeping. Probably she ought to swaddle herself in all-enveloping winceyette, if such a thing still existed. When the children had been young she'd gone for the Laura Ashley dairymaid look in nightwear, only to have Matt grumbling that he couldn't actually fancy someone who looked as if they were about to run through the fields cooing at the sheep.

Experimentally, Jess waved at herself as if seeing her reflection off on a journey to see what happened to her arms. A woman at the gym had said she had 'bye-bye arms' and explained that when she waved at anyone, her upper arms waved all by themselves as well. Not much of Jess's flesh flapped around. She was still reasonably firm in the triceps area. 'And so I should be,' she thought, prodding at the skin which she'd prefer to be a bit more dewy-textured, less desiccated. 'All those hours sweating with the weights at the gym . . .'

'If I say I'm sorry, will you come and get into bed with me?' Matt called. He had his penitent-little-boy voice on. It wasn't appealing, not in a sexy sense anyway. She thought of her mother and the 'never say no' advice. Was it worth risking that it might be true? Or was it perfectly reasonable of her not to have sex if she didn't fancy it?

'OK,' she said, returning to Matt and climbing into bed. 'That boy, Tom, he seemed to enjoy himself, didn't he?' she said. Matt stood up and took off his robe, flinging it in the direction of the door where it collapsed in a heap and did not, as Matt had probably hoped, hang itself neatly on the hook like the hat James Bond always flung into Miss Moneypenny's office.

'He didn't give a toss about the chilli. And he loved the chicken kebabs – he was very complimentary. He's a polite lad, one to be encouraged. Old George likes him too.'

163

'Mmm,' Jess agreed. 'He doesn't actually look as if he often gets a proper meal. I get the feeling he lives on junk food and handouts. He makes me want to take care of him, feed him up a bit.'

'Like a stray cat?'

'Probably. Maybe I'm just feeling the lack of Oliver around the house. And Natasha seems happy enough. Though I hope she's not . . .'

'She's only fifteen, Jess, and not daft.'

'No, I know. But fifteen's like eighteen used to be now. There's no point assuming she's not even curious about sex. I bet the boy is.'

'No, I suppose not. At the moment though, I'm the one who's feeling curious about it. Like am I going to get it? I mean I do hope so . . .'

He switched off the light and snuggled up to her, feeling his way under the purple nightdress and stroking a finger along her inner thigh. The headache was already fading and Jess wondered about what her mother had left out from the advice: there was an unmentioned (and unmentionable in those days probably) 'because' element. 'Never say no, because your body is like an old television set, everything works fine after a bit of a warm-up session . . .'

Donald the cat hurtled up the stairs miaowing as if a Rottweiler was chasing him. He raced into the attic bedroom and leapt onto the bed, shaking his rain-soaked fur all over Jess's face.

'Ugh! Donald get off!' She pushed him away and he sat beside the bed looking offended and making a start on washing his wet paws. 'You've made muddy foot-prints all over the bed,' she told him, leaning down to stroke his ears. He rubbed his face against her hand, purring happily. Cats have definite smiles sometimes, she thought as she watched him. Sometimes, overcome by the bliss of being petted, Donald even dribbled, though she was under no real illusion that he had come to see her for any other reason than that he considered it was time for her to get up and fill his food bowl. She slid out of bed and pulled on her robe, a white waffle-textured cotton one that was never quite warm enough on chill mornings, and padded out of the room and down the stairs. It was already after nine o'clock. She rarely slept that late, even at weekends. There was no sign of life from the girls' rooms, but that was perfectly normal for a Saturday morning. Whoever had said that teenagers grow in their sleep was probably right – the girls were already quite tall and, given the choice, would happily linger in bed, Walkmans clamped to their ears till they reached six feet four.

Jess collected the newspaper from the mat by the front door and went back to the kitchen. The rain was making a million tiny rivers intermingle as they trickled down the conservatory windows. As she peered through the glass, Jess could just make out a selection of empty wine bottles on the table outside – the clearing up had been abandoned after everyone in the family had brought in a couple of token items and decided it was getting too cold and dark to bother continuing with it. Her best chopping board was out there too, and a plate with a few slices of tomato being slowly marinaded in rainwater. She wondered what had happened to Paula. After Angie's choking session and Jess taking her home, Eddy had said he'd get Paula a cab and then led her out into the night.

'We were lucky it didn't rain like this last night, weren't we?' She made conversation with the cat as she picked out a sachet of his favourite duck-flavoured food from the cupboard. Donald plaited his ecstatic body around her legs, trying to hurry her up.

'OK, wait a minute sweetie!' She put the foul-smelling dish on the floor and the cat pushed his face into his breakfast.

'No magic word? No "thank you"?' she teased him as she went to switch on the kettle.

'Are you talking to the cat?' Zoe stood in the doorway in an oversized striped tee shirt with her long pale legs looking frailly thin, like seedlings that haven't had enough light.

'Of course I am!' Jess told her, getting another mug out of the cupboard for Zoe. 'Did nobody tell you it's bad manners not to talk to the people you're feeding?'

'Yeah, *people*,' Zoe mocked. 'He's not *people*.'

'I've heard you talking to him.' Jess poured boiling water into her favourite teapot: it was pink and had large bold strawberries painted on it. She always felt it was a good one to use when summer was slow getting started, as if it would encourage the weather to ripen the fruit.

Zoe picked up the newspaper and started rummaging through the various sections in search of something with cartoons. 'I talk to him when I'm telling him off, making him stop sleeping on my clothes, leaving fur and stuff.'

'You could try putting them away,' Jess suggested tentatively. It was too early in the day for the 'when are you going to tidy your room' routine.

Zoe ignored her, becoming absorbed in the rock-music pages and an interview with Simplicity whose CD she was currently playing to wear-out point.

'Er, you're up early for a Saturday,' Jess commented.

'Going shopping with Emily. We want to get out early before all the good stuff goes.'

'Oh, you've come into money have you?' Jess smiled at her. It would be only fair to let her have a bit extra on top of her allowance, after the Selfridge's expedition with Natasha.

'No, but Emily has. She hasn't spent any, well hardly any, of her whole last term's allowance and she wants me to help her blow it all on clothes. Don't suppose much will fit her though.'

'Oh? Why's that?' The tea was ready now but Zoe had sat down at the table and was looking serious. She was also chewing at the skin on the edge of her thumb, a sure sign she had something on her mind. Jess sat down opposite her and poured tea for the two of them. Matthew would just have to wait and have it cold or stewed.

Zoe shrugged and looked shifty. 'Like she's so skinny? Didn't you see, last night?'

'You're quite thin yourself,' Jess prompted.

'Yeah but I eat, she never does, or if she does she sicks it up again. That's the difference.' Zoe stood up and picked up her tea, walking quickly towards the door. 'I'm going to have a bath and get ready.' From halfway up the stairs she called down, 'Tash wants to come too, she's meeting Claire so she might like some tea as well.'

'OK, room service on the way,' Jess called back.

Zoe hadn't needed to say any more. Both she and Jess knew that. Jess had seen the performance over the hamburger the night before – she should have recognized that classic sign of an eating disorder, the meticulous delaying/avoidance ritual with food when in company. She wondered if Angie knew that Emily wasn't eating. It was unlikely: anorexics were devious, highly skilled at convincing themselves and those around them that nothing was wrong. Angie might not even notice if Emily had lost weight, even if she hadn't seen her for a few weeks, for dress-disguise was another starver's trick. She watched as the cat, full at last, clattered out through the cat flap and huddled on the step, reluctant to go out into the rain. Animals never starve themselves unless they're dying, she thought, wondering if that was as near proof as you could get that anorexia was a mental, not a chemical problem.

She poured tea for Natasha and Matthew and walked up the stairs. The bathroom door was closed and from the other side of the door she could hear the water running and a DJ on Zoe's radio being unnaturally exuberant. Jess tapped lightly on Natasha's door and went in. The blind was down and in the semi-dark there was a mildly musty scent and a hazardous heap of discarded clothes and shoes on the floor between Jess and the bed.

'Morning Tash, tea for you.' She picked her way through the obstacles and approached the bed, then her heart lurched with sudden shock as the naked top halves of not one but two figures reared up from the duvet. There was a weird snapshot moment as her eyes gradually captured the sight and her brain slowly and painfully registered that Natasha had Tom in bed with her.

'Shit,' was all Tom said.

Natasha rallied some instant defiance. 'We weren't *doing* anything!' she protested at a level that neared a shriek.

'How the hell did you get in?' Jess slammed the mug

of tea down on the little chest of drawers beside the bed before her trembling hands dropped it. She took a step back to distance herself from the two of them, stumbling on a shoe. 'We double-locked all the doors before we went to bed!'

'Er . . . sorry, we, um . . .' Tom gave a quick giveaway glance towards the window. Jess followed the look and noticed that Natasha's normally cluttered desktop was completely clear. All her school files, her unfinished homework, pen tray, stack of paper were piled up under the desk.

'You climbed in? Like a sneaky thief in the night? How dare you? Natasha is *fifteen*! I want you to get out right now! Fast! And by the front door! Don't you ever, *ever* come back.' Her voice had risen almost to a scream. She slammed out of the room, shaking, and crashed into Matthew, who was coming down the attic stairs to investigate the noise.

'What is it? What's happened?' He took her hand and led her back up to their room, sitting her on the bed carefully as if she was injured.

Jess, sobbing, pointed out of the door. 'That boy, Tom – he's in bed with Natasha. He climbed in through her window!'

Matt, unforgivably, chuckled. 'Oh very *Romeo and Juliet*,' he said.

Jess glared at him. 'What the fuck are you talking about? Natasha and that *boy* are in her bed, neither of them apparently with a stitch on and all you can do is *laugh*?'

Matthew recomposed his face. 'Sorry, but well, as you said, fifteen is the new eighteen. And at least she's on the premises, not in the back of some car down a dark alley.'

'I don't believe you're saying this.' Jess felt genuinely puzzled. 'Are you saying it's OK? We had that boy in the house as a guest, fed him, felt sorry for him, all that, and this is what he does, he climbs in through the window and sleeps with our daughter?'

'Now you're overreacting. You're making too much of a drama out of it. Sure, it was a shock. And for double sure it mustn't happen again. But . . .'

Jess got up and went into the bathroom to run the shower. She felt the need to be covered in soap, to wash away last night's sex that now just made her feel sick, picturing Natasha with Tom.

'I can't think where "but" comes in,' she said. 'You might not feel betrayed, by both of them, but I do.' She shut the door, and, unusually, locked it. From the other side of the door, just before she turned the taps on to 'full' and drowned out both thoughts and words, she heard him say, 'Oh, it's all about you is it?'

Zoe stayed in the bath till the water went cold. She hardly dared move. So they knew now. Once she'd thought that might be a relief but it wasn't at all. The good thing, the end of her having to keep their lousy secret, was ruined by her mother's anger. She'd heard how much hurt there was in her voice. Natasha had wounded their mum by having Tom in just as much as if she'd punched her in the stomach. Mum being a bit cross about stuff she was well used to – but only the usual small things like not getting up early enough for school in the mornings and having to race around, or not putting stuff away in the kitchen. It occurred to her that this wasn't at all a house where there were regular major rows. Sometimes girls at school came in in the mornings and sat around in the cloakroom saying things like 'Jesus you should have heard the olds last night!' gathering an enthralled crowd as they described earth-shattering quarrels, doors slamming, plates being broken. Sometimes they'd cry and tell about divorce or a parent who'd packed their bags and walked out.

Zoe had marvelled at the tempestuous atmospheres some of her friends lived in, had even wondered if it would be fun to exist in the brittle air of high drama like a soap opera full of disasters. It was probably why she hadn't resisted all that much when Emily had dragged her into the non-pregnancy thing. Once or twice she'd even longed for something a bit more lively to happen than the contented day-to-day existence her family seemed to plod along with. When her dad had lost his job, then she'd had something to tell them at school but no-one was very interested. When they'd asked if that meant there'd been a big row and would they be broke and have to move house, all she'd been able to do was shrug and admit that so far, no, nothing had changed. No-one had asked about it again. It really was just like television: only the worst that could happen was of interest to anyone.

Scared of the noise it would make, Zoe pulled the plug and let the water go. She shivered as she climbed out. The skin on her fingers was all puckery from being in the water too long. A girl at school had told her that dead bodies found in rivers or the sea look like that all over and she'd had dreams about that, about skin so wrinkled it resembled the texture of a pale brain. She dried herself slowly and thoroughly, delaying the moment when she'd have to come out and join in with the family. It might have been Tash who'd done the bad thing, but she was sure to cop for some of the fallout, even if it was just in terms of a horrible atmosphere.

She stroked some of Natasha's favourite coconut body lotion over her legs and then sloshed an overgenerous amount into her palms to anoint the rest of her body: Tash owed her for keeping the secret, and for being so stupid as to let Tom oversleep. The loss of a bit of body lotion was only a teeny part of what she deserved.

Natasha slammed around her room looking for the right things to wear, opening and shutting drawers and her wardrobe too fast and furiously to be able to concentrate properly. Her mum had gone well over the top and the horrible thing was that deep inside she didn't really blame her. She felt angry with everyone. She felt like crying. She probably wouldn't see Tom again – he'd be out there looking for someone else with a comfortable bed and a more reliable alarm clock. The battery had gone on hers, she'd realized as soon as Tom had given her that accusing look and pointed to the clock. No lights had showed on it. It just sat there, dead, almost asking her to hurl it out of the window.

She was hungry. It would take a lot of nerve to go down and face her mother over the kitchen table but she was going to have to do it or she'd collapse. She couldn't understand how people like Emily could go without food; she couldn't even sulk her way past breakfast. At last, dressed in suitably sober grey trousers and a comfortingly warm hooded black top, she quietly opened her door and looked out. There was no sound from up in the attic, which was bad news and meant both her parents had to be downstairs. Zoe's door was closed, but Natasha realized it was unfair to expect her to back her up, be on her side and do whatever it took to defend her. Zoe was just a kid. She hadn't wanted to know about her and Tom and Natasha hadn't wanted to tell her. She hadn't been showing off or anything, it was just that sliding a big sash window up and down and helping Tom climb in was quite noisy and with her alarm going off every morning before seven, Zoe would have been sure to suspect something.

One thing was definite, she thought as she tried to creep down to the kitchen without the stairs creaking, if Oliver had still been at home she wouldn't even have thought about letting Tom in to sleep with her. Oliver was so much the bloody Perfect Son, he'd probably have beaten Tom up for molesting his little sister. And of course, *he'd* never do anything like break into someone's house and share a girl's bed. But then he didn't need to: he had a perfectly good, warm, comfortable bed of his own. He didn't have to sleep in a broken-down car. Natasha looked out of the window, down towards the railway. She half-expected, certainly fully hoped, that Tom would be there, watching from the edge of the line and waiting to send her some sort of signal that he was thinking about her. There was no sign of him. Of course it was raining, the kind of day when no-one in their right mind would hang about outside if they didn't have to. It would have made her feel better though, to know he cared enough to make sure she was OK.

Matthew and Jess were sitting at the kitchen table reading the paper. For a second Natasha thought that perhaps it was all over, the outburst upstairs, the ordering Tom out of the house was all there was going to be to it. Her parents looked so normal, just sitting there, reading about Saturday stuff in the paper. As quietly and unobtrusively as she could Natasha made her way into the kitchen, almost sliding, catlike, along the units.

'It's all right, you're allowed food you know,' Jess said to her over the top of the *Times* magazine. 'There's some bread cut if you want toast.' Natasha mumbled, 'Thanks,' and went to put bread into the toaster. She really wanted Alpen, but felt that refusing the offered toast might be construed as impudent, challenging. Her mother was still looking cross and sort of miserable as well. Natasha felt bad. She'd rather, on balance, her mum had just walloped her. Anything would be better than this wounded look.

'Do you want more tea?' she asked, filling the kettle.

'Not for me,' Jess said.

'Oh, yeah, thanks I will.' Matt smiled at Natasha who almost cried with relief. Her dad still loved her. Her dad didn't think she was the worst, most wicked person on earth.

She took the toast to the table and sat down as far away from her mother as she could. She could hear the toast crunching into the room's silence. Now the food was in her mouth it was hard to swallow it, as if there was already a lump of something blocking the way. She couldn't bear Jess not speaking. It was way too soon to hope that everything was all right, but she needed very much to get things going that way.

'Mum?' Jess looked up and waited. It was impossible to read anything in her expression. Her eyes looked all dead, as if she didn't recognize her.

'I'm really sorry, Mum,' Natasha began. Any other words she'd been hoping to say trailed away as big tears started to tumble down her cheeks. Miserably, she went on chewing her toast.

'Sorry? Yes I expect you are, now you've been

174

caught.' It wasn't going to be easy. This had never happened before. In this house you apologized and it was all over – there was a kind of rule about not bearing grudges. But her mum looked hard and cold as if she'd run out of patience and forgiveness for ever. Surely she couldn't have used it all up on this one thing?

Natasha felt a flash of anger; after all what else could she say? Some of her usual spirit rallied itself. 'Look, Tom hasn't got anywhere to, like, live. It's still cold at night. How would you like it if it was Oliver out there living in a car? Wouldn't you want someone to take him in?' Her voice was rising now and Matt flashed her a warning look which she ignored. 'I mean, I did ask you if he could stay in Oliver's room but you said no!'

'Oh so it's all my fault is it? My fault that you, under age, are letting a complete stranger climb over the conservatory roof and into the house and then sleeping with him?'

'Jess, can't we talk about this later? Tash's upset,' Matt ventured, putting an arm round the girl and pulling her against him.

'I wasn't sleeping with him! Not like that . . .' Natasha wailed. 'Not like that! And now I might not see him ever again!'

'I don't care whether it's "like that" or not,' Jess said coldly. 'And as for seeing him again, well you're right there, you won't be. You're grounded till I decide I can trust you again.'

'What? That's not fair!'

'Well it's not *un*fair,' Matt said. 'You must admit you can't expect just to get clean away with this kind of thing.'

'Oh you're just like Mum!' Natasha roared, getting up and stamping out of the kitchen. At the door she turned back and smirked defiantly at her parents, throwing them one last bone to chew on. 'Why don't you ground Zoe too, while you're at it? She knew all about it!'

Zoe, hanging about outside the door hoping the battle level would fall enough for her to feel safe to get some breakfast, heard her sister shop her to her parents.

'You spiteful cow! I wish I had bloody told them now,' she hissed at Natasha as she hurtled past her towards the stairs. 'Don't ever ask me to cover up for you again.'

Eleven

'I handled that about as badly as it's possible to,' Jess said to Matt after Zoe had grabbed a piece of toast and left to meet Emily.

'Hmm, you could be right.' There was amusement in his voice, though for the life of her Jess couldn't think what there was to laugh about. He went on, 'I guess you could have approached Natasha with the talking option rather than the shouting one.' He was infuriating, she thought. He'd gone back to studying England's prospective test match team for that summer. He was, she thought, more concerned with whether Ramprakash would be fit enough than with whether his daughter was turning into a complete little tart.

'It's difficult to talk rationally when you're this angry. How could she do this? I thought we'd brought her up to be straight with us. Oliver worked out all right, I mean what went wrong? Or is it girls? I really don't want to think it is . . .'

'Well you're the expert,' Matt pointed out. 'You're

the one who writes about the delights of family life. And aren't you always telling me about the disasters people write to you about?' Oh thanks so much, Jess thought, go ahead, remind me I'm supposed to know all this stuff.

'From my point of view though, I'd say nothing went wrong.' Matthew folded the paper and drank the last of his tea. 'Natasha genuinely thinks she was doing the right thing. He hasn't got anywhere to live.'

'Well she didn't have to move him into her bed. And anyway, why didn't she say?' Jess started loading the dishwasher. 'We might have been able to help him find somewhere. And what about these foster people he's supposed to be with? He's only young, I realized when I saw him with her this morning, he can't be much older than she is.' She felt herself shiver at the thought of her child in bed with the boy. Natasha *was* still a child in many ways. And so were her friends. If you looked past the tummy-revealing little tops they wore, the trousers slung so low on their hips you could see the lacy edges of their minimal knickers, they were still barely touched by life's deeper and more danger-ous dramas. Natasha was nothing like some of the schoolgirls you saw at the bus stops, smoking and snogging and swearing and trading flirting obscenities with undeserving, unappealing and barely co-ordinated boys.

'Things go wrong with foster people,' Matt said. 'You read about it all the time. And she says she did tell you. She says she asked you if he could have Oliver's room.'

'Oh on the Selfridge's day. I didn't take her that seriously. You can bet your life if he'd moved in she'd have gone off him in about twenty-four hours and then we'd have had to think about how to get him out again. Surely even you can see that was never going to be a goer?'

Matt sighed and picked up the pile of paper. 'Yeah well. It's all done with now. He's gone and she's angry but she'll get over it.' He frowned at Jess. 'The point is, will you? Are you going to keep beating yourself up for being a less than perfect parent or are you going to let it drop? Because I know which we'd all prefer.'

From the back of her wardrobe, Natasha pulled out her Reef backpack that she'd used for school books till Claire had hinted (very gently but acutely) that surfer stuff wasn't too cool in London any more, and crammed in a few pairs of knickers, spare trousers, a couple of extra tops and her sponge bag. She added her make-up bag and a hairbrush and her old pink fluffy rabbit that was still good for cuddling on a thundery night or when stuff was going wrong. There was no way she wasn't going to see Tom again. No way she was staying in this house with its horrid new layer of atmosphere hanging around like a thick November fog. Being grounded was for kids Zoe's age. You couldn't keep a fifteen-year-old in, it wasn't natural. And they were about to find out it wasn't even possible. She opened her bedroom door and looked back into her room. Something wasn't right. She shut the door again, put down her bag and went to make her bed and put all her books back on the desk. It was a gesture, quite a clever one she thought, her mother would get it, even if Dad and Zoe didn't notice.

She could hear them in the kitchen, talking quite loudly which meant they were still going on about her. The door was still shut. Zoe must have closed it after her when she went to get ready to go out with Emily. She felt bad about Zoe – she shouldn't have dropped her in it – none of this was her fault. After all, she had kept the secret, she hadn't actually dobbed her in to the parents.

It was easy, just walking quite normally, though perhaps a bit more consciously quietly, down the stairs and out through the front door. It wasn't as if her parents were actually going to lock her in: if they said she was grounded it meant they had to trust her a bit – otherwise she'd just walk out when she felt like it, like this, wouldn't she? Working this out, she felt a small twinge of guilt: if the idea was for them to trust her again then even she, even in this pent-up fury, could see this wasn't the way to do it. So that the door wouldn't bang she left it slightly ajar, wedging it, to stop it slamming shut, with the free paper full of ads for in-your-dreams-priced property and visiting massage women that a year-seven kid from Briar's Lane chucked through the door every Saturday morning. This wasn't really running away, she thought, as she sprinted down the path and along the road towards the square. It was just putting a bit of space between her and the parents for a while. When you cared about someone you had to make a stand. All the same, she had to try quite hard not to feel tearful. She also wished she'd brought her big snuggly old puffa jacket with her. It might be horribly dated and Claire would pull that face she did but it would at least keep her warmer and dryer than her fleece.

She increased her pace almost to a run as she passed Eddy's house. Fearfully, as if he was about to rush out and accuse her of taking men in, of lying on his bed with Tom and creasing his duvet cover, she glanced at his window. It hadn't mattered the evening before when she'd seen him on home ground, but out here in the Grove she had that feeling that all the blank house windows knew and told all that went on. Eddy's house, having no curtains or blinds, could see more than most. At the end of the road she crossed the square and slowed her pace a little. No-one had followed her. Her dad hadn't come racing down the road ordering her to stay in her bedroom till she promised eternal celibacy, or until she was twenty-one, whichever was sooner. Nor was her mum magically waiting there to trap her and look disappointed and tell her how much she'd let them down and how bloody perfect Oliver would never have behaved like that. How would they know? she thought, Oliver was a bloke – they communicated mostly in grunts and the parents were grateful for each precious whole word. For all they knew he might have been chucked out of more girls' beds by more parents than any of them had had burnt barbecue sausages. She was almost at the allotments now. Tom would have gone back there: he'd be waiting for her. She passed the row of shops, turned the corner by the bus stop and opened the allotment gate. There was the Sierra.

'. . . looking for surf that has no bluebottles (Portuguese men-of-war). They are everywhere, even the little ones give a bad sting and a rash . . . Off for three-day surf camp in Straddie with Canadians & couple of English tomorrow. Must go, it's sangria night at the hostel again and a didgeridoo lesson. Love (I suppose) to Girls, tell them to mail me with any goss. Ol.'

'Well Oliver sounds like he's still having a good time anyway,' Jess commented as she printed out Oliver's latest missive. 'No cares in the world. I feel quite envious.'

'We haven't got much in the way of cares either, not when you put it into a world-scale context,' Matthew said from the sofa. He'd almost disappeared under the many sections of the paper. Only one, Appointments, as immaculately folded and untouched as it had arrived, lay on the floor beside him. It would look exactly the same when it went into the recycling bag. As she watched, he flung down the TV listings and stretched, yawning luxuriously. 'What do you fancy doing today?' he asked. 'Shall we see a movie? I quite fancy that one about the woman growing dope in her greenhouse in Cornwall.'

Jess laughed. 'You would! It sounds like some scheme you and the bunch up at the Leo would dream up over a few beers!'

Matt looked rather shifty at that and he had a strangely secretive smile as he over-scrupulously rearranged and refolded all the newspaper pages, confirming that this particular scam certainly had been discussed. 'Well I suppose at least if you were in prison you'd have food and accommodation provided,' she told him. 'Anyway, I think I'll go up and talk to Natasha, see if we can see a way of getting back towards normal.'

Natasha's empty room was a shock. Somehow Jess had assumed the girl would be slumped on her bed either sullenly pecking out text messages to Claire on her mobile or pretending to sleep. The neatly made bed and the carefully reorganized desk looked like a statement about being adult, about Natasha refusing to be quashed. She would organize her own life, thank you, Jess interpreted from the doorway, praying Natasha would somehow materialize magically from the wardrobe.

'She's gone!' Jess hurtled down the stairs and back into the sitting room.

'Oh, hi Jess! Who's gone?' Jess hadn't heard Paula arrive. She was sitting on the sofa next to Matthew, looking as if she hadn't had a lot of sleep. She was, Jess managed to note, still in last night's clothes and had a look on her face as if she was trying hard not to keep breaking into a very broad pleased-with-life grin.

'Natasha's gone? Where?' Matt asked.

'God, Matt, how the hell am I supposed to know? She's just not there. She must have gone off out straight after we told her she was grounded.' Jess leaned across her desk and peered out of the window into the drizzle as if Natasha might still be waiting on the front doorstep, like a small child who runs away and daren't go further than the garden shed. It even crossed her mind to check the shed: she'd noticed Natasha and Tom lurking close to it the night before.

Paula's smile was a lazy, mildly curious one. 'Oh dear! Have there been words? Your loyal readers will want to know all about it!'

'I don't think I'll be writing about this one, Paula.'

'Oh? I thought your column was all about sharing both the pleasures *and* the pains of family life. You always have before! Come on, tell me what your delicious daughter has done now? Is it a boy?' Paula had scrabbled in her handbag and was brushing her hair now. Longish blond strands floated from her brush and landed on her leather trousers. Paula, with exaggerated delicacy, gathered up the stray bits between her lavender-painted thumb and index fingernails and dropped them over the side of the sofa onto the floor, assuming,

Jess thought, that a cleaning fairy would deal with them in due course.

'It is a boy, but it'll sort itself out.' Jess didn't want to be so disloyal to Tash as to start telling the world and its friends what she'd been up to. Stuff the column, she thought, this one's private. She was worried too. If Natasha had flounced out in a teenage huff, she might decide it was too difficult to creep back in again and simply not come home.

'Anyway, I was just telling Matt . . .' Paula went on, eager to get back to the more enthralling subject of herself. 'I've come for a character reference. Your friend Eddy is quite the sweetest man I've come across in ages – oh sorry that sounds so rude! – and I want you two to tell me all about him and what the score is. He says he's single, but then he would, wouldn't he?'

'Oh he's single. I think you could say he goes in for serial singleness.' Matt laughed. 'There's three ex-wives, several children and a couple of grandchildren and I gather the old royalty cheques don't go so far these days.'

'Oh I'm not bothered about the money aspect,' Paula said airily. 'I just want to know if he's a Nice Person, someone I could think of in terms of more than, well just, sort of sex. Grandchildren though,' she frowned, 'that must make him . . . how old? . . . too old?'

'I expect he started young,' Jess cut in. 'Living the rock dream life, you know, married an early pregnant girlfriend, dumped her later for literally a younger model, that kind of thing. He's OK these days, pretty settled. He was very kind to Clarissa when she was burgled.' She smiled a warning at Matt not to elaborate on the nature of the 'kindness'. It was actually quite cheering to see Paula looking so happy.

'What, though, does he actually *do*?' Paula went on. 'I mean I asked him, of course, but he just said "this and that" and went on about expecting to make a million any day now, just like Del Boy used to in *Only Fools and Horses*, remember? I mean he must do *something*, he's too young to live like an old retired bloke, pottering about all day, don't you think Matt?'

Jess held her breath, wondering if Matt was actually going to slap Paula for her profound tactlessness or laugh at her for putting her foot so far into her mouth she'd practically digested it.

Matt stood up and headed for the door. 'All I can say, Paula, is that Eddy is full of ideas,' he said with mock solemnity. 'As are all of us who are released early, and mercifully in my opinion, from the stifling grind of daily employment.' He left the room and Jess heard him climbing the stairs. He didn't sound unhappy or unduly insulted for he was leaping up them two at a time. She heard Oliver's door open, then after a few seconds close again. Then there was the faint sound of slower steps heading for the attic.

'Oh I'm so sorry. Me and my huge mouth.' Paula put her fingers across the offending feature for a second and looked penitent.

'Oh don't worry about it,' Jess reassured her. 'He's only gone up to watch the sport on telly in peace. Just because he's out of work, he can't expect the rest of us to pussyfoot round the issue. He doesn't seem unhappy about it.'

'No? Isn't he desperate to find another job? I know I would be.'

Jess perched on the edge of her desk from where she could talk to Paula and also keep an eye on the Grove in case Natasha was on her way back. 'He thinks of it as a great opportunity,' she said. 'It's like he's finding himself, the way hippies used to.'

'Some of them still are, you should see my aunt Eileen, still seeking personal space by way of bits of art therapy and rune reading and strictly middle-class university-level spiritual retreats where she gets her karma sorted. Never done a hand's turn as my mother used to say.'

'Yes well for that you need someone who's prepared to keep you in meals and mortgage. I guess Matt thinks it's my turn and he's probably right.'

'Aunt Eileen married a merchant banker and lives near Sissinghurst, so there you are. Are you jealous?'

'What, of Matt? Of all that free time? No, it's not that. It's as if now he's opted out of work, he's sort of opted out of everything else in our lives as well. I feel very much on my own at the moment.'

Paula got up and gave her a quick hug. 'Write it all down, sweetie. Your readers need to know you're not perfect.'

'I'm not sure I need them to know that though!' Jess laughed.

Tom wasn't in the Sierra. There was nothing in it at all, nothing to show he'd ever so much as opened its door. The steering column was smashed around the area where the ignition key should go, Natasha noticed as she peered in through the dirty window, so it must have been stolen at some time and dumped there. It couldn't have been Tom though, she told herself, squashing her suspicions, he wouldn't be so stupid as to sleep in a car he'd stolen. Someone else must have done it. The city was full of nicked cars.

'Hello sweetheart, what are you doing up here?

Looking for that boyfriend of yours?' George, with inevitable hoe in hand, was watching Natasha from his scarlet shed. She grinned at him. Her grandad was cool. How wonderfully mad did you have to be to stick so fervently to political beliefs that were on their way out half a century before? And how crazy to paint your shed bright red and declare it the People's Palace of Mortlake Road?

'Hi Grandad, how's the carrots?'

'Plagued with root fly but at least they grow straight and not twisted. If only people were like that.'

'People? Why?' For the first time she realized that George looked quite severely old. She'd always taken it for granted that he was an Old Person, that's what grandparents were. But he'd always looked well, acted as if age wasn't something that was a problem. Just now she realized that he wasn't that far away from death. He even looked as if he'd been thinking about it.

'Bloody vandals and thieves, that's what I'm talking about. Val's shed was broken into a couple of nights back, all her tools stolen. She had good stuff too, not the cheap sort you get down the market that don't last five minutes. Someone had a go at Dave's as well but he's got a lock on it that would do the job on Fort Knox so they didn't get in. If people want to go nicking they should do it from those who've got it to spare, not from the likes of us. Anyway, enough gloom and doom. Come and have a cup of tea. Tell me what brings you down here. That lad hasn't been around today, not that I've seen.'

Natasha was impatient to leave, there was still time to meet Claire and she needed somewhere to sleep for the night. The idea of camping out in the Sierra had seemed romantic, daring and exciting but only combined with sharing it with Tom. Now her resolve faltered seriously at the idea of a chill and frightening night in it by herself. And whoever was doing the shed-burgling might come back. She caught herself thinking about how much her mother would worry and almost grinned at the thought that she was, deep down, feeling quite responsible, though her family wouldn't see it that way.

She followed George into the shed, dumped her heavy bag on the floor and sat in one of his battered old floral picnic chairs.

'You were lucky they didn't get in here,' she said. 'You've got a lot of stuff and it's all so clean and polished. The burglars wouldn't even get earth all over them.'

Her grandfather gave her a long look as he stirred the two mugs of tea. 'I hope it was just luck,' he said. 'I don't like to think badly of people, not people I like. Car boot sales, I blame them.'

'What do you mean?' Natasha was mystified. Car boot sales were what her school PTA had every summer to raise funds for a new minibus or a new filter system for the swimming pool. Parents turned up in their Mercedes estates and set up clothes rails with last season's Donna Karan skirts on them and boxes full of CDs that had barely been played. Clothes their smallest children had grown out of were eagerly snapped up, for the top-of-the-range quality guaranteed that wear and tear would be absolutely minimal. There were picnics during the day, too much wine was drunk and the takings were ludicrously vast compared with the Sunday morning boot sales in aid of the local hospice.

'It's where your local crook takes his swag and flogs

it to the unsuspecting punters. It's all too easy. You don't even need a car boot, just rent a table-top space and hope the cops aren't on the lookout,' George told her. 'You can shift any amount of gear that way. You should ask your mate Tom.'

'Tom? Why would Tom know?'

George laughed. 'Hey lass, he may be straight, he may not. But he sure as hell knows people who aren't.'

Later, as Natasha walked back towards the bus stop to go to Claire's house, she thought about what George had said. Tom did know how to get into houses. But he didn't take things, she was sure of it. She wasn't sure, though, how he lived. He always had money for cigarettes, never seemed to be that hungry, and admitted he lived on junk takeaways, which were cheap enough but still didn't come free, not like food at a parent's house. She huddled against the bus stop, wishing she hadn't bolted from home. It was a huge disappointment not finding Tom waiting for her. That was what was supposed to happen, surely? If he cared about her? She couldn't recall that he'd said he did. Now she felt foolish that she'd assumed, because he was happy to kiss her, to touch her, that what he'd been feeling was real affection.

She could see the bus in the distance, waiting at traffic lights. She picked up the bag and stepped closer to the pavement, ready to put out her hand for it to stop. A VW Polo swooshed round the corner, too close to the kerb, and splashed water all over her feet and the bottoms of her trousers. Chill wet fabric clung against her already cold legs. The car window was open and she heard raucous laughter. Mel, her so very long-ago best friend, was in the car, dropping a cigarette end out of

189

the window. The driver, she could just make out, was Tom.

Matt sat on the old Lloyd Loom sofa in the bedroom and thought about Natasha. He needed to be by himself to do this, to let down the puppyish façade he'd been keeping going since Jess had shrieked at the girl in her room. There was no way he'd wanted to rush in and throttle Tom, that would have meant he'd have had to see them, get too accurate a picture that would stay with him, no matter what. He'd done very well so far, quite determinedly keeping the idea a bit hazy, not picturing Natasha wound around the boy, not tangled and tumbling on the bed with him. He didn't have any of those rather dodgy 'she's my little girl and always will be' feelings that he'd heard were harboured by some men, the type who shuddered at the thought of their daughters growing up. But still, he could have done with a bit more time, a few more leisurely years in which Natasha went through the usual dating process, dragged one or two home for inspection perhaps, before he had to come to terms with her as a grown-up sexual being. This way it was all too horribly sudden. He didn't see any great value in virginity for its own sake, scorned the usual idea that it was something that was 'lost' as if it was a particular treasure. But *fifteen*, who on earth had a clue what they were doing at fifteen?

He picked up the remote control and switched on the TV. A couple of the usual punters, two British ex-footballers and a Dutchman were discussing the FA Cup Final. The Brits, he thought, looked so awkward, trussed up in stiff, dull suits and with ill-matched ties that looked as if they'd been chosen by their children and had to be worn to avoid upsetting them. By contrast, the Dutchman was easy and relaxed in a polo shirt and a beautifully cut jacket. We Brits can't do casual, Matt thought as he allowed the discussion to drift into focus and shift his brain's attention away from Natasha. In fact the Brits couldn't seem to get their heads round the concept of leisure at all. He thought about men in summer, on the hottest days wearing shorts that tended to be that bit too short, with the wrong sort of shoes or the old cliché of socks-with-sandals.

Perhaps, he thought idly, I'll set up a consultation for companies, try to teach them how to grasp the dress-down concept of office-wear, and kick-start the unthinking design-ignorant desk-man into confidence in his own taste, rather than clinging to the dreary comfort of a suit-and-tie uniform. At this point Matt tried very hard to concentrate on the football: somehow, he worried, the idea of an actual occupation had taken root in his brain. Of all the daft ideas he and the others at the Leo had been coming up with, this was one he actually thought he could pick up and run for goal with. It was too frightening.

'So can I stay with you? Just for a little while?' Natasha watched Claire putting on her lipstick. She observed closely the way Claire's mouth parted slightly and pouted, and had to stop herself copying. Claire and make-up were made for each other: mascara never flecked like dead baby flies onto her cheeks. Eye-shadow never disappeared into creases and blusher didn't make her look as if she was trying to resemble the kind of dolly you won at the fair.

'I suppose. I'll have to ask Mum though.' Claire

wasn't as welcoming as Natasha had thought she'd be. Perhaps it was because of what she'd done. She'd told her about being found with Tom and hoped Claire would help the mood to lighten, perhaps think it was funny. But Claire didn't. It crossed Natasha's mind that perhaps she was jealous, as if it wasn't what she'd had in mind, Natasha getting ahead of her like this.

'We weren't even having sex,' Natasha had felt the need to explain when Claire had been a bit cool, the cold sort not the good sort. 'I just, well he needed somewhere to stay.' It sounded lame, put like that. She half-expected Claire to ask, 'Why didn't you have sex? You might as well have done.' She didn't know what she'd say then; she'd have to admit that what she meant was 'We didn't do it *in the house*' which had been because she was in her own home, with other people around. She didn't want to tell her about when they were down by the railway, she didn't want Claire being all condemning and spoiling it. The picture of Mel in the car with Tom flashed through her mind. She hadn't mentioned that to Claire either and she was glad now that she hadn't. It involved too many more awkward questions, like whose was the car? How come Tom, who was actually only sixteen, was driving it? And was he doing all that sex stuff with Mel too?

Jess wished she and Matt had gone out now, then she wouldn't have had to spend the day wondering when Natasha would return. If they'd gone out, taken the car, it would have made it easy for Tash to come back in the house, just be there as if she'd never been away and they could find some way of all muddling along again. Instead, she'd spent the rest of the day doing mindless chores: cleaning the kitchen (including taking every-

192

thing out of the fridge, washing every shelf and reloading) with one eye on the clock, another on the job in hand.

'Has she just stormed out for a while to show that she can or has she run away?' she asked Matt eventually, when at nearly seven that evening there was still no sign of her. 'I mean suppose she's run off somewhere with Tom, should we call the police?'

Matt opened the pristine fridge and upset the symmetry by removing a couple of bottles of beer. 'And say what? "We've got a fifteen-year-old daughter who's been out most of the day"? I think they'll want it to be at least an all-nighter before they get interested, especially round here. This bit of London is full of girls of her age staying out: the middle-class ones with over-liberal parents *and* the others. Covers almost everyone. And Zoe isn't back yet either, they'd want to know why you're not just as worried about her.'

Jess opened one of the beers and drank straight from the bottle. Cleaning was thirsty work but had been suitably mind-numbing when she needed it. Certainly in the kitchen she hadn't left much for Monica to do on Monday. There was even a lamb casserole in the oven, one of those comfort-food items that was supposed to stick families, as well as your ribs, together.

'Tasha's probably at that friend's house,' Matthew suggested. 'Claire, the one I saw her with the other day.'

'I just wish she'd ring if she is. I want her to know we want her to come home. She hasn't taken her mobile, she said last week that it had run out of time – I think that was a hint that I was supposed to buy her a voucher.'

Matthew hugged her. 'Don't worry, she'll turn up.

193

Nights are still cold. She won't be out on the streets. Give her a call at Claire's, I'm sure she'll be there.' Just then the front door was slammed shut but it was Zoe, not Natasha, who came running in.

'Mum, Dad, come quick! Emily has collapsed and I can't get her to wake up! Angie isn't there, she's gone out with the bloke who delivered the new fridge and . . .' She stopped, gasping for breath. 'Come *now*!'

Emily was lying in her mother's kitchen, sprawled out on the floor with her legs at strange angles like a corpse in a bad TV drama.

'Shall I get an ambulance?' Zoe stood hopping from foot to foot, biting her thumb. 'Emily! Get up!' she yelled, prodding at the girl with her toe.

'No, don't kick her, that won't help,' Matt said. 'Let's put her in the recovery position and see how she goes from there. An ambulance might be a good idea.'

'No!' Emily opened her eyes and groaned. 'I'm OK, I'm just feeling a bit woozy . . .' Her eyes rolled in her head, quite terrifyingly, Jess thought. She took Zoe's arm and pushed her out into the hallway.

'Zoe, has she taken anything?'

'What? Like what? Only aspirins. She's always taking aspirins. She says her head hurts.'

'Has she eaten anything?'

'No.' Zoe's eyes filled with tears. 'I told you, she never eats. You were supposed to tell Angie.'

'I know. I haven't seen her since you mentioned it though.'

'But you've had ALL DAY!' Zoe wailed. 'Angie was *here* this *morning.* You could have come over. You could have talked to her! All you think about is Natasha! Suppose Emily dies?'

Then it will be all your fault was the bit Zoe wasn't

194

saying. 'She isn't going to die, not today anyway,' Jess told her. Matthew had hauled Emily up and sat her on one of Angie's slinky kitchen chairs. He looked at Jess, indicating without Emily seeing that she weighed about as much as a kitten.

'Come back with us,' Jess told Emily. 'We're going to give you something to eat and drink, nothing big or heavy, just enough to keep you upright. And then when your mum gets back I think we all need to have a talk about what's been going on, don't you?'

Emily nodded miserably and gave Zoe a feeble smile. 'Thanks a lot Zoe, now you've really landed me in it.'

Twelve

The answerphone was on. Natasha listened to her own voice (gratingly bright and overeager, as if she was about twelve) asking her to leave a message after the beep, decided she couldn't, on the spur of the moment, think of the appropriate attitude to come up with and hung up quickly.

'They've only bloody gone out, haven't they? You know, like they don't care?' she complained to Claire. They were sitting in Claire's kitchen where they'd been for the past two hours. Scattered remains of pizza base lay strewn about on the table among several empty Coke cans. Claire picked up a shaving of pizza crust and put it in her mouth.

'They could be trawling through the streets looking for you,' Claire said. 'It's only eight o'clock. You could have left them a message, let them know you're OK. *We're* the ones who should be going out.'

Natasha pulled a face and slumped over the table, her head in her hands. 'I don't feel like going any-

196

where. I'm too depressed. I can't believe Tom was with Mel, how does he even *know* her?'

Claire gathered up the pizza debris, loaded it into the box it arrived in and went to squash it all into the bin.

'You keep going over the same old stuff, Tash, you're beginning to sound like one of those whingers off *Neighbours* or something. It's getting boring. Can't we just go into Richmond or Putney and see what's going on? I want a life, I don't want to waste a Saturday night, even if you do.'

'OK, OK, I'll come.' Natasha ran her hands through her hair. 'My hair feels filthy though. I only washed it yesterday.'

'That's town living for you. You were out in the rain this morning, getting pollution poured all over your head.'

'And aircraft fuel and other stuff.' Natasha giggled. 'Eddy-up-the-road's always saying we're being bombed from holiday flights with shit and kerosene. You'll have to lend me something to wear,' she said. 'I only brought stuff to be warm sleeping in a car in, not stuff to go up the pub.'

Talking about Eddy reminded Natasha of the day she and Tom had climbed into his house. Tom might be in someone else's house right now. He might be pulling Mel onto another crease-free embroidered duvet cover. Maybe there were loads of other girls too: other people's homes where he got friendly with the mum so he could have a permanent supply of good food and somewhere warm to be. He hadn't climbed in through her window every night, and he hadn't died of cold in the Sierra, so perhaps he had a sort of rota. She didn't want to think about it. Claire was right, they should go out and get themselves some life.

*   *   *

It wasn't easy to convince Angie that there was a problem. Jess didn't blame her – it must be a nice comfortable life having her children tidied away at school in the termtime. The school was being paid to take care of Emily and Angie had trusted them to do exactly that, assuming they would not let her merely limp through the term with a growing eating disorder and then send her home to have a serious health crisis. Luke never had any problems, Angie tried to reason, and she'd brought them up the same, so what had to be so different about Emily? Emily, persuaded with difficulty to drink some orange juice, eat (tediously slowly, barely a crumb at a time) half a slice of toast and then forced to stay sitting at the kitchen table until it was too late for her to go and sick it up, was now in Zoe's room complaining that there was nothing wrong with her.

'Why did nobody say anything? Why haven't I had a letter?' Angie wailed to Jess. Jess could hear denial in her voice: if there hadn't been a letter, if whoever had been allocated the role of Emily's pastoral carer hadn't got in touch, Angie was reasoning that surely it wasn't that serious.

'But you can see for yourself. Look how her clothes hang on her, and how her face has caved in. And next time she passes out she might not be in the safety of her own home, with people who care about her.' Jess was trying to keep her patience. At the back of her mind she was still thinking about Natasha and the morning's row. Helping Angie come to terms with Emily's problems, it occurred to her that maybe they should just swap daughters, see if they could do any better with each other's than they had with their own.

At least now she knew where Natasha was, and was hugely relieved she hadn't run off with Tom. Claire's mother Veronica had phoned and said (very quietly, for fear the two girls would hear her) that it was all right for Natasha to stay one night, but after that she was going to have to tell her to go home. It wasn't the first time she'd had to be a refuge for runaways, she'd admitted. 'My older daughter's best friend once had a family, er, upheaval, and moved in for three months, which was *not* convenient, so of course, you can quite understand . . .'

Jess was uncomfortably conscious of being pushed towards expressing excessive gratitude while at the same time being warned off from expecting any more than the one stingy night's bed and board for her daughter. Claire, over the years, had spent many a whole weekend giggling nights away in Natasha's bedroom and she'd spent a damp week in a Devon cottage with them one summer. But then that was when times were good and easy, not to mention more innocent. Perhaps, Jess had thought, attempting to feel charitable, Veronica was concerned that Natasha shouldn't think she was taking sides. Less charitably, she also suspected that Veronica might not want her darling daughter to be infected with whatever bad behaviour her friend was up to. Veronica, a pillar of the local Conservative party and an eager school PTA participant, would not wish to be mistaken in any sense for a liberal parent.

'So what do I do?' Angie sat chewing her nail extensions and looking desperate. 'I'm supposed to be going out with Steve tonight. Can Emily be left? Do I have to stay in with her and get her to nibble biscuits every ten minutes?'

Jess felt quite sorry for her, but sorrier for Emily. Angie hadn't a clue about any illness that couldn't be cleared up with a couple of paracetamol and a few extra hours in bed.

'I'll find some phone numbers for you,' she said, rummaging through the filing drawer in her desk where she kept a bulging file of references that might come in useful for work. 'There are people who can help but you have to trust them. I can't pretend the process is likely to be easy. She might have to stay in a hospital for quite a while.'

'Oh she won't want to do that,' Angie laughed. 'It's the holidays. She wants to be out having fun. But then . . .' Angie pulled on a piece of her hair. 'She hasn't got the energy, really, has she? Poor girl. If only she'd said something.'

'She couldn't have. That's part of the problem,' Jess told her gently. 'If she'd been able to do that she'd have been halfway to getting herself better.' She pushed a sheet of paper at Angie. 'Here, take this, make the calls. Steve will still be around tomorrow.'

Matt finished his beer and wondered about having another one. He was quite hungry but didn't want to order food from Ben. That would feel too much like having sneaked out for a solitary supper to avoid being at home, and besides, he quite fancied the idea of going out to eat a bit later with Jess, if she could tear herself away from the house. He thought about phoning her and getting her to come and join him, but she might think it was Natasha and get frantic or furious when she found it was only him.

The Leo wasn't very busy, but then it was still quite early in the evening. On Saturdays the tables filled slowly and the place was rarely full before ten. Even Eddy wasn't in: Matt wondered if he was seeing Paula again tonight. If he started having a regular thing with her he might not be around so much, which would be a pity. If he really worked on this theme Matt could make himself feel very much like a small boy whose best mate had gone off with someone else. Eddy's won't-grow-up humour and general air of permanent bad behaviour was such an entertaining novelty after all those years spent in a job where arriving in the office twenty minutes late was interpreted as some kind of suspect political manoeuvre.

Matt strolled over to the counter. 'Hey, Ben have a drink with me.' Maybe that would stave off the hunger, especially combined with some of the olives off the bar. He'd give it a bit longer before he went back. Perhaps Angie would have gone back across the road by then, maybe Natasha would have come home, made up with Jess and decided to concentrate on her GCSE coursework and give up boys for the next year. Perhaps fat pink piggies were formation-flying over the Grove. He waved a tenner at Ben who pulled a single Heineken from the cold cabinet, opened it and handed it to Matt. 'Not for me thanks mate, got a whole evening to get through. Micky's off tonight, some cousin of his died and he's gone to see the family. Anyway, haven't you got a home to go to, or does that sound too much like a proper pub land-lord?'

'It does, and frankly at the moment I don't think I have. It's full of women having traumas. It's like living in the middle of some God-awful problem page. I had to get out, it's definitely no place for a man.'

*   *   *

On Sunday morning Natasha walked home very slowly from the bus stop. The extra few minutes were to give Tom a last chance to show up. He should have been waiting for her, lurking in the square or even behind the laurels outside Claire's house. There was no reason for him to have known she was there, Natasha knew that, but as he'd so far had a knack of turning up where she was when she didn't expect him, it didn't seem too much to hope for.

Natasha wasn't particularly keen on Sundays. It was a day that didn't really count. She always felt as if she was merely hanging around waiting for Monday when real life could kick in again. Jess was a firm believer in a proper roast lunch on Sundays; all the family had to be there, unless, like Oliver being in Australia, or when Zoe went on the school ski trip, they had a really sound reason not to be. It meant that the day was broken in half – there wasn't time to do anything before lunch except hang about sleeping for as long as possible, and the afternoon sort of drifted by into the evening filled with nothing but last-minute homework and really bad television. The parents slopped about, cooked, read the papers all day, did bits of gardening and fell asleep early in the evening, bad-tempered from too much wine. Other families went out and did things, trawled round the shops as if it was just some ordinary day, went swimming or out on visits to places. Jess and Matthew had never quite got themselves round the fact that Sunday had moved on from the static non-day it had been in their youth, and seemed to be doing their best to pass this feeling on to their children.

There was laughter coming from the square by the Leo. Natasha could hear people mucking about before she could see them. There was the sound of a can being kicked, a yell of 'Goal!' Her heartbeat's pace picked up a bit: the laughter was young, some of it might be from Tom. She turned the corner feeling as nervous as if she was about to have her BCG shot all over again, but Tom wasn't there. There was just the usual bunch of Briar's Lane year tens, including Mel who was leaning against the bench, wearing a very short black skirt (with bare legs even though it wasn't warm enough yet and she was winter-pale) and smoking a cigarette. She glanced across at Natasha and gave her a broad grin and a wave. 'Y'all right Tasha?' she yelled. Natasha smiled and nodded back. If there'd been no-one else around she might have gone up to Mel and asked her about Tom, how she knew him, how *well* she knew him. With the others there it would take too much nerve. They'd crowd round, wanting to know the full story. Mel might go challenging, ask things that made her sound hard, like 'Whad'you wanna know for?' Natasha, on balance, was glad it was just the grin and the wave. Mel might tell her things she'd prefer not to know.

George hadn't a clue that anything unusual had been going on. For this Jess was thoroughly thankful, as it meant that the atmosphere over lunch could almost border on the normal.

'So did you find him then? That young lad you were looking for yesterday?' George asked Natasha as soon as they sat down. There was a brief tense moment, for George was possibly the only one who wasn't *that* interested in her reply, and then Natasha grinned at him and said, 'No. I wasn't really looking though. Went to my mate Claire's and later we went into Richmond and met up with some friends from school. It was a bit

203

boring really.' Shrugging, she made a fast start on her roast lamb and didn't meet anyone's eye, but somehow it was acknowledged that enough information had been given about what she'd been up to and the subject didn't need to be pursued.

'Emily's in a hospital with a special anorexic unit. She had to go in last night, like an emergency?' Zoe told her as the two of them cleared the table and loaded the dishwasher. 'She's way under six stone and she's got to stay in till she's at least six and a half.'

'Jesus, poor her. Still, at least she'll get sorted.' Zoe glanced at her sister, wondering. Natasha looked miles away, her mind gone off to some place where she didn't seem to be very happy. She wished there was school tomorrow so the two of them could go on the bus together and get back to being like proper friends again. Somehow she didn't think Tom would be climbing in through the windows any more. Natasha looked as if she'd been dumped, but was just that bit too moody and distant to be asked about it. Stuff would work out though, she assumed. It had over Emily, it would with Tash.

. . . foolish parents thinking holidays give an opportunity for a few uninterrupted hours of coursework. A couple of hours in the evening, with time off for EastEnders, cups of coffee, the video that has to be watched now because it's due back tomorrow, plus several phone calls to sympathize with their friends over how much homework is making them suffer doesn't really add up to much that's down on paper. Two maths questions and Zoe requires Nurofen and a lie-down on the sofa. Natasha specializes in preparation techniques, in which the right pen, paper,

selection of paper clips, hole puncher have to be arrayed on the desk top. Some may have to be shopped for . . .

Paula wasn't going to like this. She was expecting a blow-by-blow account of whatever trauma there'd been at the weekend, not a cop-out little piece about homework in the school holidays. She'd already called twice this Monday morning to ask 'Is everything all right now?' using that voice of profound sympathy to disguise shameless curiosity. It was all Jess could do to stop her calling in, hoping to catch the entire family at each other's throats. Paula with her single life, in her perfect Kensington apartment with her clean perfect furniture, flowers of the latest and best taste and her slinky-sleek cat that never seemed to shed fur, must be feeling the lack of a turbulent family battleground and be strangely keen to acquire one second-hand.

'I'll be seeing Eddy later,' she confided to Jess on the phone. 'I could just pop round if you like, have a quiet word with Natasha, woman to woman, sort of thing.' The implication 'I'm nearer her age than you are' was unmissable. Paula appeared to be going for a new vocation: Friend to the Teenager, as if it went hand in hand with Rock Chick, or would it be Rock Hen, Jess wondered, seeing as Eddy was so far past his peak. Tactfully, Jess had dissuaded her, saying she was busy working on Nelson's Column.

'Oh goody, I'll catch up when I get the copy,' Paula had enthused, leaving Jess in no doubt that she expected a full and factual report to be shared with the *Gazette*-reading populace.

'Are you writing about me?' Natasha slid into the room while Jess was working at the computer.

'Sort of. Why?'

'Do you have to?' Natasha sat down on the sofa and flicked through Sunday's Comfort Zone section.

'No, I suppose I don't have to. Would you rather I didn't?' This day had had to come some time. It probably came to all columnists who used their family life as material: years before it had happened to Hunter Davies with his column in *Punch*. The word 'exploitation' lingered in the air.

'If you're using us for something to write about, shouldn't we get paid?' Natasha asked.

'It depends. If you were supplying the ideas and the words, then yes. But I'm the one putting all this together, arranging what I choose to use, coming up with the words and the style to express them. And,' she turned to look at Natasha properly, 'don't forget you get the benefit.' She smiled at her. 'It's not as if I rush off all by myself and spend my earnings on fancy holidays in health farms in California or something.' Though sometimes I wish, she thought. 'This column pays for you to go to school . . .'

'I don't have to go there. Now Dad's not working me and Zoe could go to Briar's Lane. I hate that school if you really want to know. Being with just girls gives you weird ideas about boys.'

'What sort of ideas?' Jess was intrigued, and also aware that they were getting neatly close to the Tom subject. If there was anything Natasha wanted to talk about, it could well be now.

'Ideas that they're actually trustable, that they're people just like us.'

Matthew came into the room at that point. 'Ha! You don't want to go thinking like that!' he laughed. 'We are *men*!' he roared, beating his chest, gorilla-like.

'We will not be tied, we'll not be tamed!'

'You will not grow up!' Jess grinned. Natasha was distinctly unamused and stood up, slamming the newspaper back down onto the sofa. 'Why don't you take anything seriously? Why do you have to make a joke out of everything? Nothing's *funny*!' she yelled, racing out of the room. Matt and Jess stared at each other as the footsteps clattered up the stairs and Natasha's door slammed shut.

'*Are* you writing about her?' Matthew asked at last.

'No, well not about the stuff at the weekend. That wouldn't be fair.'

'No it wouldn't. You know, people she knows read your pieces. It's worth being a bit careful what you say. I can imagine the school head's face if you *did* write about that boy climbing in through the window to sleep with Tash. She'd probably get expelled.'

'Well that's partly why I'm keen to branch out and write about the other things, going out on the jaunts that Paula keeps coming up with. On the phone earlier she asked me to think of a sport that I really, really hate. She seems to think I should go off and find out a bit more about it and then write a piece about how I changed my mind.'

Matt thought for a moment. 'Well, what *do* you hate?'

'Since hockey at school which was like sheer bloody torture? Nothing particularly. And don't go telling Paula about the hockey, I'm definitely never going to play wing three-quarter ever again. The only grown-up women still playing are the sort like my school arch-enemy Jenny Humphreys who flattened everyone in her path.'

'My sort of woman . . .' Matt chuckled. 'Choose something you don't have to get muddy and frightened for, then. What about motor racing?'

'That's a thought. Though it might take some fixing up. One thing I really can't see the point of is golf. All those rules about women not being allowed in some of the bars and having to give way to men on the greens, all that.'

'Well there you are then. Now, it's nearly lunchtime, come with me to the Leo and hang out for a while with my dodgy new mates.'

They were all there in the Leo: Ben and Micky of course who were working, Eddy, who from the bottles in front of him was on at least his third lager, the sorrowful-looking architect from next door to Angie, and even Wandering Wilf had taken a break from pacing the streets to amuse himself with the day's newspapers. The men looked up from their table by the window and greeted Matt effusively, calming with bizarre suddenness when they realized he was accompanied by his wife. Jess immediately felt as if she'd been cast in the role of a rather bossy minder.

'What on earth do you tell them about me? I feel as if they think I'm some kind of witch,' she whispered as they went to the bar to look at the day's menu on the blackboard.

'Nothing!' Matt protested too firmly. 'I hardly say a thing, do I Ben?' Ben, with a look of wide-eyed over-innocence, backed him up. 'Honestly, he never mentions home, truly.'

'We've got other things to discuss, believe me,' Matt added. She could see him looking over her shoulder, winking at his collection of dropout mates.

'Come and sit with us! Plenty of room over here!' Eddy called.

Reluctantly, feeling she was stepping into enemy territory, Jess sat at the chair Eddy had pulled out for her.

'How are you?' she asked, as if she hadn't heard only an hour before about the mind-blasting seeing-to that he'd given Paula the night before.

'Never better darlin',' Eddy chuckled, picking up his drink in a mock toast, 'thanks to you donating your sexy friend Paula to the cause of the sad old rocker. Tee-hee.' The others joined in the sniggering, exactly like, she thought, silly young teenage boys. Just like teenage boys in fact, they had nothing better to do or to think about. She tried hard not to contemplate what Matt would be like if he went on much longer spending his days roaming around with this lot. It was like watching someone walking backwards towards childhood.

'Poor Micky's in a bit of a state,' Wandering Wilf told her. She was quite startled, hardly able to recall that Wilf had ever been known to talk to anyone before.

'Oh, why's that?' she enquired.

'Dead cousin,' Wilf explained. 'Can't find a funeral place that he'd be seen dead in, if you'll pardon the expression.'

Matt returned to the table carrying plates with their lunch, baguettes with lavish supplies of chicken and salad and garlic mayonnaise. 'Why? What's the problem?'

Micky, overhearing himself being discussed, took a break from cleaning the glasses and came to sit with them.

'He was an old hippy, Geoff was. He wouldn't want

to be stuck in some twiddly little oakette box lined with ruched polyester. You go in those places, and it's, like, somewhere for seriously old people. All anaglypta magnolia walls and dried flower arrangements in horrible little fluted vases. And filing cabinets with fake wood fronts and horrible, *horrible* net curtains.'

'Ugh, curtains.' Eddy shuddered.

'I mean, where, *where* is the Richard Branson of the undertaking business?' Micky was on a roll now. 'Where is Terence Conran when you need him, a bloke with design sense who can sharpen the trade up a bit? Get up to speed with the kind of people who buy their sofas at Heal's and their fabrics from Designers Guild? There's a lot of us about and our mates die too, not just ancient grannies. Geoff would be spinning in his shroud if he'd seen the Georgian-style brass-effect handles on offer for his coffin.' He leaned forward, looking intense. 'I said, "Haven't you got a tasty straight-edged chrome? Something a bit more Philippe Starck?" Bloke in black thought I was crazy.'

For once, Jess could see that they had a point. She couldn't think of any undertaker's shopfront that didn't look like a relic from a Dickensian novel. It was the one high-street business that didn't seem to have moved on, certainly in her lifetime; some of them still referred to themselves as 'funeral parlours'. The word 'parlour' should have gone the way of 'scullery' and 'wash-house' by now. She remembered when her mother had died, going into the hushed front office of Shearing Brothers, Undertakers and Monumental Masons and having to ask if the clerk would mind turning off the sombre taped music that seemed to make the whole proceedings even more depressing than they already were. The carpet had been a dingy grey and black check, and although she was only the thickness of the dusty window away from a lively spring day out on the road beyond, it had felt as if time had stopped, and the air was barely breathable. The hush and gloom that were perhaps supposed to pacify fragile emotions seemed something of an insult, as if the atmosphere of supreme respect for the dead (or 'loved one' as the woman taking down the details had called her, reminding Jess of Evelyn Waugh and making her want to giggle) was entirely false.

'We should take it on,' Matt suggested. 'Smarten up the death trade a bit. Bring in something like the Ikea factor, some smart paint along with the cardboard-box and wicker-casket options. After all, you're never going to run out of clients . . .'

'Hang on a bit, in theory you've got a point but . . .' Jess could see him starting to get the kind of excitement going that he'd had over the ludicrous Cat Sat idea. It would lead to hours on the Internet and a week of one-subject supper conversations.

'But what?' Ben joined in. 'It wouldn't be a joke thing you know, there's serious mileage in this, I've been talking to Micky about it.'

'We'd have an empire in no time.' Matt was getting excited. Bits of chicken and mayonnaise were dropping all over the table as he talked and waved his baguette about. 'It's just a matter of getting the right name.'

'Dead Reckoning,' Micky suggested.

Eddy giggled into his beer. 'Nah, that would be what you call the bill, put it on the invoice heading. I think it should be something musical, like, let me think: what about Knocking on Heaven's Door?'

'It's good, but then you wouldn't get any atheists.' Jess, rather amazed, found herself joining in.

'Paint it Black?' the architect, his face still suitably gloomy, said.

Matt laughed loudly. 'How about Going Underground?'

'They'd think we don't do cremations,' Ben said.

'Final Countdown?' Eddy suggested.

'Oh I like that one,' Matt agreed.

'I'd better get back to work. Keep thinking about it though.' Micky stood up and walked over to the bar. 'Because I'm serious. I want something else to do. Can't run a back-street bistro all my grown-up life.'

'What's got into him?' Matt murmured to Ben as soon as Micky was occupied serving a customer.

'Jaded. The cousin going has shaken him and he wants to travel and things. I don't want him to go, I need a partner to run this place and I don't want to take up with someone I don't know. I need someone with a business brain like his – I can mostly take care of the food and the stock. Whatever. It'll work itself out. Things do.'

Tom was back by the railway, looking up at Natasha's window. She pulled the curtain back and waved down to him. Jess and Matt had gone out for lunch but she didn't dare let Tom into the house again. This time her dad might just decide to murder him. She hoped he'd got the message to wait for her and ran off to get her coat. Since coming home the day before Natasha had spent most of the time in her room. Her parents would be amazed to see how much of her homework she'd got done. When it really came down to it, there wasn't much else to do when you were in there all by yourself. Jess was of the completely dated (in the view of all three of her children) opinion that it was bordering on a mortal sin for teenagers to have televisions in their rooms, considering that anyone bored and on their own should occupy themselves reading a book.

Leaving her books open and spread out on the desk in an impressive display of ongoing diligence, Natasha slipped down the stairs and out of the back door. At the end of the garden she twisted the rotting fence plank sideways and wriggled out through the gap to the long damp grass on the railway's embankment. She felt quite scared to be there: from the time five years before when they'd first moved to this house they'd all been told Never Ever to go out to the railway line. She felt as if a train was going to veer off the track any second and rip her to shreds, just because she was doing the one big dangerous thing she'd always been warned about.

'Hi.' Tom had been waiting for her. She hadn't been sure he would, he might have just been hanging about there waiting for Mel or someone else and hoping she wouldn't be looking out of the window.

'Hi,' she said to him. Tom got hold of her arm and pulled her towards him, holding her tight against his chest. She relaxed and grinned to herself, breathing in the heady scent of the leather jacket again. It felt like the right place to be. She didn't care what the parents said. If Tom asked her right now to run off to Paris or even Peckham with him, she knew she'd go.

Thirteen

Jess hadn't stopped worrying about Natasha, though she knew deep down that worry in itself was a useless emotion that achieved nothing and changed nothing. It had been one of her mother's brisk sayings: 'You won't get anything done if you wait for worry to do it for you.'

On the surface, between Natasha and herself, there was a truce, but still an uncomfortable sort of not-saying atmosphere lingered in the house. It reminded her of that faintest aroma of unfamiliar cat that she'd noticed the previous spring, every time the wind sent a breeze through the conservatory, when neighbouring felines were reassessing their territory and doing their encroaching through each other's cat flaps in the night. In the circumstances it didn't seem such an inapt analogy, she thought, trying not to picture Tom risking a plummetous death climbing, with less than a tabby's agility, up the conservatory drainpipe and across the glass roof to Natasha's window.

Jess, waiting out Natasha's cool sad silence, had always assumed she was the kind of approachable mother that her children could talk to about absolutely anything. In the past she'd embarrassed them horribly, Oliver too ('God, *Mum*'), by chatting away about contraception, drugs and the usual array of don't-shove-it-under-the-carpet subjects that the average parent of the new millennium was supposed to be fully on-message about. But with this Tom thing, in all honesty she felt quite queasy at the idea of even his name being mentioned. The picture of the two pale figures rising up, Loch Ness monster-like, from the depths of Natasha's bed had left too much of an imprint on her brain, like a half-remembered bad dream. One day, she thought, perhaps I'll even find it funny. But not now.

There was no indication that Natasha was in any contact with Tom, and Jess hated herself for watching out, sneakily, for signs that she was. Her mobile phone was out of action through lack of funds and the house phone was something that Natasha and her friends hardly used these days, all of which added to the impression that she was deliberately isolating herself. The girl wasn't sliding out of the house to use the payphone by the square, or running across the road to Angie's on the pretence of finding out how Emily was doing. She was spending most of her time in her room and seemed to be occupying herself, with a diligence that bordered on the unnatural, with a maths investigation that was a pivotal part of her GCSE coursework. Jess couldn't quite put her finger on it but, if pressed, would admit that Tash seemed a bit *too* quiet. She'd ventured to Matt that Natasha might be up to something, but he hadn't wanted to know, saying that she shouldn't go looking for trouble and coming close to suggesting that if she didn't stop being so suspicious, she would drive Natasha to do something unspecified but stupid.

'So it'll be all my fault then, will it, this unknown stupid thing?' She'd felt outraged.

'Not exactly,' he'd sidestepped, which she took to be a 'yes'.

The weird hush had infected Zoe too, and she and Natasha were speaking on only-when-necessary terms. She was spending the days either out with her friends or e-mailing them, hunched over her computer keyboard as she tapped away, leaning protectively close to the screen if she thought someone was about to catch sight of her hyper-secret missives. Occasionally she'd offer a crumb of information, such as telling them all over supper that Emily was doing OK and was desperate to come home from the hospital. She said it in a way that implied she should have been asked, using a 'I don't suppose you're remotely interested but . . .' voice.

It was hard to get it right, Jess thought, feeling exhausted by the effort to keep on the right side of them both and not provoke any outbursts. If she asked Zoe questions about anything, what she was up to, even how she was feeling, she risked a 'What do you care? You're only interested in Oliver and Tash' response. Her younger daughter seemed to be relishing her new role of hard-done-by teenager. Oliver, meanwhile, was sending e-mails about the glories of carefree teenage travelling which seemed to include rainforest horseriding and bungee jumping.

'He was never that active here,' Matt commented as he read an account of a scuba-diving trip. 'Perhaps he'll start getting up in the mornings when he gets

216

back, taking up the odd sporty hobby and joining in with the human race a bit.'

'Well, he did work for six months,' Jess pointed out. 'It didn't leave much time for anything else.'

'It left enough time for clubbing, drinking and sleeping,' Matt said with a grin. 'I used to be terribly envious. Now I've got time for all three and . . .'

'And the one you don't much fancy is clubbing?' Jess finished for him.

'Well . . . I dunno, should give it a try I suppose.'

'We need to go out and do something, all together,' Jess said to Matt one night while they were making coffee in the kitchen after another subdued, unnaturally polite supper.

'We could visit Highgate Cemetery,' he suggested. 'Get a historical perspective. And then we could drop in at the Natural Death Society, the office is quite close by . . .' His words trailed away. 'Sorry, just thinking in terms of research,' he said. 'What did you have in mind?'

'So you're still pursuing the undertaking idea?' It had been over a week, she thought disloyally: given the usual pattern, he and the Leo crowd should have moved on to another million-making brainwave by now.

'Course I am. We all are. But what's all this about an outing?'

'I've got to go and do that sport thing for the *Gazette* this week, and Paula's secretary has booked me into a really smart golf club at a converted stately home in the middle of Surrey. We could all go, they've offered a free lunch.'

Matthew looked doubtful. 'I thought there was no such thing. There definitely wasn't when I was working. I don't think it's got much teenage appeal either,' he said. 'It sounds like the "Sunday run out" our parents used to take us on when we were kids. About as much fun as typhoid.'

'Mine didn't. You know George never approved of cars.' Jess laughed. 'We used to go to museums in town by tube or out to the country by Green Line bus. That was exciting, Dad never used to check if there was a bus home again so it was always a bit of an adventure.'

'Did you get marched round stately homes? We did – Blenheim and Hampton Court Palaces, Windsor, Arundel and Leeds Castles – they all blurred into one after a while. And they were all freezing.'

'No we didn't! Can you see Dad handing over money to prop up the aristocracy? He'd only have paid to see them guillotined!'

'Perhaps we could bribe the girls with something?' Matt suggested.

'Well, I've thought of that. This place is also a hotel and health spa, so I thought while I'm doing the golf lesson and talking to the people who run it, the girls could go and have a treatment or two, a massage perhaps or a facial and a manicure, something like that.'

'Mmm. And what kind of incentive can you offer me?' He nudged her across the kitchen till he'd got her pressed up against the fridge. 'If I forego the manicure do I get a massage with some seriously filthy extras?'

'Certainly not!' Jess laughed. 'It's a highly respectable establishment!'

'Oh boring. I'll just have to make do with what I can get at home . . .'

It had been surprisingly easy to get Zoe and Natasha to agree to go to Featherfield Hall. Even Natasha had

218

allowed herself to break out of her long sulk and show a bit of enthusiasm. The car had barely pulled out of the Grove before she started on a tentative shopping list.

'When you have a facial, I read in *Marie Claire* that it's really important to buy some of the stuff afterwards. Otherwise you can't keep all the good work going. So can I?' she asked. It was going to be an expensive day, Jess realized: this wasn't the kind of place where bargain-priced products were used.

'You can, but don't go mad,' she agreed. 'You only need a bit of mild moisturizer at your age.'

'Oh and cleanser and toner and something round my eyes at night so I don't get lines and some face-mask stuff would be good as well,' Natasha went on, recognizing, and preparing to exploit, Jess's attempt at bridge-building.

'Don't push your luck,' Matt warned. 'Or your mother will have nothing left from what she earns today.'

'Tash is good at that,' Zoe said. 'And if she's having things, I should too. I need really top-quality gloop: my skin is very sensitive.'

'So is my credit card,' Jess reminded her.

It was a very long time since they'd all been out together in one car as a family. The two girls slumped comfortably in the back seat of the Golf, Zoe occasionally pecking at her Gameboy and Natasha gazing out of the window as if it was a long time since she'd seen the fascinating views from the M3. Jess had another missing-Oliver moment. It would be a crush these days if he was with them as well (and he'd probably be the one driving) but she indulged in a bit of nostalgia, remembering the journeys to holidays in Devon and

Cornwall when the children were little. There'd been the downsides of course, such as the 'When are we there?' questions that had started the moment they'd passed Basingstoke and turned off on to the A303, and Tash had gone through a phase of feeling sick and having to be let out for some dramatic and exaggerated gulps of air every ten miles. She remembered Zoe's tape of nursery songs and the day, after the seventeenth rendering of 'We are Woodmen Sawing Trees', Matthew had removed the tape from its slot and hurled it out of the window somewhere near Honiton. Zoe had wailed so desperately they'd had to do a three-point turn right there on the jammed-up bank holiday A30 and go back to retrieve it from the hedge. 'That's why you often see great long shreds of tape along the grass verges,' Matt had grumbled as he'd clambered out of the nettle-strewn ditch with the tape. 'If you played them, I bet every single time you'd hear that bloody "Wheels on the Bus".'

Perhaps there was a positive side to Matthew being out of work after all: at least he now got to join in with the day-to-day family stuff. Even over the Natasha/Tom episode, he hadn't been able to cop out immediately after the weekend and take refuge in the office. She felt quite sorry that over the long years of the children growing up, his involvement with them, apart from holidays, had usually been limited to evenings and weekends. It happened to too many men, being left out so that they hardly knew which road to take if they were delivering a child to ballet or to the stables. Angie had said that part of the reason she'd sent Emily and Luke to boarding school was that she couldn't bear David giving her a vague and questioning look whenever she asked him to come with her to sports day or

220

to pick them up from the after-school drama club. She said that if they weren't actually present in front of him, David found it hard to recall that he had children at all. There'd been something of a backfiring outcome here when Angie had discovered that by kindly relieving David of the daily burden of his children she seemed to have given him the impression that she'd set him free from his wife as well, and he'd gone off to live in the kind of loft apartment aspired to by far younger men, equipped with a woman half Angie's age.

At least, so far, Matt hadn't shown any signs of wanting to go the same way as Angie's David. It seemed to be enough for him to hang about with the 'lads' at the Leo. It wouldn't be enough for long though, she thought. Smoking Eddy's home-grown after a lunch-time drinks session, playing at looking for billion-earning business opportunities and ringing up the council about carelessly placed wheelie bins and unlit skips in the road wasn't going to satisfy him for long. She took a quick look at his profile as he drove. He had a look of contentment tinged with amusement, as if he'd just recalled a joke someone had told him and was thinking of putting it into words for the rest of them to enjoy.

'I've never wanted to play golf,' he said, as if sensing that she knew he was about to speak.

'Well that's OK, you'll never be forced to.' She patted his arm in a gesture of mock-comforting.

'I know everyone thinks that's what all men are desperate to do the minute they've retired, or *been* retired, but I've never seen the point,' he went on. 'I mean what do you get from hitting a little ball round a park?'

'Tiger Woods gets lots of money,' Natasha said smartly.

'And you see the point of cricket,' Zoe added. 'Most of the rest of us can't.'

'Ah, now cricket's different. It's a glorious game and it's about teams and tradition and . . .'

'Grandad says it's about Britain's shameful imperial past,' Natasha interrupted. 'And how we enslaved poorer nations and all that stuff.'

'Well maybe it was then,' Matt conceded. 'But with either game I'll never be good enough to make money at it. I think I've only just realized that, that I'll never *excel* at anything. I think most people get their heads round that one by my age. I must be a bit slow.'

Jess pointed out a sign for Featherfield Hall and Matt turned the car off the main road.

'I'll never be an Olympic gymnast, not now, or a swimmer. I've got my head round that OK,' Zoe announced.

'Did you want to be?' Jess turned and asked her.

Zoe shrugged. 'What? Be an Olympic swimmer? No, not really. Think of the massive effort. And so boring, all those pointless lengths for hours on end.'

'Lazy sod.' Tash prodded her.

'The list of things you won't be brilliant at just gets depressingly longer as you get older,' Jess told them. 'The trick is to recognize what you do like doing at a time when you can get good enough at it for it to be fun.'

Matthew stopped the car in front of Featherfield Hall next to a sign that said 'No parking, members only'.

'It's what I've been saying ever since I got fired,' he told Jess. 'Never waste your life on something that only feels so-so.' He looked around at the view. 'Now where do we go from here?'

Featherfield Hall, courtesy of a major hotel chain

and a vast amount of smart City investment, had been restored way beyond its former glory. It looked as clean and fresh as it must have done when it was built: from its vast pillared main door to its crenellated roof the very bricks looked as if they'd been individually scrubbed back to the pale gold colour of weak winter sunlight. Neatly trained wisteria was about to break into flower beneath all the upstairs windows and a froth of clematis *montana* bloomed around the porch.

Jess peered around her as she stepped out of the car. There was no sign of golfers, no earth-scarring sand bunkers and no snappy little notices about not walking on the greens and allowing foursomes to tee off first that were the usual features of suburban golf clubs. Instead she looked out towards a long slender lake, over a Capability Brown-style landscape complete with mature trees, little bridges and in the distance what looked like a pretty mock-classical temple. It was as if someone in charge had struck a deal with nature by which the man-made element would do its best not to intrude into the landscape so long as nature didn't run too rampant in return.

'Where's the golf then?' Matt asked, surveying the view. 'I was all ready to say what a crap deal it was, wrecking a landscape with fairways and scissor-clipped little greens and that. This looks OK.'

Robin the photographer was waiting just inside the reception area. As ever he looked gloomy and as if he doubted he'd ever get a decent photograph out of the situation. He eyed Matt warily, as if wondering how much damage he was likely to do to today's assignment.

'There's a bit too much sun,' he complained as Jess

commented on the perfection of the day's weather. 'It'll be all shadows and squinty eyes.'

'Cheerful bugger isn't he?' Matt whispered to Jess as he and the girls left to go in search of less sporty facilities.

Jess and Robin were introduced to Ned the golf club professional by the receptionist, climbed into a buggy and were driven away by Ned across the landscape.

'I can't see any of the usual signs of golf going on. Is all this part of the course?' Jess said to Ned, indicating the sweeping parkland in front of them. Ned grinned at her. He was Australian, young and disconcertingly good-looking. He wasn't wearing a multicoloured diamond-patterned V-neck sweater, nor were his trousers the dreadful mustard or pea green colour she'd so often seen on TV golf tournaments. It would be hard, at this rate, to write the pithily scathing article she'd mentally planned out. She'd assumed she could do some deeply amused piss-taking and express a sort of staggering incomprehension about the whole concept of the game.

'The grounds are kept as natural as possible,' Ned explained, waving a hand to indicate the meadow-like grass speckled with early wild flowers.

'But isn't it all private, only members and hotel guests allowed in?'

'Nah, anyone can come. We get hundreds of walkers. Here we are, the practice range. Let's see what we can get you to do.' Jess and Robin climbed out of the buggy by a field in which were planted several distance markers, and Robin wandered around looking at the sky and the grass and the surrounding oak and beech trees as if the perfect composition would eventually inspire him.

'You've really never played before?' Ned asked Jess as he took a club from his bag.

'Er, no. Never held a club. Should I be wearing these shoes? Is it OK?' she asked. Two-tone lace-ups with spikes were what she'd expected to be told to wear. She'd expected to be marched into the club shop and, with deep disapproval at her favourite black trousers and comfortably floppy pale grey cotton Joseph sweater, ordered to equip herself with a lavender polo shirt, beige bum-enhancing polyester slacks and a green eyeshade. It was almost disappointing.

'You're fine. Golf doesn't need special equipment. Just be comfortable, that way you'll play your best. Now, how to hold the club . . .'

Ned stood behind her, pressed in close, arranging her fingers on the club's shaft and linking her thumbs together. It felt more than slightly sexually pleasant, she thought, having this blond young Australian squashed against her like this. She had a sudden rush of contentment with life, something that hadn't happened for quite a few weeks now, as she looked into the distance and then back down at the little white ball on the grass. It was a beautiful day, she had a beautiful family and a job she loved. Even Matt and his redundancy seemed strangely irrelevant and distant today. What more could anyone want?

'That's good,' Robin's voice called. 'Can you hold it just like that for a bit?'

'No problem,' Ned muttered into Jess's ear. Oh absolutely not, she agreed silently.

'*This is Henry Reid's message service, please talk after . . .*'

Natasha hung up and collected her 20p back from

225

the payphone. At the time when Tom had given her the number, she'd asked where he'd got the phone from. 'A mate,' he'd replied, with that same crooked grin that had made her feel so gorgeously wobbly the first day she'd met him. So either the 'mate' was this Henry Reid or Henry Reid was the unknown but rightful owner of a nicked phone. When she'd told him her own phone was out of action because she couldn't buy any more time for it till she got her next month's allowance, he'd pulled a selection of pay-as-you-go vouchers from his pocket and offered them to her. Her phone was an Orange, though, and the vouchers were not. She'd asked him where he'd got them and, there again, it was 'a mate', who'd somehow intercepted a delivery of them.

Natasha, as she walked down the corridor to the beauty therapy suite, asked herself if she minded that Tom was turning out to be a bit dodgy in the honesty department and decided that she didn't actually care. It's only because he hasn't got any money or any family, she said to herself. She just knew he wouldn't do it unless he had to. And he only went into houses of people who were pretty well off and could spare a bit for those who hadn't got it, if Angie and Eddy were examples. There was a lot of her grandad in her, she thought quite contentedly as she sat down to leaf through the latest magazines before her facial, he'd be really proud of her.

'I can quite see how people get obsessed,' Jess was saying over lunch. 'Once you've held the club the right way, understood how to connect with the ball and then clouted it a really good distance, you just want to do it again and again.'

Matt, Zoe and Natasha all groaned at once. 'Oh God, now you'll be joining a club and talking about "Ladies' Fours", whatever that is, and buying weird kit. Then your bum will get huge and you'll get a butch haircut,' Matt said. 'Just don't get any of those ideas along the lines of "This is something we could do *together*", will you?'

Jess laughed. 'No I promise. After today I'll probably never pick up a golf club again.' Or a gorgeous young golf pro, she thought with a small private sigh. Not that she really had, of course. Ned was sure to have a stunning athletically-built girlfriend somewhere in the background and his very much hands-on, flirty approach was just as sure to be one he brought out to get middle-aged women to part with the exorbitant membership fees. Still, now and then it was fun to speculate . . . 'So what did you all get up to while I was out there swinging a stick?' she asked.

'I've had an aromatherapy massage,' Matt told her, narrowing his eyes seductively at her. 'I think it's done me good.'

'And we've both had facials and our nails done,' Zoe said, holding out her hands to be inspected. 'I've had a French manicure. Tash's are a really gross blue.'

'It is not gross,' Natasha snapped at her. 'It's choice. I love it.' She stared down at her nails, admiring the blue which was exactly the near-turquoise, Jess thought, of her i-Book computer at home. It seemed strange to think that the whole day was merely supposed to be material for a magazine piece. It felt more important than that, almost as good as a holiday, certainly far more durable, as if this was an important load-bearing brick in the family structure. Natasha seemed close to normal again, though sometimes Jess

227

could catch a look of fleeting worry on the girl's face. It was to be expected really, she thought: Tom was Natasha's first proper boyfriend and it could hardly be painless that she wasn't going to be seeing him again.

George finished sweeping out the shed and hung the brush away on its hook just to the left of his second favourite spade. He liked order in his surroundings. He liked small rituals like lifting the dahlias every November when the flowering was over and storing them under sacking just as his father had taught him to do all those years ago. Hardly anyone bothered lifting dahlias these days, he thought as he lit the camping-gas stove to boil water for his tea. It was all to do with global warming and not getting proper winters any more. We get the same old summers though, it occurred to him; they couldn't have got that much better or people wouldn't keep harping on about the summer of '76.

The boy was back again. George watched from the shed window as Tom stashed the boxes in the boot of the old Sierra. He might, he thought, have a quick look in there later. After all, the car wasn't going anywhere: two of the wheels had gone missing and the other two had flat tyres. It was the sort of thing people phoned the council about; perhaps they had. But with the council being all for getting rid of the allotment holders they were probably hoping there'd be thousands of old cars dumped there so they could clear the land of both cars and gardeners in one greedy go.

Of course it could all be Tom's worldly goods, George speculated as he kept watch from the shed. He hoped that was all it was, in the boxes. Ever since Val's shed was broken into he'd had his reluctant suspicions about the boy. He wanted to think well of him. He was nice enough, didn't mind hard work, had manners to charm anyone and he'd not had an easy time. Somewhere along the line someone had put in the foundations of a good upbringing and one day he'd have no trouble talking his way into a decent job that would take him places, just so long as he was cleaned up a bit. And so long as he kept out of trouble.

Tom slammed the boot of the car shut. He wouldn't be able to lock it, George knew, he certainly wouldn't have a key. Nor, it crossed his mind reluctantly, might he have a key for the blue Peugeot parked just beyond the fence. Tom strolled over to it and climbed in. The car hiccuped and over-revved and then was off, tyres squealing as the lad put too much pressure on the accelerator. George shook his head and went back to his tea-making. It was all very well hoping for the best. It didn't mean you were going to get it.

'You're not serious, are you Dad? Please don't be!' Zoe pleaded with Matt from the back of the car. She peered into the driving mirror, trying to see if he was joking or not.

'It's just too gnarly to think about.' Natasha shuddered. 'You mean you're going to spend all your days handling dead bodies? What am I supposed to put on forms where it says "parents' occupation"?'

'Well your mother's a journalist, you can put that. You can leave me out if you're that bothered. Undertaking's a noble calling,' he told them. 'And there's always a demand for it. The one job that isn't ever going to be short of business. Especially with the baby-boomer generation getting older. All the acid casualties will be off on their final big trip.'

They were just coming into the Grove, passing the Leo. There were tables outside now that it was getting warmer, and Eddy was sprawled across one, reading a newspaper.

'I'm not sure I'd want Eddy attending to my last rites,' Jess murmured.

'Actually,' Matt admitted as he pulled up outside the house, 'the hands-on bit is the one part I don't reckon we've quite thought through. I don't think any of us are going to want to get involved with any of that. We'll have to employ people, then sit back and count the cash.'

Jess unlocked the front door and went in. There was a pile of mail on the mat and as she bent to pick it up she noticed a mobile phone lying at the bottom of the stairs. Assuming it was Natasha's she put it on the hall table.

'Because really I think we were thinking along the lines of superficial decor and design, not . . .' Matt, still on the topic of his proposed new career, was saying as he walked past her into the sitting room. 'Er, Jess? What's going on in here?'

Jess, Natasha and Zoe followed him into the room. It looked quite still and tidy, nothing different was immediately obvious.

'The telly, it was here wasn't it? You haven't moved it? And the video?' Matt asked.

'Have we been burgled?' Zoe's eyes were wide with both fear and excitement.

'I'm not sure.' Matt looked puzzled. 'Jess's computer is still here. Anyone with any sense would have taken that, it's small enough.'

Zoe ran upstairs to check her room, shrieked loudly then yelled down, '*My* computer's gone! And my CD

230

player! And someone's been in Oliver's room. I can sort of *smell* them.' Zoe's face, her eyes full of tears, appeared over the banisters. Natasha rushed up the stairs past her and went into her room.

Matt raced around the house, checking for what was missing. 'Upstairs television, the Magimix of all things, both radios, the kitchen CD player,' he reported. 'What about you, Tash? What's gone from your room?'

Natasha looked quickly round her room. She didn't need to really, she knew nothing would be missing. Her window was open, the curtain flapping lazily in the warm breeze. She could smell him too. She breathed in slowly, taking in the slightly smoky, leathery scent. While her parents thought she was still checking for what was stolen, she picked up the phone extension on the landing and dialled 'Henry Reid's' number. No-one was answering. She could hear another phone ringing, somewhere downstairs, then getting closer as someone came up towards her.

'If I answer this, I get the feeling I'll be talking to you,' Jess said, holding out the ringing mobile to Natasha.

Fourteen

Natasha didn't feel any different about Tom. She tested herself, asking herself if it was different now that he'd done this thing. She tried thinking of it as a violation of their home (her mother's over-dramatic description), as a sign that he didn't really give a flying fuck about her (her father's more down-to-basics view) and she still wanted more than anything to get out of the house and be with him, curled up together down by the railway on the warm gravelly place next to the track where the embankment was scuffed away making a hollow. Sitting there with him, cuddling tight against his leather jacket when the trains whistled by and whooshed up the wind, she felt like a fox safe in the earth. Now her parents thought he was the complete pits, the scummiest grub on the planet, even worse than they'd thought before, she knew he had to have someone on his side. There wasn't anyone else so it had to be her. He was her responsibility. She thought, fleetingly, about Mel but he'd insisted Mel was just a

232

friend, just someone he talked to now and then, bummed cigarettes from, gave a lift to, nothing special. *She*, Natasha, was the one that mattered. He hadn't taken anything from her room. He hadn't even taken her mother's computer. Tentatively, she'd tried to suggest that that showed a little bit of respect, only to be silenced by the thunderously furious look on her father's face. Zoe wouldn't stop crying. She said it wasn't about losing her stuff, which made it even worse because Natasha couldn't really work out what it *was* about.

Natasha sat on her bed and tried to feel something that wasn't just misery. When you loved someone you had to go along with it. You couldn't just choose which bits of them to like, the power of your feelings wouldn't let you, you were stuck with the whole package. The trouble was, she loved her family too. It hurt that her dad had such a disappointed look on his face. When the police came, one of them had asked if she knew where Tom was. She'd said no, and her father had given her that look, as if he didn't believe her. That was really painful. 'I'm not a liar!' she'd yelled.

'How can we be sure, any more? We told you you couldn't see or contact him, but you obviously have been,' her mother had said, so very coldly. It wasn't fair. She really didn't know where he was. She only wished she did, then she could go to be with him – and this time she'd be packing for more than just one night away. Anyone would think it was *her* who'd done the burgling. She honestly couldn't remember, when they'd asked her, if she'd said anything to Tom, whether she'd told him they'd all be out. Telling him they were all off on a jolly family outing wasn't the sort of conversation they had. Anyway what difference would it have made, she'd wanted to say, (but daren't): when Tom decided to get in somewhere he was quite capable of choosing his own moment. If it hadn't been today it would have been some other time. She even sneaked into both bathrooms to check for newly wet towels, just in case he'd taken a few minutes to have a shower while he had the chance.

'So much for being grounded,' Matthew said to Jess after the pair of sombre and not particularly optimistic policemen had gone and Natasha had stalked off to her room. 'She must have thought it was well cool, sneaking out to meet him on the sly like that. It must have been like a game to them.'

'Yes. Very romantic. Perhaps we shouldn't have tried to stop her seeing him, then it wouldn't have been so exciting.' Jess was clearing away all the mugs still half full of tea that they and the police had drunk. Making tea had seemed, as with a family death, the thing to do. No-one had really wanted any. The police officers had sipped politely at it as if it was not only part of their duty but their fourteenth of the day. Matt was now helping himself to a beer from the fridge. 'It's almost frightening that she can be so wilful and so secretive. Do you think it was Tom who burgled Clarissa's house as well? I mean he's so young, shockingly young to be making a living at it, surely.'

'There's a lot of it about, so Plod said. We were lucky the police bothered to come at all. It was only because we had a name we could give them.'

'Well, we *thought* we did. Like they said, it might not be his real name: he could be called anything and even then they still have to prove it was him. Whatever happened to good old-fashioned fingerprint taking? I got the impression that with this kind of crime, they've given up on it before they've started.'

Jess, in spite of her anger at having the house burgled, was rather touched that her computer had been left behind. It might have been an oversight, though of all the light electrical household goods he could have chosen, the pretty little i-Book was probably the most sellable item, and certainly one of the most valuable. If Tom had taken that, plus any of Natasha's possessions and not dropped the mobile phone, there was every chance that they might not have connected him with the theft.

'He's not very good at it, is he?' Jess smiled as she opened a beer for herself. (Why did men do that? she thought, always assume that beer was such a male drink that women didn't need to be offered one.) 'If he's going to make a career of crime he'll have to learn not to let any lingering good manners and inconvenient scruples get in the way.'

'Better that he gets caught now, in that case,' Matt said, 'before he turns old and hard and becomes the sort who ransacks every room, pours bleach over the carpets and shits on the bed.'

'You were still seeing him. They told you you couldn't and you just went straight out and did it.' Zoe, confronting Natasha in her room, was trying not to feel tearful again with anger.

'Sorry. I should have told you.' Natasha was lying on her bed, her hair sticking to the tears on her face.

'I didn't *want* to bloody know!' Zoe shrieked, picking up a shoe and hurling it at her sister.

Surprised, Natasha sat up and rubbed her head where the shoe had so accurately landed. 'What's your problem then? Why don't you leave me alone?'

'The problem's you! You've gone really horrible! It's like you're not the same person any more and I hate it! Why do you like him more than you like us? He's really bad news and you can't even see it!'

Natasha lay down on the bed again and rolled over, turning her back on her sister. 'You just don't understand. It's how I feel about him.'

'Well *stop* feeling it then. Be like you were before.'

'I can't,' Natasha muttered. 'I'm older now, it's what happens. You wait till it's you.'

'Me? I think I'll be better at choosing. I *know* I will be. *I* wouldn't go out with some creepy thief who climbs in people's windows.'

'I've made a chicken and mushroom pie.' Angie was at the front door holding an oblong dish covered with a tea towel. 'I thought you might not feel like cooking.' Angie had been on the phone to see what was going on before the police car had turned its flashing blue light off.

Jess led her through to the kitchen and the pie was placed on the table. All by itself beneath its cloth on the otherwise empty table there was something vaguely sacramental about it.

'That's so sweet of you, Angie. I hadn't even thought about food.'

'It's nice to have someone to cook for, especially someone who'll actually eat it and not sneak out to throw it up again. The bad news is I'm going to stay and share it with you.'

'Of course.' Jess looked at the newly blank space beside the kettle. 'He took the Magimix as well, you know. I mean what will he do with that? You can hardly sell those down the pub.'

'Car boot, small ads, Internet if he's got access – which he probably has, by way of your Zoe's computer. He'll sell it all right, the little sod.' Angie went to the fridge, pulled out a half-full bottle of white wine and poured them both a drink. It really was as if someone had died, Jess thought, having neighbours calling in with essential supplies and making free with your kitchen. It was immensely comforting.

'You know with pastry,' Jess said, gazing at the immaculate pie when she was on the outside of most of the glass of wine. 'When it says in recipes, "Roll out pastry and rest in fridge for half an hour"?'

'Yeah, what about it? I did that, with this one.'

'No, what I mean is, sometimes I read it too fast and I think they mean me, that I should rest in the fridge for half an hour.'

'Are you nuts?' Angie, who'd downed her first glass of wine extremely fast, was going pink and starting to giggle. She opened the fridge again and pulled out a new bottle. Jess reached behind her for the cutlery drawer and felt around for the corkscrew. 'Here you are. And it's all ours, Matt's down the Leo which makes a bloody change. No I'm not nuts. I just take things too literally. I fail to interpret. I saw a sign that said "CAB volunteers wanted" and I thought, why would people want to drive taxis without being paid for it?'

'So what was CAB?'

'Citizens' Advice Bureau.'

'You *are* nuts.'

'I didn't interpret Tom too well.'

'That's because you're a nice person, not all suspicious and nasty.'

'No it's not, it's because I'm basically superficial and sort of non-delving. I thought the "Keep away from fire" labels on clothes were an instruction for the wearers, a kind little reminder, not a warning that the fabric was dodgy anywhere near a match. I'm gullible.'

'Well if you're gullible, I'm as thick as a plank. For months I've watched Emily getting thinner and thinner and all I thought was "Oh good, she's losing that puppy fat at last."'

Angie, fast getting drunk, leaned closer to Jess. 'Are you wearing your nice new bra?'

'I am as it happens. Mrs Cutler would be proud of me.' She started to giggle.

'Me too. And,' Angie stood up and hiked her skirt up, 'I went back to the shop and look what I bought . . .' She revealed the marabou-trimmed pink knickers, a couple of slivers of silk held together with ribbon and feathers.

'Oh, so poor Eddy didn't get them!' The two of them fell across the table, laughing. The pie trembled in its dish. 'Shall I put that in the oven?' Jess wiped her eyes, looked across at Angie and the hysteria started again.

Then the kitchen door was flung open. 'So glad you're having such a brilliant time! You don't bloody care about anything really do you? It's all just a laugh to you!' The door slammed shut, then the front door and Natasha disappeared into the cold dark night.

She hadn't taken anything at all with her this time, not so much as a jacket or a door key. Natasha was frozen before she even reached the end of the Grove. She wrapped her arms tight round her body and made her way fast towards the square. The lights of the Leo looked like a ship on a miserable dark sea, no other

238

buildings around seemed to have any life in them. Bloody suburban death, she thought as she walked, this place is the pits. For the first time, she hoped Mel might be hanging around – she needed someone to talk to – but it was seven o'clock, there was no sound of raucous laughing, no sign that Mel existed. Everyone on the planet must be having supper, everyone with a normal family life. Everyone except her and Tom, wherever he was.

Natasha was too scared to go down to the railway. In the dark she wouldn't be able to see the live rail, wouldn't dare pick her way along the wrong side of the fence to the lovely soft hollow that she and Tom liked. Or *used to* like, she thought sadly. It probably was all past now, it couldn't be long before he was caught. She couldn't believe he'd dropped that phone by the stairs. Never, in the (admittedly short) time she'd known him, had he been even the slightest bit careless. She remembered him leaving Eddy's bedroom door open for the big ginger cat, and making sure that the window he'd climbed in through was open exactly the same amount when they left.

At the Leo, Natasha stopped and looked through the window. Her dad was there sitting at the bar with Eddy, talking to Ben and Micky. They were probably talking about her, she thought, probably having a laugh about it just like her mother. She just didn't get adults: one minute her mum was treating the whole thing as the biggest disaster that could ever happen and the next she was in the kitchen, pissed up and howling with hilarity with Angie like it was any other day. Come to think of it, Angie didn't have much to laugh about either at the moment. No wonder Emily had got herself an eating problem – she was probably, subconsciously, trying to do that thing where you avoided turning into a grown-up. And when you looked at what they were like, who could blame her?

Natasha waited by the allotment gates. Peering over the top of the fence, she could just see the Sierra. It looked even more decrepit in the dark, and reminded her of a small dead animal rotting under a tree: just a little bit more of it disappearing each day, blending more and more easily into its surroundings. She didn't need to go any closer to see that Tom wasn't there. Perhaps he wouldn't be ever again. She felt very much alone and was ashamed to find that she was quite enjoying the feeling. Oliver would have taken the piss and called her a drama queen, she thought. She missed him quite dreadfully just then. None of this would have happened if he'd been around. It wasn't that he was some kind of super-hero, just that she'd never have dared let Tom into the house in the night. Also it was quite likely that Tom and Ol would have been friends too and everything would have been less . . . well, less intense. That blokey, talking-about-football thing they all did would have been bound to take the edge off the exclusivity she and Tom had. Her parents would have thought it was healthier too.

She wondered where Oliver was, right now. It was nearly eight here in London. In Australia it would be anything from about eight to ten hours ahead of her. He'd be asleep. He might be asleep with a girl some-where, in a hostel, in her home, on a beach, whatever. Or he might be by himself, camping under a back-packer's moon out in the bush. She wished he'd come back: she wasn't making much of a job of taking over being the eldest. And it really was like a job: she was supposed to be there for Zoe and not to give her

240

parents a ton of grief and she was failing horribly. Lucky Oliver had escaped and was *free*: absolutely untroubled by responsibility and the need to please anyone but himself. They were all like that, all the males she came across in her life at the moment, even her dad who probably should have more on his mind than most.

If Oliver was here now, she thought, what would he tell her to do? As if by round-the-earth telepathy she could hear his voice: 'Go home Tash, you silly sod, just go home.' She turned round and walked back towards the square. School started again in the morning. There wasn't any point making things worse by not being there.

'. . . as if the house shrinks in proportion to the length of the school holidays. Every room has at least two abandoned pairs of shoes in it, as if staking a claim to the space on behalf of their owners. Trainers, like metal coat hangers, breed if they're left to hang about too long. Zoe's homework takes up no space at all because it is so rarely allowed out of her bag . . .'

Paula would have to lump it, Jess thought as she typed. No way was she going to write about being burgled by her daughter's boyfriend in a flurry of merry quips as if the whole thing was no more traumatic than having an unused scratchcard fall out of your pocket. Natasha had stormed off to bed the night before, with Jess conscious of her humiliation at having had to ring the bell and be let in. Paula, when she'd told her what had happened, had mostly been concerned that the burglar wasn't making his steady way along the Grove (as if he was collecting the Red Cross envelopes) on his way to

241

liberating Eddy's guitar collection, which was all he possessed by way of a pension fund.

'Do you think I should move in with him?' Paula then asked anxiously, as if her constant overnight presence was all Eddy needed to protect him from the teenage thief.

'Well, only if you really want to,' Jess told her. 'And has he asked you to? I mean, isn't it a bit soon?'

'Oh, he hasn't exactly *asked*. But he doesn't like me going home, you know,' here her voice dropped to a near whisper, '*after*. I have to go back to the flat most nights, to feed Miu-Miu and do her litter tray.' Jess imagined Eddy having to wake up from a deep post-coital sleep to do the good-manners thing of saying good night, possibly (for he was quite old-fashioned) calling for a taxi and accompanying Paula down to the front door. No wonder he'd rather she stayed overnight – he was not of an age to relish interrupted sleep.

'But what about your flat? It's so exactly the way you like it.' Jess thought of the clutter-free white space in Kensington, the slender glass vases containing scrupulously exotic single blooms and the creamy-beige suede sofa, exactly the same macaroon shade as the soft little ears of Paula's cat. The jewel-and-citrus colours of the walls in Eddy's house, on the other hand, made your eyes sting. She couldn't at all imagine Paula relaxed on the pink paisley sofa, gin and tonic in hand, with Eddy's massive ginger tomcat kneading holes into her Joseph leather trousers. Nor could she imagine her attempting to cook in his haphazard kitchen. From what she could remember, from a party the previous Bonfire Night, his cavernous lime green American fridge contained nothing but beer and pre-packed, brick-sized slabs of Red Leicester cheese in readiness to be sandwiched between the thickest possible pre-sliced white bread. Paula was more of a pesto and pasta girl, with Parmesan of translucent slivers. If she ate a cheese sandwich it would have been ordered in from Pret A Manger and contain the best Brie, rocket, organic cherry tomatoes and some quality dressing of fine olive oil and balsamic vinegar. Still, maybe it was true what they said about opposites.

'I'd rent the flat out,' Paula went on. 'To be honest, from the Grove it's just as easy to get in to the office. And besides, perhaps it's time I went in a bit less often. There are other things besides work. I know Matt's just realized that, though I don't want to have to wait to be sacked to find out.'

Oliver, when Jess checked her e-mails, was now full of the delights of Sydney.

'This place is just awesome – like all that stuff you see on telly is really here. Crossed over the famous bridge at dawn this morning on the way in and there's the Opera House, looking like something out of a movie. I was stoked. Staying in King's Cross area sharing a dormie with three guys who have to get up at five for work and none of us sleep till three anyway. This is a party city . . .'

In a reversal of the traditional postcard, Jess said to herself, 'Wish I was there.' The bliss of escape . . . Quite impossible though, she thought briskly as she shut down the computer. Besides, imagine leaving the house clear for Tom to wander back in at his leisure and extract any little valuables he hadn't had time or carrying capacity to liberate the first time.

George wished he hadn't looked. The Sierra's boot was crammed with what could only be described as light electrical goods, which were so obviously stolen that the boy might as well have written 'Swag' in the dust on the paintwork. The back seat held the bigger stuff, a couple of TVs and a computer monitor covered with a blanket, all in this unlocked car. Tom clearly trusted his fellow citizens far more than they could trust him. George hadn't seen him yet today, though no doubt he'd be turning up to shift the stuff to somewhere where he could exchange it for cash. He put the boot lid down as soundlessly as he could, so as not to attract the curiosity of Val who was fitting cardboard collars round the bases of her young cauliflower plants as a defence against cabbage root fly. He'd taken one of the smaller items from the car boot and now went into the shed to collect his reading glasses. There was one of those little gold printed name-and-address labels stuck on the side of the Walkman, the sort you ordered by the thousand. He'd seen them before at Jess's place. He put the glasses on and read the label: 'Zoe Maria Nelson' it said, followed by her address.

Natasha and Claire spent the morning break in the cloakroom, lying flat out on the benches like a couple of tramps dozing in the park. Natasha had enough to be unhappy about, she thought, she didn't need Claire giving her a hard time as well.

'Maybe your parents are right,' was Claire's verdict when Natasha told her all that had happened. 'I mean, do you really want to go out with a criminal?'

'You don't get it, do you.' Natasha sat up and stared down at her so-called best friend. 'There's more to him than just the criminal bit. I didn't even know he was when I started liking him.'

'Yeah, but you know now,' Claire pointed out,

leaving Natasha feeling as if she'd been set adrift. Nobody at all understood. She hated this school, hated its poncy assumption that everyone, really, wanted only to be nice and firmly middle-class and stuffed to the eyeballs with academic qualifications. There wasn't one girl in the school who could imagine a post A-level life that didn't include going to university at their mummy and daddy's expense. Not one of them, she thought with a certain amount of arrogance, would dream of saying, 'Oh I'm going to leave at sixteen and be a hairdresser (or a plumber or whatever).' This was a sausage machine for the professional classes; they'd all emerge with their grades more intact than their virginity, full of useless information about oxbow lakes and the causes of the American War of Independence but completely ignorant of anything that might be of practical use. Not like Tom, she thought. He might get by on other people's stuff but at least he could survive, like an animal, on his own. None of this lot, she thought with increasing exaggeration as she watched Claire re-applying her mascara, could so much as make themselves a sandwich: they thought they came in cellophane packaging from Marks & Spencer.

'I've had enough of this place. I'm going to leave as soon as I'm sixteen,' she told Claire.

Claire turned away from the mirror and looked, at last, interested. 'Oh? Good idea. I think the sixth-form college would be much more fun. I might join you.'

Natasha laughed. 'You know Claire, there's more to life than being stuffed with useless facts. When I say *leave* I mean exactly that.' She looked out of the window towards the high gates at the entrance. They reminded her of prison. Something out of place caught her attention and she screwed up her eyes. There was someone leaning on the ironwork, someone whose body shape looked thrillingly familiar. Adrenalin flooded in, and she hoped Claire wouldn't notice how flushed she suddenly was. Claire, though, had moved on to perfecting her eyeliner. Natasha smiled at her by way of the mirror and said, 'In fact I think I'll go now. Why wait?'

'What do you think the upper age limit is for joining the police?' Matt leaned back on Eddy's pink sofa, stretched his legs out in front of him and gazed down at the length of his body. It looked strong enough, firm enough to him. If it needed a bit of toning, that wouldn't be a problem. And they were short of good cops, weren't they? Most of the ones he'd seen lately looked about twelve. They must be in need of more mature ones who could trot around with the youngsters and help them be taken a bit more seriously.

'You can't join the pigs man,' Eddy slugged some more beer and took a deep toke on the joint. 'I mean you're the wrong sort. You'd give them a good name.'

'Do you know, they've offered us victim support? We can get some sort of cop-counselling because of the burglary. You get offered it for everything apparently, even if it's just your bike being nicked from outside the pub.'

'You mean, just cos they've been nice to you, you want to join them?' Wilf was puzzled.

'Of course I'd only want to do it part-time. And not weekends. And possibly not summer either.'

'Or Christmas, and definitely not New Year's Eve,' Wilf added. 'You don't want to deal with all the drunks.'

'And not traffic control. Because I don't care about

246

traffic being controlled at all.' Matt passed the joint on to Eddy. 'In fact maybe I'll think of something else.'

'Good idea.' Eddy nodded slowly and for a long time. 'You don't want to go arresting people for this either,' he waved the joint towards Matt, 'I mean you'd end up dobbing your mates in.'

'No I wouldn't.' Matt was indignant. Eddy's head shook from side to side this time, with the same deliberate slowness. 'You would you know, you'd get corrupted, you'd end up as one of them. It happens.'

'Sad isn't it?' Wilf said.

'Tragic,' they agreed.

Fifteen

Natasha's form tutor had one of those voices that seemed to assume all replies to her questions would be out and out lies. Jess could feel something rising where she assumed human hackles would be as the woman spoke to her on the phone, asking, 'Would you tell me what good reason Natasha had for being absent yesterday, during the time following on from morning break?'

No 'please' or apology for disturbing her, Jess noted. She fought down an urge to say 'And what's the magic word?' guaranteed to irritate the woman into reserving perhaps an unnecessarily dire punishment for the wayward Natasha. Instead, caught without a handy whopper ready-prepared for her daughter's defence, she admitted, 'Er, no, not offhand, I couldn't.' Pompous cow, she thought, as she tried at the same time to assimilate the gist of what the woman was getting at. So Natasha had skived off, which wasn't terrific news, and certainly from Jess's point of view was potentially hugely worrying. But the form tutor made it sound as if she was the first girl in the school's history ever to have done it and that only dire failure and disgrace could follow.

'. . . obviously not something we tolerate at Julia Perry . . .' the disembodied voice continued.

'Obviously,' Jess concurred. 'But she should be in school now, perhaps you could find her and try asking her where she was?' Surely the woman could have done that in the first place, she thought, unless of course, Natasha, now, *wasn't* there.

'Oh we have. She *said* she'd had a migraine.' Jess wanted to cut in smartly with 'Well there you are then', but the tutor continued, 'But she hadn't reported to the school nurse and she didn't turn up to any lessons after the morning break. In future, if Natasha needs to go home for any reason, she must have a note, or at the very least, a phone call from a parent.'

'Did she mention to you that we've been burgled, or that she has been having rather a difficult time at home lately?' Jess rallied, conscious that this might come across as a series of excuses but that the school perhaps should know that there might be more to Tash than simple unprovoked naughtiness.

'She hasn't said anything.' There was a wariness in the tone: 'difficulties at home' too often led to divorce and a cessation of the family's fee-paying ability.

'Has anyone asked? I remember your prospectus does emphasize a certain amount of pastoral care.'

There was a whistling intake of breath down the line. 'If a girl has family problems, obviously we do all we can to accommodate any special needs, but the fact remains Natasha left the premises in flagrant contravention of the rules . . .'

Jess, still fuming at the woman's tone, returned to her computer after the phone call. She couldn't really understand why she'd had to be involved and rather wished no-one had told her. Natasha might have walked out of school through hatred of maths and simply mooched around the shops all day. Or she might have gone off somewhere with Tom. It would be hard to work out how she'd have contacted him, though: presumably he was on the run somewhere and if the phone he'd dropped at the bottom of the stairs was the only number she had for him, then Jess couldn't see how they'd got together. Whatever she'd abandoned the school day for, Natasha had apparently been sentenced to two weeks 'on report', which meant being signed in and out of all lessons, along with having to spend all her breaks and lunchtimes wasting time on a chair outside the staffroom. At least, Jess thought, that would give her plenty of time to get her homework done.

With the idea of selecting some of the best of her articles to put together for a potential book, Jess carried the i-Book to the kitchen table and started looking at her past year's work. It was, she thought, a bit like reading old diaries, though in this case the mood was perpetually light and her articles lacked any of the self-pitying grumbling that diaries tended to contain. The tone of the articles seemed to come from a distant, enviably carefree age. There was the chirpy account of Zoe's week at Pony Club camp (hilarious, had been Paula's and the readers' verdict), a piece about the delights of having six massive, perpetually hungry to the point of midnight-fridge-scavenging, friends of Oliver's to stay (without warning) on their way back from Glastonbury, and something of a fill-in, when

250

she'd run short of ideas, about parties of men let loose in French Channel port supermarkets.

As she sorted through them, arranging the pieces in some kind of order so that she could make a Year in the Life theme for the book, it crossed her mind that Nelson's Column, in its current happy-dappy form, really was coming to a natural end. It wasn't going to be possible, or even desirable, any more, she realized, to use her own family as material. Natasha had been right; the girls (and Oliver) were entitled to privacy. She could hardly believe now that she'd thought it would be a major career catastrophe when Paula had suggested running the column down over the next few months, and encouraged Jess in the direction of a different kind of writing. Right now, with all that had happened, she was wondering what on earth she'd have done if Paula *hadn't* thought of it.

'OK, take a look at this.' Matthew dashed in through the back door, opened a large carrier bag and tipped a pile of fabric swatches onto the table. 'What do you think?' He was beaming, clearly anticipating a hugely positive response.

'Ooh such lovely colours, but what am I looking for? Something for curtains, a dress, cushion covers, what?' Jess picked through them. She recognized a couple of classic Liberty Tana lawn flower prints that reminded her of party dresses she'd bought for the girls when they were little. There were some strips of gorgeous dewy-textured silk in enough brilliant colours to run up a new Technicolor dreamcoat for Joseph, plus a larger length of purple satin.

'I rather fancied the satin myself, so I thought I'd get an extra big bit.' Matthew picked it up and smoothed it against his face. 'Mmm, feels sexy. And that colour, gloriously royal and perfectly papal. I could live with that. Not that I would be, of course.' He folded the fabric carefully and went to switch on the kettle. 'Coffee?'

'Yes please. So what are these for? What do you mean about not living with it?'

'Because I'll be dead.' Matthew gave an 'isn't that obvious?' look. 'It's a few ideas for possible coffin linings. Thought I'd run a few samples past the lads, see what they think.'

Jess dropped the swatch she'd been looking at as if it was about to threaten her own mortality. 'Matt, you're not *serious*? Tell me honestly, has it really become your life's ambition to be an undertaker?'

'Don't worry, I won't be hands-on. You need qualifications and experience for that. I'll be a sleeping partner,' he corrected. 'Hey that's really funny when you think about it,' he chortled as he poured water into the cafetière.

'Yes, very nearly,' Jess conceded.

'Oh come on Jess, lighten a little. I was just passing Liberty and thought I'd pop in, you know?' He scooped up the fabric pieces and shoved them back in the bag.

'It's starting to get to me,' he went on. 'All this having time on my hands and nothing to do with it. It's different when it's time off, because that's time off from something to get back to. This is forever-time-off and I can see it might drive me crazy in the long term.'

'You mean you aren't going to hang about in the Leo for ever, drinking beer and gossiping?' Jess teased.

'Well I wouldn't mind, I suppose. It's a very convivial place and being sociable is something I'm good at. But no-one's going to pay me to do that and even I can see the money will run out one day.' He put a mug

252

of coffee on the table next to Jess. A couple of drops trickled down the side and spread themselves into the purple satin and Matthew stared at them, looking dejected.

'I dropped in at the office,' he said quietly. 'I know I said I wouldn't but, well I thought I'd say hallo, see what they're all up to.'

'So how was it? Everyone pleased to see you?'

'Sort of.' Matt thought for a minute. 'It's hard to tell what they really think. I mean to be honest, I felt a bit like a spare part. Which of course I am. I don't think anyone knew what to do with me – when you've been fired you're just an embarrassment if you turn up again.' He gazed into his coffee. 'I wish I hadn't gone there now. They probably thought I was missing them all or that I was hoping they'd realized I was completely indispensable.'

'And are you?' Jess asked quietly.

Matt grinned. 'Fuck, no! Felt sorry for them all as it happens. But – it would have been great to go in there and say, "Hey suckers, I sure as hell fell on my feet!" I should have realized the only question each and every bugger was going to ask was "So what are you doing now?" Right now, there's no real answer to that.'

Jess spluttered into her coffee. 'You could have shown them your coffin linings, taken a few early bookings!'

'Now why didn't I think of that?'

It went against the grain to call the police but it had to be done. In spite of their being, in his opinion, agents of the nation's would-be oppressors, they were the only ones who could deal with this. George had left it overnight already and there was every chance that the boy had been back with a car that actually worked and taken everything away. He still had Zoe's Walkman of course, but that would be pretty pitiful compensation if he had to admit to Jess and Matt that he'd put off bringing in the law till all their electrical goods had gone walkabout again. What did feel good though was being able to call Jess and tell her that everything she'd had stolen had been found, presumably none the worse for being stored in the old Sierra. It was just a shame about that boy. He'd had the makings of something better than a petty thief – and not even a very good one at that.

'Hey Tash!' Zoe caught up with her sister in the school's back courtyard as they were about to leave for home. 'I rang Mum to ask about the field-trip money and guess what! Grandad's found all our stuff and we'll get it all back again!' Even as she bounced with excitement she realized Natasha was probably the last (or certainly the second to last) person that this was good news for.

Natasha stopped walking and stared at Zoe. 'Where did he find it?'

Surely she didn't really need to ask – Zoe felt confused. 'In the old Sierra of course, where your thieving boyfriend stashed it.'

'It might not have been him.' Natasha glared at Zoe. 'Everyone's just assuming.'

Zoe laughed. 'Oh come on Tasha! You know it was him! It's obvious!'

'Yeah, well . . .' Natasha shrugged. 'Listen Zoe, I need just one more favour from you, the last one I'll ever ask you, ever in my whole life, I promise.'

Zoe started backing away, scared of what she was

going to say. 'Not if it involves Tom, *please* Tash. There's been enough trouble from keeping stupid secrets already. I'm not covering for you, not any more.'

Natasha grabbed her arm to stop her running off and hauled her towards the school gate with her and pointed across the road.

'Look, he's over there, in that black car,' she hissed. 'He's waiting for me. I just want to see him for an hour, then I'll be home. I promise. Nobody else needs to know. Just tell Mum and Dad I've gone to Claire's, that's all.' She almost let go of Zoe, then renewed her grip. 'No, second thoughts, tell them we've gone to the library to look something up for homework. If they think I'm at Claire's they might phone. I don't seem to be trusted too much at the moment.'

'Well what do you expect?'

'God, Zo, you really don't get it do you?' She let go of her sister's arm and raced off, running into the road without looking and making car tyres screech. Zoe watched as Natasha hurled herself into the car and flung herself on Tom. Then she turned away, she didn't want to see. She didn't want to see or know anything, especially not another bloody secret. Didn't these people have anyone else to offload onto?

'Ever been to a fortune-teller, sweetie?' As ever, Paula's voice was crammed with enthusiasm. Every idea she had seemed to thrill her completely to pieces. It made Jess laugh every time – the exuberance was delightfully catching.

'I can't say that I have,' she admitted. 'But I sometimes read my horoscope. I forget it again immediately though so I never know if it's right.'

'Oh me too, me too. But if we sent you to a proper one, someone with the full kit, crystal ball, tarot cards, palm skills, the lot, would you try and write something down that you *could* remember and then share it with your loyal public?'

Jess considered for a moment. 'Well it depends what I was told. Suppose I heard I was going to win the Lottery on a rollover week? I'd have crowds of people outside and a thousand begging letters. Or suppose it was all doom and gloom . . . ?'

'Now, now, don't be so defeatist! Do what real journalists do: exaggerate or make it up, whichever looks cuter on the page. Right, I'll ring round and sort something out for you. Now: let me tell you about what I've been up to with your sexy neighbour.'

Jess listened as Paula, sounding more and more like a schoolgirl relishing her first good sexual encounter, told her more than she really wanted to hear about Eddy's bed preferences. It seemed he had a penchant for the sort of sex toys that Jess had last seen when she'd agreed to go with Angie to an Ann Summers party because Angie had claimed she was 'too shy', as she'd put it, to go on her own. Angie of course had turned out to be the life and soul, prancing around the floral-wallpapered sitting room in Wimbledon brandishing an unappealing and bizarrely orange dildo. The Ann Summers rep had offered it at a discount, on the grounds that the lurid colour made it a 'second'. Angie had also stripped right down in front of an uncurtained main-road window to try on an emerald green satin basque before the evening's hostess could get her hands on it and claim it as the Free Gift she was entitled to.

'So are you any nearer deciding to move in with

him?' Jess asked Paula once she'd paused for breath.

'Yes, I think I might be. He's amazingly *energetic*. And I don't just mean in *that* way.'

Jess wondered if they were talking about the same man. Any connection between 'Eddy' and 'energy' did not immediately spring to mind. She had only rarely seen him in anything other than a sprawling position, occasionally varied with a loping amble as he, like a lazy cat, paced his territory, but then maybe that was love for you. It could, as the song went, change everything.

'God I'm knackered.' Eddy folded his arms on the table-top and laid his weary, shaggy head down on them.

'Not surprised,' Wandering Wilf chortled. 'You've got a young thing in the house, well compared with you anyway – they take a lot of keeping up with.'

Eddy raised his head and met Matthew's eye. A glance was exchanged that expressed the non-likelihood of Wilf having any clue how it would be to entertain someone like Paula on a nightly basis.

'Keeping you up late is she?' Matt chuckled.

'I'm still fully functioning if that's what you're getting at.' Eddy grinned. 'But, Christ, only just. Only just.' He yawned loudly and stretched his arms high in the air. There was a clinking sound as his chunky silver bracelets resettled themselves.

'Oi, watch out!' Ben, bringing out another tray of drinks for them, sidestepped neatly, dodging the waving arms.

'Sorry mate. Oh good, more supplies.' Eddy helped himself to a beer from the tray. 'Course, the problem is, she's started hinting about moving in. I'm not good with them on the premises full-time. They start wanting to do arrangements with bits of material. I haven't met one yet who gets my thing about not having curtains.'

'That's because the whole street can see their tits when they're getting their kit off.' Ben, with no more customers to serve at this late hour of the afternoon, had sat down to join them at the table outside in the sunshine. 'It's all right for us, our private bits are lower than the window ledges.'

'Unless,' Matt thought deeply, 'we're stripping off downstairs, and the people who are looking are upstairs across the road.'

'That's just pervy. People like that will find a way of copping an eyeful one way or another. It's a kind of addiction.'

'Nah, can't be. I've done addiction and it's not like that,' Eddy decreed. 'Micky off again today?' he asked Ben.

'It's the cousin's funeral. There was a bit of a delay because nobody could agree about the best way to do it.'

'Did he sort out an undertaker?' Matt asked.

'Yep. Found a woman who makes wicker coffins. You wind up the body in pure wool . . .'

'By the yard or would a good Paul Smith suit count?' Matt interrupted.

'He wasn't the suit type,' Ben told him. 'Anyway, then you have this body-shaped wicker thing. There was a bit of trouble, Micky's sister complained it was like one of those things you take the cat to the vet in and the woman who'd made it misheard and thought she was ordering one, because she makes those as well. Tricky.' They all nodded solemnly.

258

The enthusiasm for running their own smart undertaking business seemed to have waned. Matt had left his bag of fabric samples at home and, although sure that their idea had been a good one that would, in the right hands, revolutionize the business and make someone a fortune, he accepted with little regret that it wasn't for him. The problem was, what *was* for him? More and more just recently he'd realized that the only day-to-day ambience he actually wanted to be in was that of the Leo, which in his role of constant customer wasn't perhaps entirely healthy. It was expensive too. If you started off the day with coffee and a Danish or one of Ben's ham and cheese croissants, hung about long enough for a lunchtime sandwich and a glass of wine, then brought Jess in later for supper, it all added up. He'd realized that, even if he came up with *the* gem of a moneymaking idea, he wasn't someone who would be comfortable running things from home. If the kind of business opportunity occurred that would involve setting up a desk and a computer in a corner of the conservatory he'd find it very difficult to get his head round the idea that for certain hours of the day, in the place that he associated with comfortable relaxed domesticity, he'd have to apply himself to work. It wouldn't feel natural.

Natasha knew the car was stolen, she wasn't an idiot. It was quite a nice one, a Ford something, she could see from the badge in the middle of the steering wheel, though she didn't know exactly what. It wasn't a very new car but it was very clean inside and she felt a pang of regret for the poor person who must have come out from their house or office or whatever and discovered that it had gone. It had had a lot of care. There was no rubbish in it; no tissues stuffed in the side pockets or sandwich wrappers or Pringle tubes like in her mum's Golf. The dashboard didn't have a layer of dust and there were track marks on the carpet from where it had been carefully vacuumed. It had probably belonged to the sort of person who always checked the oil and tyres when they filled up with petrol and drove her dad to impatient fury when he queued up behind them for fuel because they took such a long time to get going. He always drummed his fingers on the steering wheel and muttered 'Come on, get on with it' as the occupant of the car in front meticulously emptied ashtrays, cleared the side pockets of a couple of sweet papers and washed down the windscreen (with a special little spongey thing), all the time with the car blocking up the space at the pump. 'Now give him another half an hour to find the socket for his bloody seat belt . . .' Matt would then say as the driver eventually climbed in and started adjusting the mirror.

Just now, travelling with Tom along the road that ran beside the river, Natasha felt annoyingly guilty about her parents. If they knew she was riding along in a stolen car . . . It could have been a thrilling feeling, she'd have told Claire (till Claire went all straight and strange) that it was, but really she felt a bit empty inside and slightly depressed as if she'd been given a huge treat, something she'd been whining for for ages and then found she didn't actually like. It wasn't about Tom. She liked being with him. She loved his hand resting on her leg as he drove and she loved watching his face as he concentrated on what he was doing, sensing where the road went, what the traffic ahead was going to do.

'Where are we going?' Natasha asked Tom after she

felt she'd given him a long enough silence to get used to this car.

He shrugged and then changed gear, noisily. 'Thought we'd just find a quiet lane and stop and talk for a bit.'

That was OK with her. It was enough just to be with him: she was glad he wasn't intending to do anything more complicated. It would be bad enough going home to back up the simple lie that she'd made Zoe tell. It would be much harder if the lie was hiding an even bigger one: a lie about sex.

'This is a good place.' Tom pulled into a small car park under the trees, close to a recreation ground. After-school parents and au pairs were pushing small children on swings or watching nervously over the roundabout as bigger children jumped on and off, playing games that were too alarming and daring for their little ones. Around the edge of the playground was the grubbier evidence of use by older kids. Tasha, looking down at the ground just below the car's door, could see cigarette packets, with bits torn off the sides, a sure giveaway that someone had been here smoking dope. If she looked further, into the bushes beyond the roadside, there would probably be condoms, discarded needles, abandoned bits of clothing. It was depressing to be thinking like this. It made her feel as if she'd stopped being able to see anything as simply beautiful, but had started to smell out something sordid beyond.

'It's good, this bit of London, like being in the country.' Tom leaned back in the seat and lit a cigarette, using a flashy gold lighter that looked, to Natasha, as if it belonged to someone far richer, older and more sophisticated than he was.

261

She didn't respond to his comment, instead she pointed to the lighter.

'Whose is that?'

'Mine,' Tom told her simply.

'Is that "mine" as in "it is now"?'

'Probably. Till someone nicks it or I lose it.' He grinned at her. 'What's wrong, don't you like it here? Shall we move?'

'No, no it's fine. It isn't like the country though. It's not clean. There's filth beyond the prettied-up edges.'

'The country's not that clean. It's full of wurzels with filthy minds. Everyone thinks they're OK because they live on the land and keep to themselves.' He looked angry, Natasha could see. His eyes had gone cloudy as if he was hiding deep anger.

'Is that where you're from? Wurzel-land?' She tried laughing a bit, feeling the need to lighten things up. She wanted him to be cocky like he usually was, strong and confident the way he'd been when she first met him. It frightened her that he might be vulnerable because when he got caught, and he was sure to one day, he'd suffer. It should all go over him as if it didn't matter. Crime could just be something he did for *now*, for a laugh and to get by till grown-up life came along and he went and did something else. Surely, that was how it would happen?

Tom threw the half-finished cigarette out of the window and pulled Natasha close to him. 'No more talking,' he said, smiling at her. He started kissing her before she could argue. He tasted of smoke, smelled of oil and dust and he hadn't answered her question but it didn't matter, not now that his hand was working its way under her shirt.

'We should go,' she said eventually, knowing that if

they stayed much longer that even bigger lie would be there. 'I don't want to, but I have to, otherwise they'll know.'

'OK. Tomorrow though?'

'Yeah, tomorrow.' She nearly added 'if . . .' but stopped herself. They both knew about the 'if' factor, the 'if you haven't been caught', the 'if Zoe hasn't told', the 'if you don't have other girls to see'. They didn't need saying.

The square was filling up with after-school teenagers. Matt looked at his watch and even to his leisure-fixated brain it seemed as if he'd spent far too much of his day at this table outside the Leo.

'Better be on my way,' he said.

'You've said that three times now.' Eddy grinned at him. 'Coming back to mine for a spliff?'

'Better not. I should be home, show an interest in the girls and their school day. I think it's what home-bound men are supposed to do. Jess calls it "joining in" as if I'm on a visit from Mars doing a spot of Earth-observing.'

'Bit sort of "sexist" isn't it?' Ben pronounced the word as if it was one he'd not actually used before and wasn't sure if he was allowed to.

'Nah, she's right really. After all, she's spent all day working.'

A football whistled past Eddy's head and landed under the next table. A girl that Matt recognized as a primary-school friend of Natasha's grinned at him as she bent to retrieve it. She was wearing a very short skirt. Matt, politely, turned away as she bent down but heard an under-the-breath lusty groan from Eddy.

'You got nowhere better to go?' Ben asked the girl.

Mel expertly twirled the football in her hand and grinned at them all. 'Hi Mr Nelson,' she said shyly, then to Ben she said, 'No, got any ideas?' Ben shrugged. 'Here's good enough so long as you don't frighten away my customers.'

'What, this lot?' she said cheekily. 'It would take more than me!'

'You know, it's not a bad idea,' Matt said suddenly as Mel went back to her keepy-uppy competition with a pair of gangly teenage boys.

'What isn't?'

'This time of the day. It's a sort of down-time, isn't it. I mean, we've been coming here and staying past lunch and there's no rush of customers till the office workers are in for Happy Hour at 5.30.'

'But it's the only peace I get all day,' Ben complained.

'Get extra staff, after-school kids. And have a Happy Hour for the teenagers, though not alcohol obviously. If they want that they can go to the dodgy little shops or nick it from their parents. No, give them coffee, Coke, hot chocolate and a menu of pancakes and ice cream and biscuits. Then they'd have somewhere to go to get together after school. *And* you'd get more of the different schools mixing, which would be a good thing, stop them fighting and calling each other snobs.'

Ben looked deeply thoughtful. Matt could almost see the idea being filtered through his brain. Eddy was quiet too, as if working out where the catch was. Only the urgent wails of police sirens cut through the quiet, and the bounce, bounce of the footballs. The sirens were getting nearer, brakes were screeching.

'It's getting like bloody New York round here,' Eddy said eventually, just as a black Mondeo squealed round the corner into the square. Mel shrieked as she leapt out of its path. The car, hurtling across the pavement, skidded sideways as the driver stood too hard on the brakes, and crashed into the lamp post, bounced off onto the bench and turned over onto its side. Three police cars surrounded it, speeding across the paved area with no apparent regard for anyone who might be in the way. Officers leapt out and ran to the car.

'I hope someone's called for a bloody ambulance,' Eddy said. 'There were kids in that car.'

Shakily, as if expecting the worst, Matt followed him to the crippled Mondeo. There was still music coming from it, though the engine had, unsurprisingly, stalled. The underside of the vehicle looked like a monstrous scar, rearing up there in the middle of the square.

'There's someone trying to get out!' Matt ran the last few yards, joined a pale and frightened-looking police-man on top of what was left of the bench and peered down into the car's inside.

'We're for it if they're dead,' the young constable muttered. Matt glared at him, shoved him aside with the kind of force that came with anger and reached across to the door handle. 'Push it if you can!' he yelled, praying the occupants were in a state to comply.

'I am,' sobbed a frantic voice, 'I'm pushing it as hard as I can! It's stuck! Get me out!' Fists banged against the window.

'Jesus! *Natasha!*' Matt yelled.

Sixteen

Natasha's injuries looked worse than they were, but they didn't, according to the disapproving and pessimistic doctor, look as bad as they would in a couple of days. Bruising took time to ripen, he told Jess with an unsuppressable quotient of glee in his voice, and after twenty-four hours or so Natasha would be wanting to keep well out of the public gaze for a while. The stitches on her forehead, he warned, would also become sore as the swelling continued, her limbs would feel stiff and her body would ache as if she'd got flu and for all this she'd have to make do with nothing stronger than a couple of paracetamol.

'She was lucky to have got away without any broken bones,' he said, scowling at Jess across the bed in the treatment room at St Michael's accident and emergency department. 'These kids . . .' He shook his head slowly, leaving Jess in no doubt that in his opinion the long years of expensive medical training had definitely *not* been for the purpose of treating a bunch of young vandals who deserved all they got.

'What *about* "these kids"?' Matthew said with quiet anger.

The doctor removed his glasses, braced himself on the end rails of the bed (in readiness, Jess assumed, for when Matthew gave him a furious shove) and continued, 'Without people like these kids, who are here as a result of criminal behaviour and carelessness, the waiting times that everyone's forever beefing about in these places would be at least half what they are. You wouldn't believe how many drunks, louts, aggressive cretins who've punched each other senseless . . .'

'Er, so where do you stand on sports injuries then?' Matthew was smiling now. 'Do you make these irresponsible idiots who've chosen to risk their all in a rugby match wait at the back of the queue, just to teach them a lesson?'

'Sport is different. Sport is good for you. It would keep young yobs' minds off the so-called thrills of crime.'

The doctor was on a roll. Jess could see that Matthew, now reassured that Natasha was going to be completely all right, was about to move into a full-scale debate and needed distracting. 'Come on, Matt, let's get Tasha home. We don't want to keep the doctor from his more deserving patients, do we?'

Natasha slid down from the bed and staggered slightly. 'Did the nurse ask you if you've been drinking?' the doctor said, loading an additional dose of contempt into his voice.

'Yes and I haven't,' Natasha snapped. 'I'm just . . .' She burst into tears at that point.

'It's all right Tash, let's get you home.' Jess took hold of her arm and led her out of the cubicle and back towards the way out. Zoe was in the waiting area, reading *Marie Claire* and keeping an eye on a gaggle of police officers who were hanging around the coffee machine and telling each other jokes.

'They're waiting to talk to Tom,' Zoe whispered as they walked towards the car park.

'What, all of them?' Matt said. 'I mean how many does it take to arrest one young boy?'

'One young boy with a broken arm and possibly serious head injuries,' Jess added. 'I don't suppose he'll be doing any twocking for a while.'

'*Twocking?*' Zoe said as she got into the back of the Golf. 'What's that?'

'Taking Without Owner's Consent. Nicking cars, basically,' Natasha said.

She sounded weary. Zoe glanced at her warily as they sat together in the car. Natasha was staring straight ahead, looking as if she wanted to sleep for about a year. Her face was smeary from dried-out tears and her hair looked as if she hadn't brushed it for a week.

'Does it hurt?' Zoe asked quietly.

'Yes.' The reply didn't invite any more questions and Zoe gazed out of the window feeling tearful. It was all her fault. She should have refused to tell the lie about Natasha going to Claire's. All the way home on the bus she'd been so sure this was one secret too many and that it would be the one that made the most deeply serious trouble. When she'd got home, she'd just prayed that no-one would say, as Jess had, 'Oh just you, is it? Where's Tash?' If Zoe had only said, 'Actually, she's gone off with Tom in a car that can't possibly be his,' all this might not have happened. Or it might have been even worse, she thought. Because either way, the police knew about Tom taking the car and were going to chase it. Natasha could have been killed. Tom couldn't drive that well, no-one of sixteen could drive well enough to outrun three police cars who seemed, according to her dad, to be in some kind of competition to make the arrest.

Zoe had heard the crash from her bedroom. It was a horrible, sickening sound, all huge metallic crunch and shattering glass. It was the kind of sound that made you sure no-one in the middle of it could have survived. She'd sat on her bed feeling sick, waiting for someone to tell her the worst. She wasn't even slightly surprised when Ben called from the Leo to tell her mum that Natasha was being taken to the hospital, with Matt in the ambulance.

There was a strange calm hush in the house. Natasha, looking deeply sad and more battered by the minute (the doctor would be delighted, Jess thought), asked for a bowl of tomato soup, some hot chocolate and then went to have a long hot bath and get into bed. Jess wouldn't ask her any questions. There was no point: she was pretty sure they knew all they needed to know about what had happened. If there was anything to add, it would come out when the police questioned Natasha. At least, she thought, as she prepared a simple pasta carbonara for the rest of them, Tom would be off the scene. Permanently, if Jess had anything to do with it.

'It's all my fault, isn't it?' Matt said as soon as Zoe had gone to watch television after a quiet and morose supper.

'What, all this? No of course not, why do you think so?'

'I've not exactly been a shining example of upright

269

citizenship since the job went. I could have been a bit more of a support, backed you up when you grounded Tasha. I could have picked her up from school in the afternoons, made sure she knew we were serious about her not seeing Tom – especially after the burglary. How is she supposed to toe the line when I spend all my time avoiding responsibility?'

Jess thought about what he'd said. There was more than an ounce of truth in his words, but not much more. Teenagers made their own choices, it was part of the process. And because they *were* teenagers they tended to pick the thrill option. You couldn't put them on reins like toddlers.

'You can't blame yourself. We trusted her. If we said she couldn't do something, we assumed, perhaps naively and lazily, she'd do as we said. But she's nearly sixteen, it's a breakaway age. Hell, we haven't given her a lot to rebel about, we're pretty easy-going. Perhaps she just had to kick against the grown-up world one way or another and this was her way.'

'You mean you don't know all there is to know about teen life?' Matt leaned across and kissed her. 'You're actually fallible?'

'Of course I am!' Jess laughed. 'And come on, he was an attractive boy. She's a girl with imagination; it must have been a massive thrill that someone like him wanted to go out with her. He represents danger, the forbidden, something way beyond the boring selection on offer at St Dominic's. I just hope . . .'

'Hope what?'

'I hope she's got it out of her system.'

George waited till the morning to come and see Natasha. When Jess had phoned the night before and told him what had happened to her he'd felt quite weak with distress. It was all so stupidly unnecessary. In delaying telling the police about the stolen goods in the Sierra, it could be that he'd put the life of his adored granddaughter at risk. That was what came of putting things off, wishing that things were different from the way they were instead of facing reality and acting on what was actually true. Now, he couldn't think why he'd waited before making that call to the police. Perhaps he'd been hoping that things would be different when he'd had a night's sleep. However old you got, he thought as he walked up the Grove with the huge bunch of flowers for Tash, you never stopped hoping that the president of the immortals would make things all right overnight.

'Hallo Grandad.' George was surprised when Natasha opened the door. 'Ooh are those for me? No-one's ever given me flowers before! Come in.'

'Well you poor girl, you do look a bit battered around the edges.' George gently kissed her swollen, purple cheek. 'I'm glad you're up and about though, I thought you'd be lying around in bed and resting.'

'It's only because I didn't *have* to get up,' she said, grinning at him. 'I'm a teenager, I only stay in bed when it annoys people, like most of Saturday mornings when Mum wants me to tidy my room or do homework or something truly gross like that. Come and have a cup of coffee, Mum's in the kitchen, sorting through all her old work stuff.'

'Hi Dad, come to see our invalid?' Jess, glancing at her father, couldn't miss the change in him. He looked older, more frail somehow, as if he'd shrunk slightly in the past couple of weeks.

'Are you all right?' she asked, looking through the

cupboard in search of a packet of biscuits, as if just the smallest amount of quick-fix food would restore him to his former vigour.

George sat at the table, idly turning over the loose pages from Jess's file of past work. 'I'm well in myself. I've got a confession to make though.' He hesitated, coughed a little and then rallied. 'I found all your stolen stuff the night before I rang the police. If they'd known, they might have caught . . . you know, before . . .' He hesitated, unable to continue. Jess sat down next to him and put her arm round him. 'It's all right, they were already looking for Tom. The stuff wasn't really relevant – and we got it back, so it made no difference in the end. You really mustn't worry about it.'

'The crash wasn't anyone's fault,' Natasha said. 'Except the police, they just panicked Tom, I mean there were three lots of them all with the sirens going. All he could do was go faster.'

'Well, he could have stopped.' George, let off the hook, seemed instantly more sprightly, almost back to his normal rather confrontational self. 'I mean that would have been the honest thing to do, wouldn't it? Or just not steal things in the first place?'

'Yes, but . . .' Jess began then stopped. What was the point? They all knew, even Natasha, where honesty ranked with Tom.

It was all over the school. Girls Zoe had never spoken to in her life, even girls from the sixth form, kept coming up to her and asking if it was true that her sister had been in a crash in a stolen car. It was that day's sensation. Girls from Julia Perry's occasionally became pregnant, frequently severely anorexic and sometimes went in for a little light shoplifting. They didn't tend, generally, to go out with genuine hard-case criminals. The fact that Natasha had done so, blatantly and disastrously, had sent a vicarious collective thrill through much of the school. Guiltily, Zoe couldn't help at least half-enjoying the second-hand glamour of the situation.

'So is she OK, like she's not going to be scarred or anything?' Claire asked Zoe in the lunch queue. 'Shall I come and see her? Will after school today be all right?'

'I suppose so.' Zoe shrugged. 'Why don't you ring her?' In fact, why haven't you called for absolutely bloody ages, she wanted to ask, not at all taken in by Claire's renewed enthusiasm for her sister's company and welfare. Zoe wasn't stupid, she knew there'd been a rift. Claire and Natasha, in the past weeks, had definitely not been together so much. Claire had started hanging around with the group in her year who were known as the ball girls. This was nothing to do with tennis but was all about attending as many upmarket parties as possible and keeping a coloured-in chart listing the leading boys' boarding schools and the best snoggers therein. Only a few weeks before, Natasha and Claire had been equally damning in their scorn for this childish and silly-girl pursuit, but as Zoe listened to Claire's avid questioning for details of Tash's accident, she could see the unmistakeable blotching of a love-bite on her neck. Claire probably couldn't remember, Zoe assumed with possibly overjudgemental contempt, who it was who'd given it to her: she knew quite well that with the ball girls it was a matter of clocking up the numbers. Pondering the girls in her own year at the school, she could think of only a handful, apart from herself, who definitely *wouldn't* be a ball girl in a couple of years' time. It didn't seem a lot to look forward to.

The fortune-teller was everything Paula had promised, although her premises were uncompromisingly domestic. Jess had anticipated being shown into a musky, exotic den, festooned from ceiling to floor with splendid drapes of moss green velvet, and offered a seat at a table hung with gold-fringed cloth. Instead she was ushered into a shabby sitting room with a faded floral carpet in shades of orange and blotchy hessian wallpaper, the colour of ground ginger, which must have been up since the mid-Sixties. The fire was a gas-effect one, ruling out, Jess assumed, any staring into it to read pictures in the flames. A pair of massive scuffed leather chesterfield sofas took up most of the space. Between these was a low table covered with a purple satin cloth, which, reminding Jess of Matthew's choice of coffin lining, rather unnerved her. On the cloth was a gratifyingly archetypal selection of the tools of a fortune-teller's trade: a pack of tarot cards, a crystal ball (into which Jess peered, hoping she might discover she had The Gift) and a little silver dragon figure which contained something that was causing whiffs of scented smoke to come from its mouth. Even pessimism-supremo Robin, who'd been in earlier to photograph the set-up, must have found something to please him here.

'Coffee? Herbal tea?' Bella the mystic (in jeans and a tight pink tee shirt) offered as Jess settled herself next to a massive tabby cat.

'Er, no thanks, I'm OK.' Jess smiled and stroked the cat which stretched itself out to its full length and took up most of the sofa.

'This must be about the biggest cat I've ever seen,' she commented as Bella sat down opposite her and started shuffling the tarot cards. Her nails were spectacularly long, Jess noted, and painted with pale blue shimmery varnish and her hands were loaded with thick silver rings studded with chunky opals and amethysts.

'He wasn't very well, as a kitten.' Bella smiled fondly at the cat. 'So I treated him with reiki healing. It makes them grow, you see, all that stroking. Would you like to try it? Reiki? It helps with emotional problems as well as physical.' Jess turned the offer down as politely as she could, making a light joke about not wanting to grow any more thank you, which seemed to go right over Bella's head. She did wonder though if it was really that obvious that she wasn't currently in the most settled frame of mind, or if Bella was truly psychic. Ashamed of her cynicism, for Bella was gentle, hospitable and genuinely certain of her powers, Jess found herself seeking out the party-trick aspect of the business: surely it was easy enough to guess that any suburban working mother/journalist was going to have the odd emotional problem. There were whole hospitals in the area set up for just that kind of sorting out; Yellow Pages had several pages of private counsellors well able to afford the cost of the advertising.

'I can't tell you anything you couldn't work out for yourself really,' Bella said as she laid the tarot cards out. 'We lose the habit of trusting our intuition far too early. It needs nurturing, just like other skills do. We're all born with the ability to see into the future. Those people who somehow didn't get on that plane that crashed, the ones who say "I had a feeling about that", they're clinging onto the last of their power.' She looked up suddenly at Jess. 'You have a man in your life who is a very powerful support to you. He is on your side, an indispensable help.'

'My husband?' Jess couldn't help sounding incredulous. 'Quite possibly.'

Bella nodded solemnly. 'You would be the one to know, not me.' She gave a little smile, full of suggested mystery, and Jess again felt guilty for her lingering doubts. Bella had seen Matthew drop her off at the house on his way to take Natasha to the doctor to have her stitches out. It could easily be an exaggeration of how 'helpful' that could be.

The cards did not promise massive unexpected riches, that the girls would be married off into the royal family or that Matthew would be any nearer finding something useful to occupy his time after the next few months. 'Money will not be a problem for you,' Bella told Jess as, the cards finished, she began backing up her findings with a palm reading.

'Is that because I'll be so rich I won't *need* to worry or because I'll be so poor I won't have the burden of wondering how to deal with wealth?'

Again came the smile full of secret knowledge, as if the information could be trawled out of Jess's own brain if only she could kick-start the right dormant cells.

'Oh and there'll be travel,' Bella said, by way of a farewell.

'Isn't there always?' Jess laughed, wondering if she should start thinking about booking a holiday, which would be more than rash with Matt no nearer to thinking about finding a job, or if the four-mile journey home counted. It was certainly all the travelling she'd be doing for now.

*   *   *

'It's just like on *Casualty*. They move pretty fast when you get brought in by ambulance,' Matt was telling his usual audience at the Leo.

'They do but I don't recommend dialling 999 if you've only got a cut finger though,' Micky said.

'I feel a bit sorry for the kid, Tom, you know,' Matt admitted over his first beer of the day.

'Why? He nearly killed your Natasha. I'd want to wring his evil little neck.' Eddy made wringing movements with his hands, then grimaced. 'Bloody arthritis,' he said, 'I'm awash with glucosomites and cod liver sodding oil and it's still a bloody pain in the morning. If Paula gets frisky before the first Nurofen kicks in it's fucking agony. So why do you feel sorry for him? You turning into a social worker?'

'No, it's because he's got to go back into custody. Turns out he was on the run from a sort of young offenders' halfway house and had a string of previous going back to sometime around his twelfth birthday. Now he's gone into a serious lock-up. Young lads kill themselves in those. You always imagine kids like him, you think they're some kind of alien beings that you'll never come into contact with, but well, he was quite nice really. It's a shame.'

'Jesus Matt, you're softening up in your old age.' Micky shook his head in despair. 'You'll be looking for a proper job next.'

'Me? Never! I want something where I can do just what I'm doing now.' He raised his glass in a toast to Ben behind the bar.

'You should take over from Micky then; he's off to see the world at the end of this summer. I might have to sell up,' Ben said gloomily.

*　　*　　*

Natasha didn't want to go back to school. The bruises had started to go down and she could now bear to touch her skin enough to cover the worst of the marks with make-up. But it was a strain, the way her parents were being so perpetually nice to her, and she really needed to escape. She could understand that they were hugely relieved that she hadn't been killed but there hadn't been even the slightest bit of blame, not even the hint of a telling-off. Somehow it made her feel worse – a massive row would have been better all round; there wouldn't be this strange whispery atmosphere in the house. They kept asking her if she was all right. All she could say was 'Yes I'm fine, honestly,' and hope they wouldn't give her that look, that probing, 'how do you *really* feel' look that was pushing her to confide things that she was quite sure they didn't really want to know.

There was nothing *to* confide, that was the truth. Tom had gone now, so end of story. There wasn't much chance of her ever seeing him again. For the first few days after the crash she'd made sure she was the one who picked up the mail from the mat in the mornings, but he hadn't written. It was his left arm that would be in a sling, and she didn't even know if he was left- or right-handed. Perhaps he hadn't had much of an education though, she thought, perhaps writing wasn't something he was good at. She hardly knew anything at all about him, really, when it came down to it.

Natasha was glad to have Zoe with her when the next Monday came and she couldn't put off going back to school any longer. On the bus, one or two of the younger girls nudged and whispered and pointed but they were easy to ignore. Zoe was doing her best, chatting away about Oliver and trying to imagine where he was and what he was doing. When they arrived, Claire was waiting by the gate, claiming Natasha as her friend again in a way she hadn't done for quite a while now.

'You don't actually look too bad.' Claire scrutinized her closely, gently running a finger over the bright pink scar just above her eyebrow where the stitches had been.

'You sound disappointed! Did you hope I'd look all beaten up and be walking on crutches?' Natasha laughed. 'Tell me what I've missed.'

Claire shrugged. 'Nuffin. Usual stuff, a new maths investigation and they've sorted out a geography field trip for next term: Swanage, surprise, surprise. My sister went there and she said the whole place is *stuffed* with geography field-trip people trying to accost the residents for stupid surveys and counting cars.'

'Can't wait.'

Jess had been half-expecting the phone call. She knew this was going to be one deed of misbehaviour too far for the Julia Perry School. The school was very keen on 'standards', the head said as Jess doodled on a Post-it note and only half-listened. Standards were to be 'upheld', which inspired Jess to draw a flagpole with a skull and crossbones at half mast. Natasha's position in the school was to be reviewed, apparently. Jess and Matthew would be informed in 'due course' (she added a pirate ship) of the decision that came out of this process.

'It doesn't matter,' Jess heard herself say as she sketched in Captain Pugwash. 'She and Zoe will be leaving the school at the end of the summer term.'

After she'd hung up, Jess went into a sweaty panic. 'Where did that come from?' she asked Matt, who'd just strolled in from the Leo. 'I've just told the head of Julia Perry that Tash and Zoe will be leaving the school.'

'What, before they're publicly flogged and thrown out? Good thinking,' he laughed.

'But what about them? Where will they go? Won't they be furious?' She shouldn't have done this, she thought, not without consulting the girls. Natasha was halfway through her GCSE courses. But then no-one had ever questioned the assumption that she was likely to get the desired full-house score of nine A* grades, so surely she'd be all right anywhere.

'Furious? Those two? You really haven't been keeping your eye on the ball have you, Jess, they hate it there. They're only sitting it out because that's where all the nice rich little middle-class girls like them go to school from round here. Though, where did you have in mind for them?'

'Briar's Lane, they mostly seem to do OK there.'

'Good idea.' He hugged her. 'And your dad will be delighted. It's one small step towards your party membership card.'

At least that day was over. Hundreds more to go. Natasha trudged home, lugging the eternally bulging bag of homework. She made her way from the high street into the square. Mel was there, sitting by herself on the twisted and battered bench opposite the Leo that had been restored to its approximate right way up by Eddy and Ben after the crash.

'Y'all right Tash?' Mel called. 'Want a cig?' She

offered the packet. Natasha shook her head but went to sit beside her.

'I've got a message for you. I saw Tom,' Mel told her.

'Where? At the prison?'

'He's in a Young Offenders, quite a long way out. I went on a visit.' Mel crossed her long pale legs and stared at the floor.

'How did you manage that?'

'He wrote and asked me, sent me a VO.'

'And that's a . . . ?'

'Visiting Order.' Mel giggled. 'I felt like one of those women off *Birds of a Feather* lining up with all the mums and girlfriends.' Then she looked at Natasha. 'Er, he says he's really sorry and he hopes you're all right.'

'Does he want me to see him?' Natasha's voice, even to her own ears, sounded flat and dull.

'Er no, that's the bit you might not like. He says it was just for then, it was great but you should find someone else.'

Natasha stared at the mottled grey paving stones. She felt tears pricking. 'So he was with you, as well as me, all the time.'

Mel put her arm round Natasha and hugged her close. 'No. We were just mates. Truly. I think he really loved you, but he'll be gone for ages. And we're young.' She grinned at Natasha. 'Come on, you'll be OK. And so will he in the end. He's got a nice mum, you know, I met her up the prison. He's just a bit wild.'

'A bit!' Natasha giggled.

'OK, a lot!' Mel laughed.

'. . . *a helpline for those who think they're the Worst Parents in the World. We suffer in silence, too scared of being judged to confess our failings to even our closest*

*friends, lying that everything's fine and keeping all the
problems locked up behind the prim suburban windows. We are isolated and nail-biting, sure that
everyone else's fifteen-year-olds are immersed in
coursework, intent on cracking the central dilemma in*
Macbeth *while ours are marauding the streets up to all
kinds of no good. We wonder will tonight's collection
point be the police station again, or perhaps the hospital this time for a welcome change of venue . . .'*

Well, Paula had wanted the truth. This would be the
last Nelson's Column that involved Jess's family. It
wasn't a confessional, certainly not in the sense that
she'd shopped Natasha to the Sunday-paper-browsing
public, but it was an admission of parental imper-
fection on an uncomfortably grand scale. It would, she
knew, ring a lot of bells. The broadsheet readers of
Britain surely shouldn't have to do their agonizing all
in secret, having to put up with jolly columnists like
her pretending that the worst that could happen after a
teenager's night out was that they'd use the parental
minicab account to ferry five friends to various homes
over a forty-five-mile radius. Everyone knew, deep
down and in the turbulent cage of their own homes,
that things got an awful lot worse than that.

. . . After all that's happened the girls shouldn't have to
wait till they hit nineteen and have done their A levels
to see this place. Tash and Zoe would love the surfing.
Even you and Dad could do it here. Western Oz is just
the best place. I'm running low on cash so if you feel
like getting on a plane I could show you round for a
price (short term only, I got stuff to do, people and
places to see) . . .

*   *   *

'It's a bugger of a long way. Tell me you won't die of boredom or thrombosis before we get there,' Matt said to Jess as the safety-belt sign went off.

'I promise I'll try not to,' she reassured him. It *was* a long way, just about the furthest you could go in the world. Jess could hardly wait to see Oliver again; he'd be there, he'd told them, with a car to take them to the hotel. Natasha hadn't been sure: will he want us lot turning up, really, she'd wondered? Good question; but Oliver was easily bought with the promise of temporary escape from the privations of hostel life, with the temptation of hotel rooms with constant water supplies, with not having to eke out his precious savings for a few weeks. Then he'd be on his way again, on the backpack trail onwards to New Zealand and the snowboard season. Jess wondered what he'd look like now, how tanned he'd be, how much the sun would have bleached his hair.

From the seat behind, Jess could hear the pecking sound of Zoe's Gameboy. There was the familiar bass thud-thud of music from Natasha's headphones. She sipped her champagne (so you should avoid alcohol on long-distance flights, she'd read, but this was such a one-off) and looked at the menu.

'We're doing the right thing you know,' Matt said, taking her hand.

'I know. No doubts at all. They can go to school again in September. They won't miss much. And it was obvious the Julia Perry High School were highly relieved to see the back of them.'

Matt chuckled. '"We have to think of their peers. Influences, you know, so important."' He mimicked the ponderous tones of Natasha's form tutor who had found it so hard to pretend she was sorry Tash was leaving.

The stewardess approached with the drinks trolley. 'Any thin Celts?' she asked Matt.

He turned to Jess, perplexed, for a translation. 'It means "Would you like another drink?"' she told him.

'Oh right, er, no thanks,' Matt said, trying not to laugh.

'When you're doing your stints in charge at the Leo, you won't say that to your customers will you?' she said. 'Promise?'

'Promise? Certainly not. Now I own half the bar, I shall do exactly what I like in it,' he told her with a grin. 'It's a glorious phrase and I shall make a point of using it whenever I can.'

THE END

EXCESS BAGGAGE

Judy Astley

A Proper Family Holiday was the last thing Lucy
was expecting to have. But as a penniless and
partnerless house-painter with an expired lease on
her flat and a twelve-year-old daughter, she could
hardly turn down her parents' offer to take them on
a once-in-a-lifetime trip to the Caribbean. She'd
just have to put up with her sister Theresa (making
no secret of preferring Tuscany as a holiday
destination) and brother Simon (worrying that
there might be some sinister agenda behind their
parents' wish to take them all away) with their
various spouses, teenagers, young children and
au pair.

In a luxury hotel, with bright sunshine, swimming,
diving, glorious food and friendly locals, any
family tensions should have melted away in the
fabulous heat. The children should have been
angelic, the teenagers cheerful, the adults relaxed
and happy. But . . . some problems just refuse to be
left at home.

0 552 99842 7

BLACK SWAN

THE RIGHT THING
Judy Astley

Funerals are strange things. Kitty hadn't really
wanted to go to this one – an old school friend she
hadn't seen for years – and she hadn't bargained
for the way it made her think of the past. In
particular, it made her think of the baby she had
given birth to when she was eighteen, the baby her
parents had insisted she give away for adoption.
She'd called her Madeleine, and she remembered
her every day, what she was like, if she was happy.
But now, reminded of how cruelly short life can be,
she had to see her – just to make sure she'd done
the right thing.

Life had turned out pretty well for Kitty. Secure in
her marriage, with her two teenage children and a
house within sound and sight of the Cornish surf,
she counted herself among the lucky ones. But the
hole left by that first baby wasn't getting any
smaller, and she decided to make the first, tentative
steps towards filling it – although she, and all her
family, were quite unprepared for the upheaval
which followed.

0 552 99768 4

BLACK SWAN

JUST FOR THE SUMMER

Judy Astley

'OH, WHAT A FIND! A LOVELY, FUNNY BOOK'
Sarah Harrison

Every July, the lucky owners of Cornish holiday homes set off for their annual break. Loading their estate cars with dogs, cats, casefuls of wine, difficult adolescents and rebellious toddlers, they close up their desirable semis in smartish London suburbs – having turned off the Aga and turned on the burglar alarm – and look forward to a carefree, restful, somehow more *fulfilling* summer.

Clare is, this year, more than usually ready for her holiday. Her teenage daughter, Miranda, has been behaving strangely; her husband, Jack, is harbouring unsettling thoughts of a change in lifestyle; her small children are being particularly tiresome; and she herself is contemplating a bit of extra-marital adventure, possibly with Eliot, the successful – although undeniably heavy-drinking and overweight – author in the adjoining holiday property. Meanwhile Andrew, the only son of elderly parents, is determined that this will be the summer when he will seduce Jessica, Eliot's nubile daughter. But Jessica spends her time in girl-talk with Miranda, while Milo, her handsome brother with whom Andrew longs to be friends, seems more interested in going sailing with the young blond son of the club commodore.

Unexpected disasters occur, revelations are made and, as the summer ends, real life will never be quite the same again.

'A SHARP SOCIAL COMEDY . . . SAILS ALONG VERY NICELY AND FULFILS ITS EARLY PROMISE'
John Mortimer, *Mail on Sunday*

'WICKEDLY FUNNY . . . A THOROUGHLY ENTERTAINING ROMP'
Val Hennessy, *Daily Mail*

0 552 99564 9

BLACK SWAN

A SELECTED LIST OF FINE WRITING
AVAILABLE FROM BLACK SWAN

THE PRICES SHOWN BELOW WERE CORRECT AT THE TIME OF GOING TO PRESS. HOWEVER TRANSWORLD PUBLISHERS RESERVE THE RIGHT TO SHOW NEW RETAIL PRICES ON COVERS WHICH MAY DIFFER FROM THOSE PREVIOUSLY ADVERTISED IN THE TEXT OR ELSEWHERE.

14721 4	TOM, DICK AND DEBBIE HARRY	Jessica Adams	£6.99
99822 2	A CLASS APART	Diana Appleyard	£6.99
99564 9	JUST FOR THE SUMMER	Judy Astley	£6.99
99565 7	PLEASANT VICES	Judy Astley	£6.99
99629 7	SEVEN FOR A SECRET	Judy Astley	£6.99
99630 0	MUDDY WATERS	Judy Astley	£6.99
99766 8	EVERY GOOD GIRL	Judy Astley	£6.99
99768 4	THE RIGHT THING	Judy Astley	£6.99
99842 7	EXCESS BAGGAGE	Judy Astley	£6.99
99734 X	EMOTIONALLY WEIRD	Kate Atkinson	£6.99
99854 0	LESSONS FOR A SUNDAY FATHER	Claire Calman	£6.99
99537 1	GUPPIES FOR TEA	Marika Cobbold	£6.99
99839 7	FROST AT MIDNIGHT	Elizabeth Falconer	£6.99
99795 1	LIAR BIRDS	Lucy Fitzgerald	£5.99
99759 5	DOG DAYS, GLENN MILLER NIGHTS	Laurie Graham	£6.99
99848 6	CHOCOLAT	Joanne Harris	£6.99
99887 7	THE SECRET DREAMWORLD OF A SHOPAHOLIC		
		Sophie Kinsella	£5.99
99697 1	FOUR WAYS TO BE A WOMAN	Sue Reidy	£6.99
99753 6	AN ACCIDENTAL LIFE	Titia Sutherland	£6.99
99952 0	LIFE ISN'T ALL HA HA HEE HEE	Meera Syal	£6.99
99819 2	WHISTLING FOR THE ELEPHANTS	Sandi Toksvig	£6.99
99872 9	MARRYING THE MISTRESS	Joanna Trollope	£6.99
99720 X	THE SERPENTINE CAVE	Jill Paton Walsh	£6.99
99723 4	PART OF THE FURNITURE	Mary Wesley	£6.99
99834 6	COCKTAILS FOR THREE	Madeleine Wickham	£6.99
99651 3	AFTER THE UNICORN	Joyce Windsor	£6.99

All Transworld titles are available by post from:

Bookpost, P.O. Box 29, Douglas, Isle of Man IM99 1BQ

Credit cards accepted. Please telephone 01624 836000, fax 01624 837033 or Internet http://www.bookpost.co.uk. or e-mail: bookshop@enterprise.net for details

Free postage and packing in the UK. Overseas customers: allow £1 per book (paperbacks) and £3 per book (hardbacks).